DREAD INK

BRYAN SMITH

Grindhouse Press
PO BOX 540
Yellow Springs, Ohio 45387

Grindhouse Press #105
ISBN-13: 978-1-957504-19-3

In memory of Rachael Wise.
Thinking of old times.

THE
HALLOWEEN
BRIDE

1

THE SKY ABOVE DARKENED WITH the first faint tinge of twilight as Deacon Croswell sat on the little front porch outside his rental house and smoked what he was certain would be the first of several Marlboros. He smoked the cigarettes with the filters broken off to get a richer tobacco taste. The wording of the warning printed on the side of the paperboard pack was the most dire-sounding he had ever seen—SMOKING CAUSES EARLY DEATH.

Deacon took a long drag off the unneutered cigarette, held the smoke deep in his lungs for as long as he could, and then slowly exhaled. Wisps of aromatic smoke rose into the air and dissipated in the chill October breeze.

The smoking was a new thing. He had long considered it a nasty habit, one he had no intention of ever taking up. But that kind of thinking was a relic of a time that had passed. He no longer cared whether something was good for his health. In truth, he no longer cared about much of anything. His world had become a very dismal place, his existence colorless and drab, devoid of even the faintest trace of anything resembling joy. This was his dark period, as he

1

suspected he would think of it many years from now, providing he actually survived it. Oh, he wasn't actively courting death. There was no strong suicidal impulse within him. This was what he always told the people close to him to assuage their concerns, and it was the truth. No one was ever going to happen across his remains after he'd put a bullet through his head or drowned himself in a bathtub after slitting his wrists.

But the darkness inside him was real. It was the reason he would now do things like smoke cigarettes or walk around outside in the middle of a thunderstorm. Yes, he wouldn't take his own life, but that didn't mean he wasn't willing to flirt a bit with the reaper. And when he was being completely honest with himself, he could admit the only reason he didn't pursue his end more actively was an abiding fear of what—if anything—came after death.

At twenty-five, he was a young man, but he had suffered a deep emotional trauma, the kind that would strain the coping skills of just about anyone, regardless of age. Deep melancholy had enveloped him since the middle of the summer.

July 16.

Before that day he had been a happy guy, a hopeful person in general. He had been content with his lot in life. The world had made sense. Everything was as he'd always imagined it would be. He had a good job and even better prospects for the future. His had been an almost eerily charmed existence. Best of all, he'd had the love of a beautiful, intelligent girl. In the last days before the end of his old life, he had started thinking about how he might want to propose to her.

That would never happen now.

Because Anna was gone.

Except that no, that wasn't quite the right way to put it.

Deacon grimaced as the last little bit of the cigarette he'd been smoking singed his fingers. He opened his fingers and let the glowing nub fall to the sidewalk, where he crushed it beneath the heel of his shoe. He shook another one out of the dwindling pack, lighting it with his Zippo. The Zippo was an item he'd purchased the same day he'd bought his first pack of smokes. He'd always wanted one, even before he took up smoking. Tough guys in movies often used them, and he'd always liked the distinctive clicking sound the Zippo made when it was flipped shut. And now he had a legitimate reason for owning one. Like everything else these days, however, he derived little actual pleasure from it.

Anna was gone.

Yes. That was the simplest way to put it.

But the real truth was starker than that.

Sudden tears blurred Deacon's vision, smearing the suburban landscape and briefly lending it a surrealistic aspect, the smudges of dark color resembling something from a macabre painting. The nearest streetlight clicked on, and in that moment it looked like the angry, glowing eye of a demon. Deacon pushed the tears away with the heel of a hand. Things came back into focus quickly, but the world still looked like a haunted place, an impression that struck him as almost ghoulishly apt.

Today was the day before Halloween.

And the love of his life was dead, some three and a half months in the ground.

She had been walking along the side of the road that bright and beautiful summer day. The supermarket where she worked part-time was a fifteen-minute stroll from their neighborhood. A car would get her there in just a couple of minutes, but she liked the opportunity to stretch her legs. And it was such a short walk. Deacon had never considered it a real cause for concern, a thing he would later recall with tremendous bitterness.

Anna was halfway to work when a car that might have been a Ford Tempo or Taurus (or something else similar) veered off the road and ran her down. According to witnesses, the car had previously been moving along in a perfectly straight line at a reasonable speed. Then the driver abruptly accelerated and whipped the vehicle over to the road's shoulder. Anna had no time to react before the car's front end slammed into her and sent her broken body skidding dozens of feet along the side of the road. The car was back on the road and speeding away barely more than a second later, too fast for the few who'd witnessed the incident to get a license number or a definite fix on the make or model. Witness accounts clashed in other ways, including whether the driver was a woman or a man with long hair. The one thing they were all in agreement about was that Anna had been deliberately targeted. It was no accident. She had been murdered.

The police worked the case hard for several weeks without turning up any viable suspects. The car used in the attack couldn't be linked to anyone Anna had known and the vague description of the suspect also led nowhere. In the end, it seemed likely she had been the unfortunate victim of an act of completely random violence. The lead detective in the case was a man named Jack Vincent. The last time Deacon had talked to Vincent, the detective had speculated about the killer's motivations. He believed the perpetrator was your basic thrill-seeking psychopath. He (or she) had likely set out that day with the intent to kill someone. The victim could have been anyone at all. Anna had unfortunately been in the wrong place at the wrong time.

Coupled with the essential unfairness of it all, the prospect of never having anything resembling resolution or closure almost broke Deacon. Rage consumed him for many weeks. During that time he had endless vivid fantasies of tracking down the killer and exacting revenge, all of which unfolded like scenes from lurid B-movies. He wasn't a violent man by nature and hadn't been involved in anything like a real scuffle since middle school. Even in the darkest depths of his despair, he knew thinking this way could never bring him anything like real peace. So the rage burned itself out and in its wake came the numbness. He thought the numbness might last a lot longer.

Maybe for years.

Or maybe his "dark period" would last the rest of his life. He suspected he couldn't endure this way indefinitely. He might even become truly suicidal at some point. But maybe it would be like so many people told him. Time would heal the wounds, or at least soften their sharp edges.

Deacon winced as the second cigarette singed his fingers. He stared at the glowing nub as he let it tumble to the sidewalk. This was another thing he never used to do, these trances he would go into now. He would get lost in his head and lose significant chunks of time. Sometimes it was just a few minutes. Other times he lost hours. He supposed it would worry him if he still gave a shit.

He sighed and reached for the pack again.

And that was when something at the farthest edge of his vision snagged his attention.

2

HIS HEAD SWIVELED TO THE right and he saw a woman dressed in black come strolling down the street. She wore an elegant-looking black dress. She also wore a black hat and her face was hidden by a veil. A black choker encircled her porcelain-white slender neck. Long satin gloves, also black, covered her arms. A corsage of black flowers was affixed to one of her wrists. She looked like an elegant phantom as she passed through the warm glow of the streetlight.

Deacon might have thought the woman was returning home from a funeral if not for the fact the neighborhood wasn't adjacent to any cemeteries. A resident here couldn't just walk home from a graveside service. But the black flowers made him certain her outfit was some kind of costume, though Halloween wasn't until tomorrow. Perhaps she was just taking it out for a dry run of sorts. Twilight might have struck her as an ideal time for such a thing. The thought made Deacon glance at the sky. It was closer to dusk now. In a short while it would be full night.

She was beginning to move past his house now. An impulse caused Deacon to rise from his sitting position and move to the sidewalk, where he stood and watched her go by. Something about her compelled his attention and he wasn't sure what it was. Halloween had always struck him as a lot of good, innocent fun, but this year he had been immune to the holiday's charms. It wasn't difficult to understand why. He was still reeling from his loss and, his mild flirtations with the reaper aside, things morbid or macabre held little appeal for him.

But that nameless, hard-to-pinpoint something within him was responding to something equally hard to identify about this woman. Whatever it was, it was something beyond the standard way a man feels drawn to an alluring woman. The woman in black was slender and somewhat shapely, but beyond that it was difficult to discern anything about her appearance. This was largely because of her attire, which made gauging her age difficult. She didn't move feebly, which only told him she wasn't exceptionally elderly. She could be anywhere from twenty to sixty, perhaps even slightly younger or older. He would have to get closer to make a better determination. With this goal in mind, he took a few steps down the sidewalk toward the driveway as she began to move past his mailbox.

Deacon stopped in his tracks.

What the hell am I doing?

The woman's head turned his way. For a moment that seemed longer than it was, the eyes behind that dark veil looked right at him. A shiver rippled through his body. His heart thumped harder during this moment of silent inspection. The oddest impression came to him as her head swiveled away from him and faced forward again—that the creature lurking behind that veil wasn't human.

He knew the notion was ridiculous, though there were some obvious reasons why it had come to him. His fragile state of mind was the biggest one. The other thing was the imminent arrival of Halloween. That he'd paid the approach of the season for goblins and spooks little mind thus far meant nothing. The trappings of the season were so ubiquitous they'd seeped in and tinged his thoughts regardless of his apathy. And this had rendered him susceptible to the power of suggestion. The woman in black was no ghost or inhuman creature. She was just an ordinary woman caught up in the spirit of the season.

That sense of being noticed and marked by something not of the natural world was nonetheless hard to shake. A meek voice from a remote, paranoid corner of his brain ventured the opinion that he was lucky to still be alive, that the woman in black might have killed him had she not had more important things to do.

Deacon shook his head.

Stop being ridiculous.

She had moved beyond the driveway by the time he became aware of the children trailing after her. They followed her in side-by-side rows of half a dozen. A row of little girls walking along the edge of the asphalt bordering Deacon's yard and a row of little boys on the opposite side of the street. The children were also dressed entirely in black, the girls in little black dresses and the boys in black shorts and formal-looking black shirts. Like the woman leading the strange procession, the girls wore hats with veils hiding their faces. The boys wore black hats with very wide brims tilted low over their ghostly white faces. Their funereal garb made it clear they were somehow associated with the woman in black. The children appeared to take no note of Deacon whatsoever, which was completely okay with him as they sort of scared the living shit out of him. It was eerie how they were moving in perfectly straight lines. There was an almost militaristic precision to it. These were kids. It wasn't natural. They should be taking in their surroundings, turning their heads this way and that, maybe occasionally stumbling then stepping back into line.

These kids, he thought. *They're not really here.*

They're . . . ghosts.

And so is the lady in black.

The rational part of his mind tried to assert itself again. He was clearly still allowing the spooky vibe of the Halloween season to color his perceptions to an absurd degree, an effect heightened by the recent tragedy in his life. Well, maybe so. There was an undeniable thread of logic in this idea.

There was just one problem with it.

How did I not notice the kids until now?

Because he should have seen them much earlier, given their proximity to the woman in black. The boy and girl at the head of each line trailed her by less than a dozen feet. There was a slight bend in the road in the direction from which they had come, but there was nothing that should have obscured his view of the children. It was as if they had materialized out of nowhere during that moment when the veiled woman had been looking at him.

And there was no way that was possible.

Right?

As Deacon stood there on his sidewalk attempting to puzzle it out, his ears began to pick up the rising buzz of an engine. He realized he'd been hearing it for several seconds before becoming consciously aware of it. Headlights appeared in the distance an instant after he realized what he was hearing. They came swooping around another bend in the road, and then the car—a dark sedan of some type—was bearing down on the woman and the children. It was moving along at a fast clip, too fast for a winding, narrow residential street like this one, especially with the onset of evening.

Deacon started running across the yard, shouting desperate warnings and waving his hands, hoping against hope the reckless driver would have time to see the woman and her young attendants before it was too late. But the car never altered course as it came roaring down the street. An image of Anna walking obliviously by the side of the road on a bright summer's day came unbidden to his mind. He hadn't been there when she died—hadn't seen that moment of gruesome impact firsthand—but it was all too easy to imagine. The conjured images had taunted him for months, defying his best efforts to shunt them away. And now a similar scenario was playing out right in front of his eyes. That he was being forced to bear witness to such a thing so soon after Anna's death was like a giant middle finger from God. The universe was torturing him. He was being punished for some forgotten or unknown sin.

The car was upon them. Its headlights lit up the stretch of road in front of Deacon's house, and the woman's form was a stark silhouette against the glare. She did not appear to cringe or even break stride until the car struck her and mowed down the children. Deacon dropped to his knees, tears filling his eyes, the horror of it all overwhelming him. The car slowed down for a moment as it moved past his house, and he had a sense the driver was looking at him.

Deacon felt a chill run down his spine. The car that had run down Anna had been a dark sedan. He swiped at his eyes and struggled to stand, his shaky legs betraying him on the first attempt. He tried again and finally got upright. The car's engine revved. By the time he could see again, it was speeding away, disappearing around the next bend in the road. He saw its taillights recede and then vanish as it turned down a side road.

He was staggered by a sense the perpetrator of this fresh atrocity was the same murderous piece of shit who had killed Anna. This was the overheated, rage-fueled part of his psyche surfacing again. This part of him resisted logic and rejected any alternate explanations without even considering them. Logic often had no place in matters of life and death. Anna's murderer had returned to kill again. Not only that, but he had slowed down to take a look, to savor and drink in the spectacle of Deacon's resurgent grief. Incontrovertible proof of this wasn't necessary. He felt it in his bones.

It's someone I know.

This was another thing he felt with absolute certainty. It wouldn't wash from the perspective of the law. They had chased down all possible leads in that area. But Deacon didn't care. The killer was someone he knew. Why the police were unable to identify who that person was, he didn't know. And it didn't matter. He would do whatever he had to do to track that person down and mete out some kind of justice. So what if he had never been prone to violence? This person was a monster.

He had to be stopped.

Killed.

He had this thought in mind when he realized something was wrong. The neighborhood was too quiet. He heard the low buzz of the nearby streetlamp and the distant barking of a dog, but there was something else he should be hearing. It took him another beat to realize what that missing element was. He had been too preoccupied with the mystery of the assailant's identity and thoughts of vengeance to note it until now. But when it did come to him, the shock of it jolted him. *The woman. The kids.* They had been hit. Struck down. The street should be filled with the agonized wails of the injured, but there was only that eerie, almost total silence.

Deacon was still staring off in the direction of the departed car. He turned slowly to his left. No broken bodies were lying in the street. His head swiveled farther to the left. The procession of dark-clad apparitions was still marching down the street. They were about to go around the next soft bend in the road. The car had not hit them. It had driven *through* them. Because they weren't there, at least not in physical form. The driver probably hadn't even seen them. This insight did nothing to shake his certainty regarding that person's identity, but he nonetheless knew it was true.

The killer hadn't seen them because they were dead already.

They were ghosts.

The reflexive denial that had accompanied this thought before did not recur. They were ghosts. No doubt about it. No one else could see them, but for reasons he didn't yet understand Deacon *could* see them. His heart beat faster again and the October chill raised fresh goosebumps on his arms. And yet he wasn't afraid. He knew he should be terrified, but he just wasn't. That would come later.

An impulse divorced from conscious thought set Deacon's feet in motion.

He stepped into the street and hurried after the walking revenants.

3

THE DEAD PARADE TOOK A winding course through the large suburban neighborhood, frequently turning down side streets before again continuing for a while down longer thoroughfares. The neighborhood was old and sprawling. Some sections of it dated to around the Second World War while others had been added as recently as the 1990s, which was why the layout of the place was somewhat disjointed. This also accounted for the diverse array of architectural styles. The older houses were smaller and modest in appearance, with little thought given to anything other than functionality. A few of the newer houses were almost ostentatious by comparison, including a few that looked like scaled-down Victorian manors.

Deacon had never taken this long a walk around his neighborhood. He felt like a kid who had gone off exploring. It reminded him of how he used to spend hours traipsing around the large expanse of woods behind his parents' house. Back then he would lose himself in imaginary adventures. He would pretend he was stalking Bigfoot, or he would skulk from tree to tree, carefully peering around the trunks as he played at being a soldier eluding the enemy. This thing he was doing tonight was kind of like that. It was an adventure, too. But there was a big difference. This time the danger might be real.

Another person, say someone who had not recently ceased caring much about his well-being, would likely not have elected to follow a procession of ghosts. A sensible person would have immediately run back inside the house to bolt all the doors and shuttered all the windows. Because he should be frightened out of his wits right now. Ghosts were supposed to be scary. All the movies Deacon had ever seen about them were clear on this count.

Okay, so he wasn't afraid of them for whatever reason, but he also wasn't certain *why* he was following them. They didn't appear to be going anywhere in particular, or so it seemed from their circuitous, apparently random path through the neighborhood, nor were they doing anything all that interesting. Yes, the mere fact of their existence was pretty damn interesting in itself, but following them around endlessly as they marched could become dull after a while. More than once he considered turning around and heading back home, but the prospect of sealing himself away in that empty house held even less appeal.

On occasion, though, something did happen to spice up the proceedings. Now and then a car would come along and blow through them just as the sedan had in front of his house. The ghosts would disperse in a cloud of black smoke before rapidly reassuming the illusion of a physical form. This would happen in a space of seconds, almost too fast to see. Other times they would happen across another live human being out for an evening stroll. Some of these people would acknowledge Deacon with a nod or raise a hand in greeting. But not one of them ever seemed aware of the ghosts. The first time one of these people—a plump older lady in a workout suit—walked through them, it made Deacon laugh. His amusement stemmed from the fact that this was so much like scenes from countless movies he'd watched over the years. But the woman interpreted his reaction as derisive laughter directed at her. She shot him a nasty look before hurrying away from him. Deacon felt bad about that, but explaining himself would be pointless. It would just make him sound like a crazy person.

He wondered about that.

Maybe I am *crazy.*

Common wisdom held that ghosts didn't exist. Deacon had always counted himself among the non-believers. Before tonight his opinion had been that a belief in the supernatural was indicative of either an uneducated mind or a mind plagued by irrational magical thinking. People who believed in any form of life after death just weren't equipped to deal with the harsh realities of existence. The idea that they would just rot in the ground and not continue elsewhere in some other form terrified them. It was the world's oldest coping mechanism, a beautiful lie people told themselves so they could sleep at night.

Except that, he had been wrong all along.

If nothing else, this parade of ghosts was proof of some form of afterlife. The only alternate explanation was that his sanity had cracked somewhere along the way. But the problem with that idea was that he didn't *feel* crazy. In fact, despite his dark frame of mind, he had never felt more connected with reality. What he was seeing wasn't a hallucination. At no point in his life had he exhibited symptoms of schizophrenia or any other serious mental condition. He also believed he wasn't experiencing some abrupt psychotic break. There would be other telltale indications, he was sure.

The ghosts were real.

He didn't know why no one else could see them and it didn't matter.

They were as real as the ground beneath his feet.

Acknowledging this inevitably led his thoughts back to Anna and caused him to further ponder tonight's confluence of strange events. He now knew death didn't necessarily mean a person's essence was forever extinguished. This meant it was possible Anna still existed in some form. Whether that was as a ghost here on Earth or as a soul ascended to Heaven or some other alternate plane, he didn't know.

The important thing was that she still existed. Not just as a corpse moldering in the ground, but as a conscious entity.

Somehow, some way, she . . . *continued.*

The thought earned him a fleeting moment of staggering joy. The feeling was so intense he almost dropped to his knees again right there in the middle of the street. He had felt nothing remotely like it since before the sixteenth of July. But other implications tempered the feeling. There must be some reason the ghosts had appeared to him on the same night Anna's killer had decided to cruise by his house. Maybe the woman in black was somehow connected to Anna. His eyes opened wider at the thought she might *be* Anna. It wasn't out of the realm of possibility. The ghost's height and body shape were about right.

However, as tempting as it was to believe the apparition he'd been following was his dead lover, he didn't buy it. It was a feeling deep in his gut. She wasn't Anna, he was sure of it, but she was somehow connected to her. The idea had no foundation in verifiable fact, but that same deep instinct was strong in this assertion. Maybe he was seeing her because she had come to lead him to wherever Anna was now.

Deacon frowned.

Does that mean I have my own rendezvous with death tonight?

On that count, his gut was silent.

If that *did* happen, it was a good time for it, with the annual celebration of all things dark and macabre imminent. The neighborhood was bristling with houses dressed up for the season. There were pumpkins on almost every porch. Many yards were festooned with elaborate Halloween decorations and displays. As the procession turned down yet another side street, Deacon spied ersatz ghosts fashioned from white sheets and hay stuffing, black silhouettes of witches and plastic skeletons adorning doors, and an excessive amount of fake cobwebbing stretched over rails and porch corners. One porch was bracketed on either end by cutouts of Freddy Krueger and Leatherface.

As Deacon moved past the house, the cutout of Freddy appeared to turn its head and track his movements. That was freaky, but he was able to dismiss it as an instance of runaway imagination fueled by a trick of the dim lighting. However, when a white sheet ghost in another yard rose from its perch atop a bale of hay and floated upward into the air, he knew it was time to give up rationalizing any aspect of what was happening. The neighborhood was becoming a playground for all things supernatural as the evening lengthened. The ghost procession was only one element of a larger picture. There was a whole world of similar entities. Deacon suspected the spirits were always there, occupying some thin space between the mortal world and the mysterious other planes of existence, a space just beyond mortal powers of perception. For Deacon, however, that veil had been lifted.

There had to be a reason for that other than random occurrence. He only hoped he would find out what it was soon.

Deacon felt a chill as the procession turned down still another street, a deeper one than the nip in the October air could account for.

There was something perceptibly different in the atmosphere in this section of the neighborhood, a low electric charge he felt in his bones and the fillings in his teeth. But that wasn't the only thing different here. A glance at the street sign as he turned the corner told Deacon they were now walking down Willowblack Lane. It was a strange name, but he immediately saw that it was an appropriate one. There were willow trees in several of the yards. Oddly, though, the leaves of the trees were very dark instead of green, almost . . . black. He had never seen anything of the sort before. It made him think of the corsage affixed to the woman in black's wrist.

But there were far stranger sights on Willowblack Lane, a name he was certain he'd never heard before—and not because he didn't know every nook and cranny of his neighborhood. He soon began to suspect this was a secret street, one accessible only to supernatural beings and those occasional mortals—like himself—who were deliberately lured to it. All the houses here reminded him of spooky manors in old-time horror movies, with many Gothic architectural touches such as spires and pointed arches. Ornate iron gates blocked access to some yards. Overhead, thunder rumbled and white flashes intermittently lit up the sky. But Deacon suspected this was only for show, an atmosphere-appropriate light and noise display. Despite the thunder and lightning, there was no rain, and it'd been a clear, cloudless night prior to taking that turn down this peculiarly haunted street. The whole experience was like wandering around the appointed horror section of some giant movie studio lot.

The name of the street bothered him. He couldn't help reversing it in his head. Black willow. It was uncomfortably close to *black widow*, which of course made him think of the veiled lady in black, who could purposefully be leading him to some grim fate. Maybe he was overthinking it and conjuring implications with no actual correlation to the reality of what was happening. Then again, he was following a bunch of ghosts down a spook show street. It was possible he wasn't being nearly paranoid *enough*.

Yet somehow he still wasn't afraid.

Not yet.

The street teemed with many other sights and sounds of horror. Shrill screams resonated in the night. Creepy capering shadows appeared in the brilliantly lit windows of some houses. The door to one house blew open with a dramatic bang and a shrieking woman ran outside, followed by a large, grinning man in a blood-stained butcher's apron. The big man clutched a bloody meat cleaver in one of his enormous hands. He chased the woman down and tackled her on the sidewalk outside his house. The cleaver went up and down, blood flying as the razor-sharp blade punched through tender flesh. Deacon didn't let it bother him. He knew it was all part of the show. So was the black cat sitting atop a mailbox that arched its back and hissed at him as he walked by. He didn't believe a real woman had been butchered in front of his eyes. Or if it was real, it was just a repeat showing of something that had happened long ago, a reel of film playing on an endless loop. He had no doubt he would see the same thing again if he stood outside that particular house long enough.

The procession began to slow as it neared the end of the block. The last house on the left was the tallest Deacon had seen on Willowblack Lane. It featured the same kind of Gothic architecture common to the houses on this street, but it was several stories taller than any of the others. And it was far darker than the rest. The materials used to construct it looked as black as the leaves of the willow trees in the yard. Like many other houses here, the yard to this one was bordered by a tall iron fence, but in this case, the ornate gate was standing open. The iron arch above the open gate was emblazoned with a three-digit number—716.

As in 716 Willowblack Lane, presumably.

Deacon was unsurprised when the woman in black left the street and walked through the gate, leading the procession of ghost children up a winding path toward the imposing house. He paused for a moment on the sidewalk outside the gate and stared up at the towering black manor. As he looked at it, another flash of lightning lit up the sky, illuminating the house's jagged dark outline. The house was dark inside, too. The only light visible burned in a single window on the top floor. A shadowy form passed across the curtained window and lingered there only briefly before disappearing again.

The procession was halfway up the yard before Deacon elected to continue following them. He had felt his first tickle of real fear while staring up at the house. Maybe most of what he'd seen on Willowblack Lane existed for shock purposes only, but he suspected some genuine menace lurked within the walls of this place. In the end, he decided to keep going because he felt like he had been led here for a reason. That didn't mean he might not come to harm here, but he wanted to find out what that reason was anyway.

He heard a flutter of leathery wings as he stepped through the gate, flinching as a bat squeaked in his ear before flapping its wings again and flying away. Deacon watched it go and almost felt like laughing. All the Halloween and old-time horror tropes were on display. It was as if he had been granted access to the world's greatest haunted theme park, one replete with the most convincing 3-D animatronic creations money could buy. But this was no theme park. The things in this realm weren't special effects. They had real shape and substance of some sort, regardless of whether they could inflict actual harm.

The woman in black climbed a tall set of concrete steps to a long porch stretching from one end of the house to the other. She never broke stride as the front door swung open in front of her, disappearing through the dark doorway as the children followed her. Deacon hesitated a final time as he reached the bottom step and stared into the perfect blackness beyond the open door. A powerful sense that this was his last chance to turn back and rejoin the normal world overcame him. But the moment passed quickly and he began to climb the steps. He still needed to know why he was here. Also, he had a hunch he wouldn't be allowed to depart Willowblack Lane without having seen this through. He would be imprisoned here forever, perhaps even die here. In time he would become just another part of the eternal spook show. It wasn't an appealing prospect. There was only one way out and that was through this door. How he knew that he couldn't say. It was just another of those things he felt as clearly as the tick of his pulse in his throat.

Deacon stepped through the door into the deep darkness. Once inside, however, the blackness became less absolute. He stood in a large foyer adjacent to several even larger rooms cloaked in darkness. Shadowy forms flitted about in the darkness, their vague outlines occasionally discernible because some of the forms carried flickering candles. To his right, a winding staircase crawled upward along the inner walls of the house. Candles glowed in sconces lining the stairway. The woman in black and her young attendants had gone that way. He saw the faint form of the last little boy turning upon reaching the second-floor landing.

A creaking of unoiled hinges signaled the closing of the door behind him. The heavy door slammed into its frame with a loud bang of finality. It also caused a puff of dust to rain down from the rafters. The spirits that inhabited this place weren't big on housekeeping. He coughed and waved away the cloud of dust. Then he let out a breath and began to climb the staircase, moving fast to catch up to the procession. He slowed as he made the second-floor landing. The children were less than a dozen feet ahead of him now. He shot a glance down a long hallway before following them up the next flight of stairs.

More candles were burning in sconces down that way. He heard laughter and moans. Some of the latter struck him as sexual, while other times the moans seemed a product of pain. His imagination furnished an image of someone imprisoned within one of the countless rooms, a person tied to a bed who was being flogged with a cat o' nine tails. He thought about that further and realized the moans could be a product of ecstasy *and* pain. The thought awakened a prurient part of him that had been largely dormant since Anna's death. He considered taking a walk down that hallway to peek inside doors until he found the source of the moans. It alarmed him to find this part of him *wanted* to see naked flesh being lashed with a whip. It was odd because he'd never been an S&M enthusiast. Another alarming possibility occurred to him—that the house was reaching into his brain and implanting these impulses. An absurd idea on the surface, but it was one no crazier than anything he'd witnessed.

Turning away from the long hallway required a significant exertion of will. It was as if something down there had almost gotten its hooks inside him. He felt the pull of whatever it was reluctantly sliding away as he began to climb the next flight of stairs. A glance upward revealed that he'd lost sight of the ghosts and he again willed himself to move faster. This house was full of malign spirits that would love to seduce and corrupt him. It would be all too easy to fall victim to them, especially if he continued to allow himself to be distracted. He had to remain focused on the main goal—following the woman in black. He was sure she had some purpose in leading him here other than hurting or torturing him. He might have been wrong about this, but he felt the number above the gate outside gave the notion extra credence, corresponding as it did with the date of Anna's death. That couldn't just be a coincidence.

Deacon again caught up to the tail end of the ghost procession. This time he kept his eyes straight ahead and refused to look down any more hallways, gritting his teeth and filling his head with white noise any time he heard particularly intriguing sounds emanating from those directions, which was often. The procession ascended flight after flight of stairs. Deacon lost count somewhere after ten. It began to seem as if the house must be as tall as a skyscraper, though he knew that wasn't possible. Or was it? He remembered being struck by how big the house was as he stood outside and stared up at it. There was no doubt the house was enormous. It had seemed several times as tall—at least—as the next tallest house on Willowblack Lane. But certainly not tall enough to contain so many floors and endless flights of stairs.

Unless, he thought, *it's bigger inside than outside.*

Like Doctor Who's TARDIS, or like the house in that book Anna had loaned him once, the one where a bunch of young assholes got lost while driving through a mountain range and wound up at the creepy manor home of a monster disguised as a human. It was yet another seemingly ridiculous notion he found he couldn't reject. There was no denying the truth of it as they continued to ascend additional flights of stairs. After a while, he realized the really strange thing was how he wasn't becoming physically tired. He had climbed at least a dozen and a half flights without getting winded. He was a young guy in decent shape, but he should be gasping for breath by now. It made him wonder whether he might be dead already. Maybe only ghosts could find their way to Willowblack Lane. That might have been the key to this whole odd situation. It would explain so much.

Except he didn't feel dead. He was aware of the beating of his heart and could feel his breath going in and out. Those things alone should have been enough to bury the notion, but then he wondered whether the sensations might be illusory, nothing more than persistent echoes of a mortal existence that had ended. The ghost equivalent of phantom limb sensations. But wouldn't he remember *how* he had died?

He thought so.

And yet there was nothing like that in his memory.

That didn't mean it hadn't happened, of course. Maybe the experience of death was so traumatic the actual circumstances of it got blocked from your ghost memory. Thinking about it was giving him a headache. Wait . . . could ghosts *get* headaches?

He groaned in frustration.

Deacon was saved from having to think about it any further when he reached the next landing. At long last, the procession had reached the top floor of the house. The woman in black was leading the children down a long candlelit hallway. Deacon followed them. Most of the doors on either side of the narrow passage were closed, but a few stood open. Soft candlelight was detectable through these openings. His curiosity flared up again and he was unable to resist peeking inside one of the rooms. A nude woman with pale skin was stretched out across a bed. The top half of her face was covered with a black party mask, but she smiled when she became aware of Deacon's scrutiny, beckoning him into the room with an extended forefinger.

She was the most beautiful woman he'd ever seen. Her long hair was an alluring shade of blood red. It was fanned across the white pillow beneath her. He ached to run his fingers through it, could almost feel how silky soft it would be. Deacon wiped moisture from his mouth with the back of a hand and took a step toward the door.

He yelped and jumped when a cold finger prodded his lower back.

He turned around and saw one of the dead children looking at him. It was one of the boys. With his head turned upward, his face was no longer hidden beneath the wide brim of the hat. What Deacon saw there made him feel like screaming. His flesh was rotting, his tongue was black, and maggots squirmed in his eye sockets. Deacon directed a glance at the stretch of hallway behind the boy and saw that the rest of the procession, including the woman in black, had disappeared. He made himself look at the dead boy's face again when the ghost began speaking in a surprisingly clear, almost delicately precise tone.

"You can't go in there. The woman on the bed isn't for you."

Well, damn. Probably for the best anyway. I think she's not what she seems.

Deacon cleared his throat. "Um . . . okay. Where did your friends go?"

"Into the Nothing."

"The what?"

"The Nothing."

"That's what I thought you said. What does that mean?"

The child ignored his question. "You are to close your eyes and count to ten. When you open them again, you are to go to the last room at the end of the hallway. There is something for you there."

Deacon frowned. "What are you talking about, kid? What's waiting for me? Why don't I just go down there right—"

The child's tone was resolute as he interrupted. "Close your eyes and count to ten."

Deacon closed his eyes. He was disturbed by a fleeting sense this had happened against his will, that something had reached inside him and taken control long enough to compel obedience. He tried telling himself he had merely acceded to the kid's wishes to shut him up and get down to business. But he suspected this wasn't true.

He counted to ten and opened his eyes.

The dead boy was gone and the hallway was empty. The door to his right was closed now, the thing pretending to be a beautiful woman safely hidden away behind it. But Deacon remained where he was a moment longer. He saw a slanted wedge of bright light up ahead at the presumed end of the impossibly long hallway. The light marked the room he was to enter, he was sure of it. Whatever he'd been brought here for was inside that room. He wanted to know what it was, of course, but he couldn't help feeling a deep apprehension about it. The creeping sense it was somehow connected to Anna returned yet again.

But he couldn't stand here forever.

So he let out a breath and started down the hallway again. The sound of his breathing seemed very loud in the deserted passage, as did the creak of the floorboards beneath his footsteps. Other sounds spooked him as he continued down the hallway. Doors eased open behind him with low creaks. There were whispered come-ons and invitations. He couldn't quite make out the words, but he caught their meaning anyway. They contained promises of great pleasure if only he would come inside. One time, however, he heard a bloodcurdling scream followed by a terrified woman's shrill, desperate cry for help. Her terror sounded real, but Deacon knew it was only more manipulation. The things living here would do whatever they could to lure him into their traps. More than once he became certain something had slipped out of a room and was following him. One time he was sure he felt the breath of some infernal beast tickling the fine hairs on the back of his neck, but when he whirled around to confront his pursuer the hallway behind him was empty. When he turned around again and resumed his trek down the hallway, he heard a faint exhalation of mocking laughter.

He picked up the pace after that and did his best to stay focused on the bright wedge of light at the end of the hallway. It occurred to him that breaking into a run might be the smart thing to do, but he was unable to act on the impulse. Something was restraining him, restricting him to a fast walk. But it didn't feel as if that alien something had truly taken control over his body. It was more subtle than that, more akin to being held on a leash. That something wanted him to go to the room, but it also wished for him to endure the unique trials of negotiating this passageway. There was a troubling hint of sadism to it.

However, when it seemed like the hallway would go on forever, there was an abrupt sense of its length retracting, and the door seemed to come rushing toward him. There was also a sense of being whisked along at high speed on a moving walkway as that slanted wedge of light zoomed closer. When this sensation ended abruptly seconds later, the open door—and the beckoning light inside it—were less than a dozen feet away from where he stood.

He approached the wedge of light with great trepidation. There was something in that room he was meant to see, but now that it was within reach, fresh doubts arose regarding whether he *wanted* to see whatever it was. Again, however, he dismissed his apprehensions and willed himself to resume moving forward. This was about sheer pragmatism as much as anything else. The things in the rooms behind him had more or less behaved during his journey down the hallway because something had compelled them to do so. He had a feeling that wouldn't be the case if he attempted a retreat without first entering this room. The beasts would be let off their leashes. *Something* would get him. And he was sure whatever got him would delight in torturing him in the worst ways possible for as long as possible.

He arrived at the door and peeked inside.

He frowned.

What he saw was a sparsely furnished room of average size. The trim and fixtures all looked very old, as did the slightly uneven floorboards. The walls were a hideous shade of mustard yellow. The room was illuminated by a single bright bulb that dangled from a long cord in the middle of the ceiling. A small wooden table was set against one of the walls. Atop the table was a television, a boxy old one with a rabbit ears antenna. The television was on, but its screen showed only a pattern of white snow.

A wooden chair had been placed directly in front of the television.

There was nothing else in the room.

Deacon heaved another nervous breath and reluctantly entered the room.

4

ONCE HE WAS SEVERAL FEET inside the room, Deacon felt a rush of air as the door slammed shut behind him. He jumped at the sound of the door banging into its frame. Curiosity sent him to the door to test the knob. He knew what would happen, but he felt the need to verify his hunch, which was proven correct when the doorknob refused to turn. An impulse to batter the door with his fists and shout to be let out came and went in the blink of an eye. He would not be released until he'd fulfilled his purpose here, whatever the hell it was.

The television's pattern of snow disappeared for a millisecond, replaced by a jittery image Deacon had only glimpsed from the edge of his vision before it disappeared again. He moved closer to the television and peered intently at it. Time stretched. Minutes passed without the image recurring. He wasn't even sure what he'd seen, except for the vaguest impression of treetops against a bright sky. There had been something else, but it was escaping him. The image hadn't held long enough.

He was about to give up on the television when he heard a scraping of wood against wood. He then felt the edge of the chair against the backs of his legs. Deacon did a slow turn and scanned every corner of the room. He was still alone, at least as far as he could tell. There might be things lurking just beyond his perception because, despite the room's apparent emptiness, the chair had moved.

Clearly he was meant to sit in it.

He was getting a little weary of being manipulated by the mysterious forces at play here. But resistance wasn't a viable option. He'd learned that lesson well enough already.

So he sat.

The television's pattern of snow went away. Deacon leaned forward in the chair and frowned at a jittery image of a road. The image was in black and white. Beyond the road stood the trees he'd glimpsed before. There was something familiar about them, but before he could figure it out the picture rolled, a horizontal black bar rising from the bottom to the top of the screen a few times. In those moments, he saw the image in confusing fragments. The road on top of the trees, then the reverse, and back again. It was like what watching a television with bad reception must have been like decades before his birth.

The picture finally stopped rolling.

Deacon leaned forward again. Moments later, he realized why the image seemed familiar. He might have recognized it earlier, but the black and white picture had thrown him. He had assumed he was seeing something from long ago, but that wasn't the case at all. As he watched, the camera began to pull back, allowing for a wider-angle view of the road. His heart started pounding harder in his chest. He had a sick feeling he knew what he was about to see. He didn't want to see it, but he felt powerless to look away.

A car whooshed by on the screen and the camera began to turn, this time focusing on the side of the road. Deacon's heart lurched at the sight of a beautiful young blonde woman. She had a subtle smile on her face and was walking along as if she didn't have a care in the world. Then the image of a car filled the frame for an instant before its front end slammed into the woman and sent her body sliding down the roadside at high speed. A perfect shot of the car's rear end was briefly visible before it veered back onto the road and sped away.

Deacon's hands curled into shaking fists. He gritted his teeth so hard it felt as if the molars might split apart from the pressure. The psychic impact of what he had watched had him on the verge of hyperventilating. Somehow this strange black house at the end of Willowblack Lane could capture moments from the past and deliver them to this broken-down old television. This should have been impossible, but he knew what he had seen was real. That pretty blonde had not been an actress hired for her resemblance to Anna. It was her, and he'd just watched footage showing the moment of her death.

Before he could think too much about that, the image on the screen began to rewind. There was a fuzzy white line across the middle of the screen as the dark-colored sedan rapidly reversed course and Anna's broken body came up off the ground. The picture then paused for a moment. Deacon took another look around the room. As expected, there was no one standing behind him operating a remote control. Whatever was controlling the images on the screen was something that couldn't be seen.

The image was taken off pause the moment he faced forward again. The camera angle shifted yet again, pulling back to focus on the road. When the sedan came into view this time, what Deacon saw was a close-up shot of its interior. The witnesses had been right about the driver's long hair. Now, however, he could see that the driver had been a young woman. Her hair was a dark shade of auburn. The way it hung in the frame obscured some of her face, but he was able to discern enough of her features to trigger a faint feeling of recognition. The woman's identity didn't come to him right away, but he was again sure she was someone he had known, maybe someone he hadn't seen in a very long time.

Deacon's brow furrowed as he struggled to remember her. But the name remained just beyond the reach of his memory. This must have been someone he'd known only in passing. He thought this because he was a young man who, for the most part, was in full possession of his faculties. His memory couldn't possibly be this bad.

He banged a fist against his hip in frustration.

Then he gasped in sudden fright when he felt a hand fall lightly on his left shoulder. He craned his head around for a glimpse of the hand and let out a shuddery breath when he saw the woman in black's satin glove. His heart started racing at the realization she was right behind him. She had materialized out of nowhere, just as the ghostly children had on the street in front of his house. Her other hand molded itself against the back of his head and forced him to face forward again.

Deacon shivered as he sensed her leaning closer to him. He shivered again when her veil brushed his ear. "You know this woman." Her breath as she spoke made him cringe. It was redolent of the grave, a musky mix of rot and corruption that made his skin crawl. "She murdered your beloved."

The repulsion she stirred in him was reflexive and almost overwhelming. Choking back the bile that kept trying to rise into his throat wasn't easy, but he managed to do it. His disgust wasn't as important as the subject under discussion. He swallowed hard and forced out a reply: "Tell me her name."

She chuckled, a dry, creaking, sinisterly unnerving sound. "I can provide that information, but first you must answer a question."

Deacon stared at the maddeningly familiar visage frozen on the screen. He needed to know that woman's identity. The knowledge was worth any price. "What do you want to know?"

Another of those unnerving graveyard chuckles. "Would you like to be reunited with your lover?"

The answer to that was obvious and Deacon opened his mouth to say the words, but he hesitated at the last moment, wondering how that could even be possible. Anna was dead and there could be no reversing that. Right?

The gloved hand squeezed his shoulder. "You can be together again. This I promise you."

Deacon's discomfort deepened with the possibility that the woman in black had looked inside his mind. She might merely have intuited his thoughts. Even non-ghouls could do such things back in the normal world. But Deacon had a feeling this was something more than that. And there was something else to consider. The spirit might be toying with him, taunting him with promises of things it had no intention of delivering for the sheer sadistic fun of it. He was in a dangerous place surrounded by dangerous things. It would be a mistake to assume the woman in black was any less malicious than the rest of them.

The dead thing squeezed his shoulder again, her touch conveying a sense of insidious intimacy. He wanted to bolt out of the chair and get away from her, but he knew she would not allow it. The attempt might even earn him some form of dreadful punishment. She laughed softly and he was sure she had looked into his mind again. "If you want no part of this, I will return you to your home and wipe your memory of these events. However, make no mistake . . . I can deliver what I promise. Now give me your answer."

Deacon sighed.

In the end, it didn't matter whether the woman in black was lying. If there was even the slightest chance he could be with Anna again, he had to play along.

"Yes. I'd like to be with her again."

Another creaky chuckle and rush of putrid breath. "Good."

The woman in black told him two more things.

She gave him a name, one he recognized after an additional moment's thought.

And she assigned him a task.

~

Deacon's eyes fluttered open and he was again on the little porch outside his rental house. The pack of cigarettes and the Zippo were next to him on the top step. A dizzying sense of disorientation gripped him for a moment. His head was swimming and he felt as if he'd come out of a deep sleep. But the memories of what he'd seen on Willowblack Lane remained vivid in his mind. They didn't fragment and fall apart the way dreams do a few moments after returning to consciousness. He nonetheless briefly allowed himself the dubious comfort of believing none of it had been real. All that spook-show weirdness being a nightmare was infinitely more logical than the idea any of it had happened.

There was something in his clenched right hand. He opened it and frowned at a crumpled piece of paper. Something was written on it. Before examining it more closely, he glanced up and down the street and saw no one in the vicinity. If some joker had come along and pushed some message into his hand while he was out like a light, he or she was long gone.

He didn't believe any such thing had happened anyway.

He straightened out the piece of paper and squinted at the name scrawled upon it in black ink: *Marie.*

His frown deepened as he pondered the name. After a moment, though, his features smoothed out again as he remembered what the woman in black had whispered in his ear.

Marie . . .

Marie Cavanaugh.

She was a person he hadn't thought about in a very long time. But he was thinking about her now, oh yes, very dark thoughts indeed.

THE HALLOWEEN BRIDE

After a while, Deacon gathered his smokes and lighter and went inside his house with the intent of going to bed early. He wanted to be as rested as possible when he woke up tomorrow.

He had a big day ahead of him.

5

DEACON GLEANED ALL THE ADDITIONAL bits of information he needed with some Internet research. Early the next afternoon he drove out to a neighborhood he hadn't visited in a long time. It was a smaller neighborhood than the one he lived in now, a smattering of middle-class homes tucked away in a largely undeveloped corner of semi-rural land on the opposite side of town. He had been out here two other times in his life, back in his sophomore year of high school. That was when he had very briefly dated the girl who would murder Anna years later.

The way the houses were situated on that winding stretch of tree-shrouded road worked to Deacon's advantage. There was a significant amount of distance between most of them, and the house Marie had inherited from her late parents was set far enough back from the road that there was no need to park his car out of sight somewhere else and walk to it. He pulled into the semi-circular concrete driveway and parked next to Marie's maroon Ford Taurus.

Deacon got out of his car and walked around to the front of the Taurus, where he squatted and studied the vehicle's dented front bumper. There were dents in the grille, as well. He had no doubt the dents were from the impact of Anna's body hitting the front of the car. Marie probably hadn't bothered to get the damage repaired because, for one thing, it wasn't that glaring, and also local auto body repair shops might have been advised to be on the lookout for cars matching this one's description bearing this kind of damage. It would probably be safe to get it fixed now. The police had given up looking for the killer a while ago. Anna's friends and family had started telling themselves it had only been a terrible accident after all.

But Deacon knew better.

He stood up and turned away from the Taurus to stare at the front of the house. There were no lights on inside as far as he could tell, but that wouldn't be necessary with the bright light of the afternoon sun shining down. No one seemed to be staring out at him. He saw no forms outlined in the windows. A grinning Jack-o'-lantern was propped atop an upended bale of hay in a corner of the porch. It was the sole Halloween decoration.

Deacon approached the porch and climbed the steps to knock on the screen door. The door behind it was opened a moment later and Marie peered out at him through the glass window with an expression that betrayed only mild curiosity. There was no wariness in her casual posture. The little smile tugging at the corners of her mouth hinted at pleasure. It took Deacon a moment to realize she was happy to see him. He had to work hard to hold back an eruption of hate. If she sensed his inner struggle, she gave no indication of it.

"Well, well, well," she said in a clear, faintly lilting voice. "Deacon Croswell. Good to see you again. God, it's been how long?"

She had recognized him immediately, even after all this time. Given what he knew now, this wasn't surprising. She had been keeping tabs on him all these years. "Since high school," he said, struggling to keep his tone even. "Not quite a decade ago."

Marie laughed heartily, her pale cheeks flushing with good humor. "Really? So long ago? It seems like just yesterday."

She flipped long auburn locks out of her face and smiled. Marie looked far better than he remembered. She was tall for a woman, maybe a couple of inches shy of six feet. Back then she'd been awkward, but she had filled out and grown into her body in a way he might have found devastatingly attractive in a woman who wasn't a murderer. She wore stylish clothes and her hair looked like she had it tended to regularly at an expensive salon. A woman in her position shouldn't seem so perfectly relaxed. Deacon didn't get a stupid vibe from her. She had to know he had guessed she was Anna's killer, which was why her whole calm and assured demeanor was so infuriating.

There was an obvious explanation.

She didn't consider him a threat.

Well, that was an attitude he would have to fix.

He forced a smile. "Look, Marie, could I come in? There's something I'd like to talk to you about."

She laughed softly. "Oh, I bet there is."

Deacon frowned. "What's that supposed to mean?"

Her smile turned mischievous and she arched an eyebrow. "Like you don't know." Her tone was light and playful, as if they were two old friends engaging in a familiar bit of banter. It was another odd piece in an increasingly strange puzzle. She unlocked the screen door and pushed it open. "Come on in."

Deacon pulled the door open wider and followed her into the house. Again, displaying her utter lack of concern, she put her back to him and led him through a series of rooms that stirred very dim old memories. When he spied a long sectional in the living room, he paused briefly and let his gaze linger on it. An image from some eight years earlier surged out of his subconscious mind and snapped into clear focus. He saw Marie sitting on the edge of the sectional. Her head was hanging down and she had her face in her hands. She was crying because he'd told her he wasn't interested in seeing her anymore. Thinking about it failed to produce any sympathy for her. He had broken up with her a long time ago. After only a couple of dates. It was absurd that she'd remained fixated on him for so long based on so little.

Deacon tore his gaze away from the sofa. He frowned. Marie had disappeared. He found her in the kitchen, where she was busy opening a bottle of wine, using a stainless-steel corkscrew. Two empty wine glasses sat on an island in the middle of the kitchen. She looked up and smiled when he came into the room. "There you are. I thought you got lost."

"I was just . . . reminiscing." He indicated the wine glasses with a tilt of his chin. "Is one of those for me?"

"Of course." The cork came free of the bottle with a subdued *pop*. Marie twisted the cork off the corkscrew and dropped it in a waste basket under the island. Deacon glanced at the corkscrew. She saw him looking at it and arched an eyebrow. "Come now. That wouldn't make a very effective weapon."

Deacon tried out another phony smile and attempted a tone of nonchalance. "Why would I want a weapon?"

Marie filled both glasses to the halfway point and set the bottle down. "Because I killed that harlot you've been seeing the last two years. Why else?"

Deacon's false smile slipped and he again had to work hard to keep a lid on his anger. He didn't want to let it out until he had achieved some level of understanding about why she had done what she had done. Her use of the word "harlot" was informative. It told him there was an unstable personality beneath the placid veneer. He'd known this already, of course, but this was the first tangible proof of it. What he didn't know—what he *needed* to know most—was how anyone could hold onto this level of bitterness as long as she had.

"Why did you kill her?"

She pushed one of the wine glasses across the island. "Have a drink."

He picked up the glass and eyed it curiously before looking her in the eye. "Is there poison in it?"

She wasn't smiling now. In fact, she looked sort of angry. "You saw me opening the bottle, Deacon. I couldn't have poisoned your drink. Besides, I would never hurt you."

Deacon grunted. "Huh. That's interesting. Because it seems to me you've already done a pretty good job of hurting me by killing the woman I loved."

Marie sniffed disdainfully as she picked up the other wine glass. "You didn't really love her. You only thought you did. You're meant to be with me. I told you that the night we made love. Remember?"

Deacon opened his mouth to deny it, but then he did remember. It had been one of the more awkward of his early sexual experiences. Marie was maybe the fourth or fifth girl he had been with—he'd never had the trouble hooking up with girls common to so many boys that age—but he had been her first. And she had been very emotional in the aftermath. Now that he thought about it, she had been a very emotional girl in general, crying at the drop of a hat or suddenly flying into an uncontrollable rage for no discernible reason.

He took a chance and tasted the wine. It was good. "I get it now, I think. You're just crazy, aren't you?" He took a pointed look around at the expensively appointed kitchen, taking in all the gleaming, brushed steel surfaces. The range stove, the refrigerator, the oven hood, and the rest. "You inherited this place from your folks, right? It's nice." He smiled. "Did you kill them, too? I bet you did."

Marie stared at him in total silence for several long moments. That calm veneer was completely gone now. The calculating sociopath beneath the surface had revealed itself at last. "So what if I did? I got away with it. Just like I always have before. Just like I always will."

Deacon put the wine glass down. "So it's not just Anna, is it? Or your parents. You enjoy killing people. And you get a kick out of manipulating people from afar. A rekindling of the flame with me was never possible, and you knew it, but it was enough for you to wreck my life and savor the fallout."

She stared at him in that cold, utterly emotionless way again for a while, but then some of the warmth stole back into her features as she willed her mask of humanity back into place. She smiled. "So many insights you have, Deacon. It really is amazing. Let me ask *you* something. How did you find me out? I was sure you'd forgotten all about me, that you'd never connect me with what happened."

Deacon's smile this time was genuine. "You'd never believe me if I told you. It'd make *me* sound like the crazy one."

Marie shrugged and affected a look of boredom. "You don't have to tell me. It doesn't matter much, does it? You didn't take your suspicions to the police. Not that you could prove anything anyway. Believe me, there's not a speck of DNA evidence left on that car. You don't have a gun, which means you didn't come here to kill me. I don't see anything to worry about here."

"Maybe I plan to beat you to death with my bare hands."

This provoked her heartiest laughter since their initial interaction at the door. "Please. I love you, Deacon, but you're a bit of a wimp. I'd kick your ass."

Deacon didn't refute this. She was probably right. He was a couple of inches shorter than her and slightly built, while she had the whole Amazonian goddess thing going on.

He shrugged. "I don't doubt that. But you're wrong about one thing."

Her expression exuded smugness. "And what would that be?"

"I *do* have a weapon."

They both saw the double-bladed axe at the same time. One moment it wasn't there, the next it was within easy grabbing distance for Deacon. The axe was a gift from the woman in black. She had promised it would be there when he needed it and so it was. He lifted it off the island and hefted it, testing its weight as Marie shot backward from the island and slammed into the edge of the counter behind her. The solid heft of the axe felt good in his hands. Marie's eyes were wide and she was shaking her head in stunned disbelief.

Her terror pleased Deacon.

She deserved to feel afraid.

She let out a breath that was right on the edge of a whimper. "Where the hell did that come from?"

He smiled. "It's another of those things you wouldn't believe if I told you. And, frankly, I don't feel like explaining it because I'm tired of talking to your psycho ass. So I'll be killing you now, okay?"

She screamed and took off running as Deacon came around the island and took a swing at her with the big axe, getting out of the way in time as the deadly blade sliced a vicious arc through the air. Deacon had swung the blade as hard as he could and the momentum generated by the miss almost caused the handle to come flying out of his hands, which would have been nothing short of disastrous. It was all too easy to imagine Marie snatching it off the floor and turning the tables on him. And he had no doubt she would unhesitatingly proceed to chop him into very many tiny, bloody pieces, long-standing psychotic love obsession be damned.

He followed her through an archway into a short hallway. She disappeared through an open door on the left, veering into what turned out to be a bedroom. He saw heavy manacles attached to the posts of a wrought-iron bedframe, the sight of which gave him a moment's pause as he wondered whether she had intended to one day chain him to this bed. It seemed a very real possibility, but he didn't have much time to mull it over. Marie had reached a chest of drawers on the opposite side of the room. She had the top drawer open and was rooting through it, probably searching for a gun or other weapon.

Deacon let out a primal, alien-sounding roar of fury and came charging across the room at her. She shrieked in fright and whirled around too fast, fumbling her grip on a large-caliber revolver. She dropped it and it hit the carpeted floor with a heavy thunk as the double-bladed axe came whistling through the air again. This time she was too stunned by the savagery writ large in Deacon's twisted features to get out of the way in time.

The big blade punched into her stomach, sinking in to the handle. He yanked it back out with a grunt of exertion. Blood gushed from the wound. Bits of chopped viscera were visible through the large rent in her flesh. Marie cried out as she dropped to her knees. She looked up at him with eyes shiny with tears, shaky hands raised in supplication. Her tears pleased him. So did her pain.

He shifted his grip on the double-bladed axe and swung it again, unleashing another furious roar as the weapon arced toward Marie. This time the blade chopped through her throat and separated her head from her shoulders with shocking ease. The severed head went flying. It hit the floor and tumbled until it hit a wall. Marie's jagged neck stump pumped a staggering geyser of gore into the air for a second or two until her corpse fell back against the chest of drawers and went still.

Deacon wasn't a born killer. Nor was he some insane madman. He was just a guy who had avenged the murder of the love of his life. Just guy who had done the job he'd been given. A reflexive sob tore out of him moments after Marie was dead. He started shaking and moved to the bed to sit on its edge until the tremors had ceased. Some more sobbing accompanied the tremors. Despite this, he felt no regret at all. He'd done nothing less than what needed doing.

When he had himself under control again, he got to his feet and went to a closet in a corner of the room. He pulled the door open and scanned its contents for a suitable container. He'd accomplished the biggest part of the job the woman in black had assigned him, but it wasn't complete yet. It looked like he'd have to search elsewhere until he spied something that looked perfect at the back of the shelf above the clothing rod. He raised on his tiptoes and strained to reach the cardboard box. His fingers snagged an open flap and he dragged it to the edge of the shelf. He was then able to pull it down and dump its contents on the floor.

Deacon frowned. He needed to get on with things, but his curiosity got the better of him. He knelt and set the box down long enough to sort through the array of wallets and handbags, most of which contained credit cards, various forms of I.D., some cash, and an assortment of personal photos belonging to people he didn't know, though he was sure they all had one thing in common—they had been murdered by Marie Cavanaugh. There was no definitive proof of this, of course, but he guessed he could probably find some if he did some more hunting around the property.

It made him feel a little better about what he had done.

THE HALLOWEEN BRIDE

He stood up and took the empty box over to where Marie's head had landed. Grimacing, he wound his hand around a length of her long auburn hair and lifted the head off the floor. After easing it into the box, he folded the flaps shut, grabbed the double-bladed axe, and got out of there.

6

DEACON WAS NOT QUITE HALFWAY home when he realized he hadn't taken the time to clean up any evidence that might link him to Marie's murder. He frowned as he strove to estimate just how much of that there might have been. He remembered touching the edge of the screen door, for one thing. And there was the wine glass, as well as a few of the wallets and handbags. Some usable fingerprints could no doubt be lifted from those items, but Deacon wasn't sure it mattered. The police had already failed to link Marie to him once, thanks to the tenuousness of their long-ago connection. There was no reason to suspect that wouldn't happen again. And he was sure his fingerprints weren't in any law enforcement database.

He nonetheless wondered whether he ought to turn back and spend some more time at Marie's place, long enough to eliminate even the slightest trace of a connection. If she had a computer—as everyone did these days—it might be a good idea to take it with him. No telling what might be on that thing. If he hurried, the risk of discovery at the scene would be nil, as he was certain she'd lived alone.

As he weighed whether he should do this, he glanced at the box resting on his passenger seat. A level of disconnect from what he'd done had settled in during the drive. Thinking about it now, the enormity of it hit him anew. He was driving around with a severed human head in his car, one that wasn't neatly sealed away in the trunk, at that. Also, there was blood all over the front of his white button-down shirt. There was more blood all over his hands and face. Some of it had gotten smeared on the steering wheel, and he was sure more traces of it were on the seat beneath him and elsewhere.

He shook his head and laughed in a weary, humorless way.

His car was a rolling evidence box. He had to get home and get cleaned up. The longer he remained in the car under the present circumstances, the greater the risk. He realized now he should have taken the time to wash up before leaving Marie's house. Obviously he'd been too rattled in the wake of committing the grisly act to think straight. But oh well, it was all a bunch of blood under the bridge now. And if later tonight things played out the way the woman in black had promised, none of it would matter anyway.

Deacon arrived home some fifteen minutes after reaching this conclusion. He pulled into his driveway, parked, and glanced at his rearview mirror for a look at the street in front of his house. It was still broad daylight and getting out of the car looking like a bloody mess would be risky. But there didn't appear to be anyone in the immediate vicinity. So he grabbed the box, heaved a breath, and got out of the car.

He had a scary moment where he nearly stumbled climbing the two steps to the side door stoop. Visions of dropping the box and the head tumbling out to the ground wheeled through his mind in the seconds it took to grab the rail to the right of the stoop and get righted again. He then let go of the rail and stood there for a moment cradling the box in both arms, his heart hammering in his chest as he struggled to get a grip after the close call. A sound somewhere between a whine and a brittle laugh escaped his lips. Clearly he was more on edge than he'd realized. Getting into the house and hiding away until he had nerves under control was becoming more important by the moment.

So he shifted his grip on the box and got a hand free to pull open the screen door. He was about to slip his key into the lock when he noticed the small, formal-looking white envelope tucked into the crack between the frame and the door. He pulled the envelope out and looked at it. His name was printed on the back in neat block letters. He puzzled over it a moment before deciding he had bigger things to worry about just now. After shoving the envelope into a hip pocket, he slipped his key into the lock and opened the door.

Once he was finally inside, he put the box on the kitchen table and dropped his keys next to it. He then went into the little living room at the front of the house, where he parted plastic blind slats to peer out a window. This still being relatively early in the afternoon, the streets weren't yet filled with roaming trick-or-treaters and their parents. He suspected he wouldn't see the first of them for a couple more hours. In the meantime, it would probably be smart to take some steps to dissuade them from approaching his house.

He started shedding his shirt as he walked out of the living room, pausing for a moment to drape it over the back of a chair in the kitchen. That done, he went down the hallway to the bathroom, where he washed his hands and used soap and a washcloth to scrub the blood from his face and neck. After ducking into the bedroom to pull on a plain white T-shirt, he returned to the front of the house for another peek through the window.

The street was still empty.

Deacon opened the front door and knelt to snatch up the pumpkin he'd set there a week ago as his token nod to the season. When he stood up, he saw a young woman in black tights and a sweatshirt walking down the street with her dog, a black Labrador straining against the leash. The woman saw him watching her and raised a hand in greeting. Deacon responded with a nod. She wasn't anyone he recognized, but her presence was proof he'd done the right thing by cleaning up before poking his head outside again. He couldn't help noting how her smile slipped some as he backed into the house and kicked the door shut. She had no reason to find his behavior suspicious, of course, but she was probably wondering why he was taking the pumpkin—which had already been carved—inside so early on Halloween day.

The hell with it. Let her wonder.

Back in the kitchen, he set the pumpkin on the table, pulled one of the chairs back, and dropped heavily into it. He felt kind of beat. Murder took a lot out of a guy. He considered getting up to take down the bottle of whiskey he kept in the cupboard by the sink. A stiff drink or two would do wonders for his nerves. But he put the idea on hold when his thoughts returned to the little white envelope.

THE HALLOWEEN BRIDE

Frowning, he pulled it out and tore it open. There was a white card inside it. He opened it and stared disbelievingly for a moment before he began to smile.

It was a wedding invitation.

7

THE HOUR WAS NEARLY AT hand. It was time to head out into the deepening dusk and make his way back to Willowblack Lane. Deacon wouldn't have anyone to follow to the hidden street this time, but the invitation had contained cryptic directions. He was to journey by foot to a street whose name he knew, where he was to "wait for the crack to appear."

Whatever that meant.

The lack of specificity beyond that was troubling, but he had little choice but to trust that all would become clear so long as he did as instructed. It wasn't as if he could call the woman in black and request additional details. Nor could he simply blow off the remaining part of the task she had assigned him. He had gone through too much for that.

And the potential reward was, literally, worth anything to him.

By six that evening he had a few fortifying shots of whiskey crawling through his bloodstream and was about ready to go. The lights were out in most of the house. The darkness and the lack of decorations out front had so far been enough to keep the kids away. But he didn't want to push his luck. It was time to get going. He put the whiskey bottle back in the cupboard and went to the table to retrieve the box.

Deacon hesitated as he glanced at the blood-stained shirt still draped across the back of one of the chairs. An idea so mad it surely had to be a sign of decaying sanity occurred to him. This was Halloween. It was the one time of the year when a man might openly carry a severed head and walk through his suburban neighborhood without anyone batting an eye. Anyone who saw him would assume the blood on the shirt was fake. And unless someone examined it very closely, the head could pass for a very realistic Halloween prop.

The idea was more than merely risky.

It was foolhardy. Dangerously reckless.

This was undeniably true.

Having thought of it, however, Deacon knew he would do it anyway, so taken was he by the audacity of the notion. He was likely about to leave his old life behind forever. So why not go out in style?

Smiling, he swept the bloody shirt off the back of the chair and pulled it on over the plain white T-shirt. He left the button-down shirt open in the front as he opened the box. "Hi there, Marie. Want to go for a walk?"

Marie didn't reply.

No surprise there.

Deacon took the head out of the box and wound a length of Marie's lustrous auburn hair around his right hand before carrying it to the side door. He heard voices in the street as he stepped outside and then saw flashlights and shadowy forms indicating multiple sets of trick-or-treaters. Kids were laughing and shouting and generally having a good time. Some of them ran ahead of gently scolding parents in their haste to get to the next house.

The double-bladed axe was still in the back seat of Deacon's car. He got it out, propped the long handle over his shoulder, and walked out to the street. Some kids and the adults chaperoning them had neared his driveway. A little girl of about seven or eight shrieked and pointed at Marie's dangling head. She then ducked behind the legs of a man who might have been her father. Two boys in not very convincing zombie makeup giggled and mocked the girl's terror. A woman standing near the man chastised the boys for making fun of her.

The man was squinting behind wire-rimmed glasses. Deacon thought he was studying the severed head a little too closely. It started to unnerve him after a moment, but then the guy chuckled and shook his head. "Tell the truth. The nagging harpy had it coming, didn't she?"

The woman slugged him in the shoulder. "Alex! Your daughter is terrified. And that's not appropriate."

The man winced and rubbed his shoulder, but he was grinning. "Oh, lighten up. It's Halloween." He was still grinning when he shifted his attention back to Deacon. "That thing is wicked realistic. I bet you paid an FX pro to have it custom-made."

Deacon relaxed some. He could tell by the slight slur in his voice that the man was a little tipsy. And his first comment had been nothing more than a case of getting into the spooky spirit of the evening. The wife—he guessed she was the man's wife, anyway—had been upset by the remark's casual misogyny as much as anything else. Deacon had gotten lucky here, but he knew it wouldn't be a good idea to encourage this group's continued scrutiny. The success of the charade he was attempting rested upon his ability to keep moving. People catching fleeting glimpses of the head as he passed them in the street would probably be okay. Extended interactions of any kind might end with him dodging the police as he tried desperately to make his way to Willowblack Lane. His course of action now was obvious—he would have to scare the living daylights out of that little girl.

A maniacal grin stretched across his face as he waved the axe around. "Oh, yes! I killed this back-talking, no-good wench of a woman." He belatedly realized he'd adopted a bad cockney accent and considered ditching it, but then he got a look at the girl's face as she peeked around her father's legs and realized it was enhancing the effect he was trying to achieve. "Took her head clean off with one swing of my trusty axe, I did!" He waved the axe again, thrusting it in the general direction of the girl and her daddy. "And I'm coming for you next, little girlie!"

The loud cackle he unleashed then was every bit as maniacal as his grin. The girl let out a shrill screech of pure terror and threw her arms around her father's legs.

Deacon cackled some more.

Mission accomplished.

The woman directed a withering scowl at Deacon. Seeing it made his grin slip the tiniest notch, but he managed to keep it in place until after she had begun to shoo her kids down the street. The dad went with them, but he signaled his approval of the show Deacon had put on with a thumbs-up gesture. Deacon had a feeling the guy was a bit of a son of a bitch to his family a lot of the time. Also, he felt bad about having put such a scare into the girl.

On the other hand, it had gotten the job done.

And, thankfully, the family was moving off in the opposite direction of the way he needed to go.

Deacon settled the axe handle on his shoulder again and set off down the street. Though his garish "costume" drew a predictable amount of attention, there were no more of those uncomfortably long exchanges. He was moving at a fast pace, which helped discourage anyone who might feel inclined to chat him up. People pointed at the head, but it was clear no one believed it was real, just "realistic", though there was one kid who loudly proclaimed his opinion that it was a shitty fake. This kid looked like he was in his early teens. He had a little pack of friends with him, who all looked like they were in the same age range. There were no adults with them. They fired off a few more insults as he walked by them. Damn snot-nosed brats. Deacon had to suppress an almost overpowering urge to get in their faces and give them a good ultra-close-up view of the "fake" head. They would probably shit their britches. However, while this would be gratifying, he knew such a confrontation would be self-destructive. They undoubtedly all had cell phones and would be on the line to 911 within moments.

So he kept his head down and stalked away from them at an even faster clip, ignoring their mocking laughter as best he could. Pretty soon they were gone and he was able to stay focused on the task at hand. He needed to get to Mulberry Street. That was where this supposed "crack" would appear. He wondered about that again as he threaded his way through the milling groups of little pretend spooks and superheroes. When he had followed the ghost procession onto Willowblack Lane, there had been no sense of anything different until he was walking down that street. He had just taken a turn around a seemingly ordinary corner and then there they were. Was that how it would be this time? But then why had he been told to wait for the crack?

He sighed.

The answer would remain elusive until it was right in front of his face. It would be best to let it go until then. He was anxious enough as it was. Though no one had caught on to his ruse yet, he couldn't help feeling it was only a matter of time. He had been walking for almost twenty minutes. The need to get out of sight before someone recognized the truth had him contemplating a retreat to his home via a series of backyard shortcuts, but that option was also rife with danger. There were lots of dogs in this neighborhood, many of which wouldn't hesitate to attack a stranger intruding on their territory. Or some trigger-happy redneck might unload on him with a shotgun. These were daunting scenarios, no doubt. Not that he ever seriously considered retreat. His course was set and he meant to see it through to the end. This other stuff was just a lot of mental chatter, the paranoid part of his brain working in overdrive.

Then, at long last, he arrived at the corner of Mulberry Street.

Deacon stopped at the corner and stared at the street sign for several moments. His gaze then went to Mulberry Street itself, a brightly lit stretch of residential road not notably different from any of the others he'd seen tonight. It certainly looked nothing like Willowblack Lane. There were no black willow trees in the yards, nor was anyone being killed in the street. Also missing in action was the dramatic thunder and lightning display of the previous evening. He did see additional groups of trick-or-treaters going from door to door. Some of those doors opened and on occasion he heard supposedly scary—but mostly cheesy—sound effects issuing from speakers of varying quality, but nothing with a truly otherworldly vibe.

He heard the tread of multiple sets of feet behind him and whirled around hoping to see the woman in black and her attendants, but it was just another group of trick-or-treaters carrying plastic pumpkins and candy bags, this time accompanied by a lone adult male. The kids were yammering amongst themselves nonstop and paid Deacon little attention as they took the turn at Mulberry Street. The adult glanced at Marie's head, frowned, and acknowledged Deacon with a wary nod as he followed the children down the street.

Frowning, Deacon turned and watched them go.

He was troubled by the sense that this dude could be trouble. There was something about him, a sober seriousness, that made him almost sure of it. This was a man far more observant than the average citizen and probably much more diligent about reporting possible suspicious behavior. He became convinced of this when the guy pulled a cell phone out of his pocket and put it to his ear as he glanced back at him. Deacon's heart started thudding in his chest. His anxiety was kicking into high gear. For the first time he felt truly conspicuous being out in the open like this with his grisly trophy.

How long would it take a cop car to get here?

Probably just a few minutes, if the 911 operator took the man's call seriously. But the operator might suspect it was a crank call. Any other night that might not happen, but this was Halloween, a night traditionally devoted to mischief. The operator might also suspect the man was overreacting for the same reason.

A guy with a big double-bladed axe, you say?

So what?

It's Halloween.

Deacon nonetheless wondered whether it might be time to cut and run, even if it meant missing out on his opportunity to be reunited with Anna. The police would be along shortly regardless of whether the operator believed the man's account of the situation. They would have to check it out on the off-chance he was telling the truth. And he had no desire to go to jail.

At long last, however, the thing he had been waiting for finally appeared, saving him from that dire fate.

He laughed.

He couldn't help it.

A jagged, vertical black line about two feet wide split the world apart in the middle of Mulberry Street, a literal crack in the fabric of reality. The crack rose from the center of the street and continued into the sky high above, farther than Deacon could see. If you looked at it from the wrong angle, you wouldn't see it at all. He could walk around it the same as he'd walk around a telephone pole. The sight of it was astounding. He was positive there had been nothing like this the last time, but what did it matter?

It was here now.

No one else seemed aware of it. A lone trick-or-treater passed near the gap, but the boy didn't even look at it. Because it was the kind of thing no sane person could ignore, Deacon suspected he was the only one who could see it. Perhaps the woman in black had been the only one who could see it yesterday.

Deacon heard the buzz of an engine behind him and the shrill blip of a siren. The police had arrived. Mr. Observant must have been very convincing on the phone.

Time to go.

A strident voice shouted at him to stop and put the axe down, but Deacon kept going. The shouted voice barked at him one more time, but it cut off in midsentence, no longer audible to Deacon because he was no longer in the mortal world.

He smiled.

He was back on Willowblack Lane.

8

THUNDER CRASHED AND LIGHTNING FLASHED, but still no rain fell on Willowblack Lane. Deacon felt that sharper chill he remembered from his previous visit to the street. But there were a few notable differences this time around. Some of the houses had changed, having sprouted new wings, spires, and towers with gabled roofs. The nearest house on his right was one he remembered looking like a Victorian mansion, but now it looked more like a castle, complete with a moat and a drawbridge. The dwelling was set farther back from the road than it had been before. A closer look showed the transformed property retained some of the characteristics he remembered, including a section with a high arched roof partly visible through the castle's slatted iron gate. It was as if the house he'd seen last time had merged with something else to form this new hybrid house-castle. The main thing Deacon took away from this was that reality on Willowblack Lane was malleable and probably ever-changing.

He saw additional evidence to support this conclusion as he resumed walking. Willowblack Lane largely retained the look of a residential street—albeit one with significantly more personality than the average street in the average neighborhood—but one lot to his left was now occupied by a cylindrical high-rise building with lots of reflective glass windows. The name on the side of the building was MISKATONIC RESEARCH. Something about that triggered a faint spark of recognition.

Also, like before, occasional screams rang out, and a few times these were followed by brief bits of drama that played out like gory scenes from movies. A huge, lumbering beast chased a curvaceous blonde woman out of a dark alley and pounced on her in the middle of the street. The creature growled at her, opening its huge, wolf-like mouth to reveal rows of long, pointy teeth glistening with saliva. The thing tore one of her arms off and a pool of blood spread across the dark asphalt. The woman was still screaming as Deacon walked by them. She turned her head to track him as she muttered gibbering pleas for help. Deacon had difficulty taking her pleas seriously for several reasons, not the least of which was the fact that he was carrying an axe and a woman's severed head. Why would anyone look to *him* for help?

No, this was just for show, another example of Willowblack Lane's macabre playfulness. He encountered one more instance of the same prior to arriving at the black house at the end of the street, only this time he was forced to become an active participant in the drama. An inexplicable patch of fog materialized. It wasn't dense enough to reduce visibility to zero, but it did obscure the approach of the person who stepped out of a shadowy yard and began to follow him. The stalker had a light tread and Deacon didn't hear the muted click of the man's heels until he was almost upon him.

When he did realize he was being followed, Deacon spun about and saw a man attired in the garb of a Victorian gentleman emerging from the swirling fog. He wore a long cloak and a top hat. Clutched in his gloved right hand was a long and very sharp-looking butcher's knife. There was a dark stain on the base of the blade, perhaps a left-over bit of some poor prostitute's blood. The man raised the knife high above his shoulder as he came at Deacon.

Deacon dropped Marie's head and got the axe off his shoulder in time to block the first thrust of the Ripper's knife with its handle. The Ripper flashed him a vulpine grin and drew back for another thrust. Deacon danced backward and the knife sliced harmlessly through the air. He changed his grip on the axe handle and went into a batter's stance as the Ripper came at him yet again. When his assailant was within range, he swung the axe with all his might. The trajectory of the swing was perfect as one of the blades ripped through the knife-wielding bastard's neck and took off his head. The severed noggin went tumbling down the fog-shrouded patch of street as the now-headless Ripper took a few staggering steps before pitching over and falling heavily to the pavement. His fingers clawed weakly at the street once and then the corpse went still.

Damn, Deacon thought. *I'm getting pretty good at this head-removing business.*

Maybe that would become his official "thing" here on Willowblack Lane.

Watch out for The Decapitator!

It was a morbidly amusing notion, but Deacon was cognizant of the need to get to his destination before some other predatory refugee from the annals of horror and mayhem could come after him. He didn't know whether they could actually harm him, but he had no interest in testing that out. There was a possibility the Ripper had been placed in his path as an intentional obstacle. Perhaps the woman in black had decided to throw a few final tests his way to further prove his worthiness.

He retrieved Marie's head from the street and broke into a run. The faster he got where he was going, the better. The frenzied pace inflamed the ire of the things lurking in the shadows on Willowblack Lane. He heard panting and the heavy pad of many beasts behind him. There was also a good bit of growling and sinister laughter. He felt the breath of some large, slavering thing against his neck just as the black house finally came into view. He rejected the urge to turn around and confront his pursuers with the axe. In the time it would take to do that, they would have him. He would be driven to the ground and his body would be torn apart. All he could do was will his feet to move faster and pray for a miracle.

The creatures continued to pursue him as he got closer to the house, but somehow they never quite caught up with him. There was something in that suggestive of a lack of genuine danger. He couldn't possibly move swiftly enough to elude things like the beast that had taken down that woman. It reinforced the idea that the woman in black was merely testing him some more, which was sort of obnoxious, but what could he do about it?

A few hair-raising moments later he finally arrived at the sidewalk outside the towering black house. He stood hunched over there a moment longer, thinking he would need to catch his breath, but he wasn't winded at all. Apparently there was something in the air here that gave you super stamina powers. In the next moment, he realized the sounds of pursuit had ceased. He glanced in the direction he'd come and saw only an empty street. A wave of relief came over him, but he knew he couldn't stand here basking in it.

He stepped through the open iron gate and started down the twisting path of rocks embedded in the ground. The house was as tall and imposing as he remembered. A well-timed brilliant flash of lightning lit up its towering, jagged black outline. The same thing had happened last time. He had imagined he'd be a little less intimidated now, but this was not the case. The place still looked scary as hell. And he was about to willingly walk through its front door. This struck him as proof he'd finally lost any flimsy scrap of good sense he'd had left.

I lost my mind a while ago, he thought. *I've only been in denial about it until now.*

Deacon climbed the tall set of concrete steps to the porch, apprehension gripping him the closer he got to the moment of truth. If the woman in black had been telling the truth, he was within moments of seeing Anna again, a thing he would have believed impossible before yesterday. Given all he'd seen and experienced since then, there was no reason to believe she wasn't capable of delivering on her promise. But just because she *could* do it, that didn't mean she actually *would* do it. She might have been gaming him all along for the sheer thrill of it, indulging in a powerful ghost's idea of wicked fun.

Well, maybe so.

Anyway, there was no going back now.

Deacon banged the base of the axe handle against the door and waited for it to open. An uncomfortably long moment elapsed during which nothing happened. He was lifting the axe to bang the handle against it again when the door began to swing slowly inward. This happened with the loud creaking of unoiled door hinges Deacon now knew was the fashionable choice for Willowblack Lane residents. Door hinges that didn't creak loud enough to set your ears on edge were faulty door hinges.

As before, the door appeared to have opened of its own accord. Deacon heard a low sound of organ music emanating from somewhere inside the house. The piece of music wasn't something he recognized, but it had the stately feel he associated with weddings and memorial services. There was no one waiting for him in the large foyer, at least not that he could see. Shaking off a final spasm of trepidation, Deacon heaved a breath and stepped into the house. The door slammed shut behind him, producing the expected cough-inducing puff of dust.

He took a look around and saw he'd been right.

The foyer was empty.

Well, shit.

Deacon hadn't expected a welcoming party, not exactly, but this emptiness was disconcerting. After standing alone in the foyer a few moments longer, he decided to follow the sound of the organ music. The rooms he walked through were, as expected, cloaked in shadows, but each room had at least one flickering candle in a wall sconce, allowing him to proceed without tripping over his feet or banging into anything. That sense of the house being significantly larger on the inside than outside returned as the volume of the organ music remained low, at one point becoming nearly inaudible. He decided he'd gone the wrong way and backtracked through a sitting room, where he opted to take a new direction by going through a door he'd ignored before. It opened into a long hallway, although thankfully one not nearly as long as the one the woman in black had led him down last night. At the end of the hallway was a door that stood halfway open. Beyond that door was a large library. Expensive-looking floor-to-ceiling bookcases obscured every inch of wall space. The shelves were crammed with leather-bound volumes. It was tempting to take a look at some of the titles—who wouldn't be curious about the kind of literature that appealed to ghosts?—but the organ music had grown louder the moment he was inside the library.

Anna was close. He felt her presence. Now that he was within psychic range of her, it was as palpable as his own breath.

Deacon continued through the library toward another partly open door at the far end of the big room. The door swung open ahead of him and he saw a brightly lit large room. It looked like the grand ballroom of a fancy hotel. The room had a very high ceiling and balconies that ran along the walls. A number of chandeliers hung from the ceiling. The organ music swelled to a crescendo as Deacon stepped through the door.

Dozens of male and female ghosts in various forms of fancy dress turned his way as he came into the room. For a moment, Deacon felt uncomfortable in his casual attire. The blood-stained button-down shirt hanging open over the plain white T-shirt felt particularly conspicuous. But most of his discomfort was forgotten when he turned his head and saw who was waiting for him at the far end of the ballroom.

Anna.

She was in the most gorgeous ankle-length white wedding dress he had ever seen and her face was hidden behind the bridal veil, but he knew it was her. A tall old man clad in a dark suit stood near her. Clasped in his folded hands was a thick book with gilt-edged pages. Deacon assumed this man was the wedding officiant.

Another man—this one wearing a butler's livery—stepped out of the crowd of spectators and approached Deacon. He coughed into a loosely closed fist and nodded at the double-bladed axe. "I'll take that, sir. You'll no longer need it."

That was fine with Deacon. There probably wasn't much of a future in the decapitating business anyway. He lifted Marie's head and gave it a gentle swing. "And what about this?"

A voice behind him said, "I'll take that, darling."

The woman in black.

Deacon turned around and saw her standing not three feet away from him. Being this close to her sent a shiver down his back. She was attired exactly as she had been the day before, except that she'd changed out her black corsage for one that was blood red. This was likely symbolic of something, but Deacon didn't care to spend any time contemplating it. He handed over Marie's head. The woman in black took the head and cradled it in both hands, handling it with apparent reverence. She made a sound of appreciation and looked at Deacon through the veil. "It will make a wonderful addition to my collection. You've done well, young man."

Deacon cleared his throat. "Um . . . thank you?"

He winced at the rising inflection that turned this into a question rather than a statement, but the woman in black appeared not to notice. After handing off the head to another servant, who whisked the grotesque murder souvenir out of the room, she took Deacon by the arm and began to guide him across the room, toward where Anna stood waiting for him. The crowd of spectators parted, giving them plenty of space. Deacon didn't like feeling the ghost woman's satin gloved hand on him any more than he had the last time, but he figured he could endure it for as long as it took to reach Anna. He'd gone through far worse to get to this point. A minor case of the heebie-jeebies was nothing by comparison.

Deacon was shaking a little by the time the woman in black relinquished his arm. By then he was standing next to Anna and they were both facing the stern-faced officiant. The man's wispy gray hair was plastered to his skull with some kind of grease. Cold dark eyes peered out at the couple from behind old-fashioned round spectacles. He flipped open the book he was holding and Deacon caught a glimpse of a red pentagram imprinted on the front cover.

He frowned.

Well, that's not in the least foreboding . . .

The officiant cleared his throat and began to read from the book. The words he intoned in his deep, rumbling voice included references to the eternal grace of a dark lord and admonitions to the betrothed to remember they should always strive to cause suffering for others whenever possible to render glory unto Satan. Deacon found this all disturbing in a detached way, but the bulk of his focus remained on Anna. He was overjoyed to be with her again. If that meant he had to become a devil-worshipping servant of evil, so be it.

The officiant paused as ring bearers approached the couple.

Deacon and Anna accepted the rings. They then recited the vows read to them by the officiant. There was something very slightly off about Anna's voice. Deacon recognized her inflections at once, but there was a strange, slight catch at the end of each sentence, followed by a shuddery inhalation of breath. But he was too intent on reciting the vows correctly to give this much thought.

The officiant snapped the book shut. It was done.

He did not smile when he said, "You may now kiss the bride."

Deacon, however, was smiling as he leaned close to lift Anna's veil. This was the moment he had been dreaming about and now it was finally here. His smile began to melt as he continued to lift the veil and glimpsed her face. An impulse to let the veil drop back into place rocked him, but a deeper need to see what was beneath it prevented this. When the veil was up, Deacon had to choke back a scream.

It was Anna beneath the veil.

No doubt whatsoever about that.

But she looked as she must have looked on the mortician's table. Her flesh had a bluish tinge and her jaw was crooked, knocked out of true by the crash. There were lines of stitches along the curve of her neck, down one cheek, and across her forehead. One of her eyes had been replaced by a glass orb. Her blue-tinged smile was simultaneously the saddest and most hideous thing Deacon had ever seen. He didn't want to kiss her. He wanted to run.

But that wasn't an option.

The officiant cleared his throat. "You *must* kiss the bride."

The voice of the woman in black was right by his ear. "Kiss your beloved." That musky odor of the graveyard sent another shiver down his back. One of her satin-gloved hands insinuated itself against his lower back. "Kiss her, or I claim you for myself."

Deacon was shaking harder than ever.

Many of the spectators crowded closer, their lust for blood and pain palpable.

Deacon let out a shuddery breath and drew Anna into his arms, pressing his warm lips against her cold ones. A tear leaked from the corner of her one good eye as her arms encircled his waist. A jolt of pain ripped through the center of his body as she held him. He recognized what was happening too late to do anything about it. His lips remained merged with Anna's as the woman in black twisted the knife inside him. He experienced a moment of profound sadness and loss, but it was short-lived.

The woman in black extracted the knife from his back.

It didn't hurt as much now. Hardly at all, in fact.

The officiant smiled for the first time, though the expression failed to touch his cold, cold eyes. "I now pronounce you husband and wife."

Deacon and Anna kissed again, far more enthusiastically than before. Whistles and applause arose from the crowd of spectators. The organ music started up again, jauntier this time, and a shower of confetti rained down on the happy couple as they walked arm-in-arm out to the center of the ballroom floor for the traditional first dance.

As they rotated across the dance floor, the organ music stopped and transitioned to a swing rhythm performed by a big band. Where the band had come from, Deacon did not know, nor did he care. He glimpsed them now and then from the corner of his eye, a conductor leading a group of seated musicians on a stage. All Deacon cared about was that he was with Anna again and they were married, just as the fates had intended all along.

He was happier than he'd ever been in his entire . . .

THE HALLOWEEN BRIDE

He smiled as he twirled Anna around yet again and then drew her back to him.

Well, "life" wasn't quite the right word anymore, now was it?

No. And that was just fine.

Champagne corks were popped. Bubbly flowed. There was laughter and good cheer. Somewhere else in the house, someone was screaming.

And that was just fine, too.

Everything was just fine here in the house where the screaming never stopped and the haunted revelry went on forever.

BLOODRUSH

1

AFTERSHOCK

AWARENESS. DIM AT FIRST. FLICKERING moments of confused consciousness. The world was darkness, informed only by the grayest sense of existence, of *being*. Then smells, the first real sensory input from the world outside this cage of foggy consciousness. An array of pungent aromas assailed his nostrils, most strongly a scent of . . . sick. Puke. Somewhere very near. The almost overpowering odor made his nostrils twitch and his eyes water. The return to consciousness gathered momentum. The tactile world returned. He felt something solid beneath him. Something pressing against his face. It was . . . it was . . . oh yeah . . . a floor. Rough hardwood planks. His fingers twitched, clawed weakly at the pitted wood. Left-hand fingers only. No sensation on the right side yet. Which was vaguely worrying, but a faint signal from somewhere within the murkier depths of his subconscious indicated this particular symptom was not indicative of a debilitating injury. Which was great news. Totally awesome news. But all other indicators so far pointed toward a situation loaded with an array of negative factors. A clusterfuck, in other words.

The crawling, grasping fingers of his left hand touched something wet.

Something sticky.

He lifted his fingers out of the wetness and focused what he could of his still much diminished will on bringing those fingers toward his face. It was a slow and complicated process. Seemed to take forever. As if it was happening in slow motion. Except, no, that wasn't quite right. Slow motion would be akin to the speed of light compared to this. He thought of a saying something he used to hear. Something someone close to him used to say often. *Slower than Christmas*. Yeah. This was slower than Christmas. Wait. What the fuck was Christmas again? Huh. Oh, yeah. Decorated tree. Lights. Songs. Gifts. Everybody drunker than shit. And no one drunker than his old man. Another moment of slowly-dawning insight. *Dad. It was dad who used to say that thing about Christmas*. Said it all the time, applying it to anything that taxed his patience even a little. It had irritated him so much as a kid. Like, come on, pops, come up with some fucking new homilies already. But it felt oddly applicable now. It almost felt as if time was moving in reverse. As if . . .

As if . . .

darkness

DARKNESS

Nothingness.

And then . . .

His head jerked up a fraction of an inch. His eyes fluttered but did not quite open. *What . . . what . . . what's going on here?*

He remained very still, focused his concentration again. The very last bits of sensory information came floating back. The sick smells. The wetness on the floor.

I should really open my eyes.

Even as some terrified part of him rebelled against the notion, he willed himself to do it.

Focus.

Concentrate.

His eyes fluttered again, but only a little. He bit down on his lip, amped up his concentration. A sound disturbingly like the growl of a wild animal emanated from deep within him. He had to open his eyes. So much was still cloaked in darkness, even the most basic things. A sense of who he was. Or of *where* he was. Nor did he have any idea what had happened to him. He might have fallen and hit his head on the end of a table. Or he might have been the victim of some kind of attack. He could be bleeding to death right now.

Who am I?

What the hell's going on?

"Am I dying?"

He froze for an instant, surprised to have heard the voice. Then he realized it was his own voice. Curiously, this did not reassure him. Or maybe that lack of reassurance made perfect sense. What if he'd been attacked in his own home by an intruder. Some scumbag looking for drug money. *Okay*, he thought. *Say there's an intruder. Maybe he thinks I'm dead or close to it. And maybe in that case I should stay very, very still, play possum.*

It was no doubt the right course of action.

If there was an intruder in the vicinity.

But what if he was bleeding out all over the floor? He could die while waiting for this hypothetical intruder—who might not exist at all—to leave.

He absolutely fucking had to open his eyes RIGHT FUCKING NOW!

He opened his eyes.

Saw the blood-soaked fingertips of his left hand hanging limp right in front of his face. Full consciousness came screaming back in an instant. All thoughts of playing possum vanished in the same instant. A horrified roar came out of his throat as he braced his hands firmly against the floor and propelled himself into a sitting position.

He was in a house. Bright sunlight spilled through a large bay window, illuminating a vision straight out of hell. His breath came in short, sharp gasps. Sweat glistened on his face. Bile touched the back of his throat. His head jerked sharply from side to side, his eyes moving crazily in their sockets as his mind struggled to catalog and comprehend the scope of the horror. But true comprehension wasn't possible. Everywhere he looked, he saw blood. He was in a living room. He saw a couch, a coffee table, a throw rug, a recliner. Blood spatters stained all these things. Other blood spatters described crazy arcs across the walls and the floor. The blood was bad. Very bad. Except that it sort of . . . smelled good, which was many different levels of fucked up. And there was so much of it. But the blood wasn't the worst thing. The worst thing was the bodies. Or, rather, the pieces of bodies.

One of them belonging to his girlfriend of the last several months. *Yesterday*, he thought, struggling against the urge to collapse back to the floor and curl into an insensible ball of human uselessness. *Just yesterday I was looking at engagement rings, and now . . .*

And now . . .

Her head was on the coffee table, wedged inside a basket containing magazines. The rest of her was somewhere else. Maybe elsewhere on the floor, with all the other pieces of bodies. Or maybe somewhere else in the house. It was hard to tell.

He remembered some of it now, including who he was.

And some of what he had done.

David Rucker opened his mouth wide and screamed until his lungs were raw.

2

RECOGNITION

HE CURSED HIS STUPIDITY. HIS weakness. Because when you got right down to it, that weakness was the reason he was sitting slack-jawed and horrified in the middle of a sea of blood and puke. It was why he was surrounded by the ripped-to-pieces bodies of Janine and her family, the people who should have been his in-laws a few months hence.

His imminent proposal of marriage to Janine Martin had been a sort of open secret. Everyone knew it was coming. Members of both the Rucker and Martin families had been making sly, winking references to it for months now. They were perfect for each other. It was what everyone said. Hell, it was what they'd said to each other countless times. And today their engagement was to have become a reality. He had planned to do it here at the Martin homestead, on bended knee in front of Janine's entire family. It was to have been the kind of sweeping romantic gesture he'd hoped to make a regular part of life with his beloved.

He stared at the stump of her ripped-off head and choked back a sob.

BLOODRUSH

What a joke that seemed now. No. Not a joke. An *insult*. He knew now he'd never been worthy of her love. She was gone. Irretrievably *gone*. She had died in unimaginable agony. And it was all his fault. All because he'd been so fucking *weak*.

An image flashed into his mind—those glass cases at the jewelry shop. It was there, during his hunt for the perfect ring, that fate had taken that first bitter turn. In hindsight, it was easy to pinpoint the precise moment when he'd lost his soul forever. It was seared into his brain. He would never forget it, even if he lived for another million years.

The thought chilled him.

He would not live for another million years.

Or even another second.

Because, technically speaking, he'd been dead since yesterday. He remembered that now, too. And how he'd died. And, in remembering that, a chain of other memories began to unlock, link by link . . .

3

THE LAST DAY OF DAVID RUCKER'S LIFE

BRIGHT OVERHEAD LIGHTING ENHANCED THE glitter of the jewels displayed beneath the thick panes of glass, making some of the finer stones sparkle with breathtaking radiance. His eyes zeroed in on one displayed prominently in the center of the nearest case. Ensconced in its cushion of black velvet, it seemed to emit beams of the most beautifully incandescent sunshine. He imagined slipping that stone on the slender finger of his wife-to-be. He could see her melting at the sight of it, beaming as tears of joy spilled down her cheeks.

He belatedly realized someone was speaking to him.

"Sir? Sir?"

He glanced up, saw a smiling, smartly dressed woman on the other side of the case. "Yes?"

"I see something has caught your eye. Would you like a closer look?"

"I . . . uh . . ." His gaze drifted from the stone to the little white price tag beside it. Written in blue ink was a figure so astronomical it seemed impossible, the stuff of science fiction. No way could a number that high exist. He suppressed a flinch. His love for Janine was beyond quantifying, but the perfect stone for expressing that love was far out of his financial league. This was the kind of rock a Bill Gates or Donald Trump would give someone. And even those guys might flinch a little. It was disappointing, but—

A weird sensation tickled the back of his neck. A very light, feathery feeling. It was there and then gone. He frowned and touched his neck. Nothing there.

"Sir? Is something wrong?"

He realized he'd gone several moments without speaking. He felt strange. Just the slightest bit woozy, as if he'd had a glass or two of wine. His eyes watered a little, the brilliance of the stone morphing, becoming an indistinct blob of white light. He had to stop staring at it. He stood up straight and blinked slowly at the saleswoman.

"I'm sorry, I, uh . . ."

He felt it again.

That very delicate, feathery sensation at the back of his neck, again very brief, lasting no more than a second. In the next moment, he became aware of a secondary sensation, this one mental instead of physical. It was a feeling of being watched.

He turned away from the frowning saleswoman. She was still speaking, but her voice became fuzzy, her words indistinct. A pretty girl with pale skin and black hair sat on a bench a dozen yards or so outside the jewelry shop. The bench was nestled against the base of a gently trickling water fountain located in the center of the shopping mall's main atrium. The girl was wearing combat boots, a short black skirt, and a black jacket over a plain black t-shirt. Her lips, however, were very red, like the color of freshly spilled blood. Even from this distance, he could see that her eyes were the most vivid blue he'd ever seen. The color was so vivid he suspected she was wearing colored contacts.

She was looking right at him. When she was sure she had his full attention, she crooked an index finger at him and bent it back toward her.

Come hither . . .

He again felt that slightly woozy sensation. He shook his head to clear it and only then realized he was already walking toward her. The instant, unthinking obedience didn't strike him as worrisome right away. He was distracted, consumed with the problem of finding a way to do right by Janine without putting himself permanently in debt.

The decision to approach the girl had occurred on a subconscious level, was perhaps in part driven by a need to get away from the expensive stones on display in the jewelry shop and the maddening dilemma they presented. The girl wanted to talk to him and he was happy to oblige her. He told himself he would've been grateful for any kind of distraction. That was all she was to him.

A distraction.

A temporary diversion.

Nothing more.

Sure. Of course. He wondered if he knew her somehow. He didn't recognize her, but he supposed it was possible. He smiled sheepishly as he came to a halt in front of her. "Hey. I'm sorry, but do we know each other? Because I can't—"

Two things occurred simultaneously.

He realized she wasn't smiling. Indeed, she had no discernible expression at all.

In the same instant, she patted the empty expanse of bench beside her.

"Sit down, David."

He sat. Again, there was no conscious decision to obey. He became aware of a rushing sensation in his ears. At first, he figured the trickling of the water fountain had amplified somehow, but then he felt that wooziness again. It felt like he was deep underwater. Too deep. With his eyes and mouth open wide and the surface somewhere far above him. His vision blurred.

The odd sensations abruptly ceased.

He gasped. "Whoa. What the . . . fuck. I felt like I was . . . like I was . . ."

Drowning.

Huh, he thought. *Strange.*

He realized then that something outside the realm of what he thought of as the normal world was occurring. It should have frightened him. He knew that. And, on some remote level, he did feel a faint concern, but the feeling was so far away it didn't matter.

Right now, nothing mattered but this strange girl.

"How . . . how did you know my name?" His voice sounded strange to his own ears. He couldn't pinpoint why at first, but then it came to him—he had spoken with a child's wonderment. "Do I know you?"

She didn't say anything.

The silence unnerved him, added to the already overpowering sense of surreality. It was a space that needed filling, so he filled it.

"You made me come over here. *Compelled* me. I know it sounds crazy, but I know what I felt." He raised a hand to his mouth, wiped moisture away from the corners of his lips. "Why did you do that?"

"I can make you do anything."

He believed it. "Okay."

"I could make you kill yourself. Right now."

A shiver passed through his body. "I believe you."

"I could make you kill the people you love. Even Janine."

"No." This time he didn't bother questioning how she knew something she should not know. She could read his mind. She knew things. Fine. About this, though, she was wrong. She had to be. "You couldn't make me do that. Ever."

For the first time, there was a perceptible change in the set of her features. Her left eyebrow—which had a single, almost understated piercing through it—arched ever-so-slightly. "Oh?" Her inflection, however, remained flat, unchanging. "Do you really think that's true, David?"

Suddenly, he didn't want to answer the question. So he asked a few of his own. "What's going on here? Who are you? What are you doing to me?"

Her head swiveled away from him. She stared straight ahead. "I'm going to give you a choice. A simple matter of picking your destiny. You'll choose your path with your own free will. I will not coerce you."

David sucked in a big breath and blew it right back out. He was close to panicking. Shoppers were passing by in front of him. Men and women. Children. Teenagers. Back and forth, going here and there, many of them passing within a few feet of where he sat with this odd young woman. Every one of them was utterly oblivious to his predicament. He put a hand to his chest, felt the rapid beating of his heart. It was going too fast, like the double-bass drumming common in the death metal music he loved when he was younger. Almost too fast to discern individual beats.

She touched his knee. "Calm down."

His knee turned to ice.

Except that it didn't. Not really. It just felt that way. The chill conveyed by her touch went down to the bone. He shivered. His heart rate began to slow almost immediately. His breathing became more regular.

He swallowed hard and shook his head. "What the fuck? How do you do that?"

She ignored the question and repeated her previous brief speech about a choice he had to make. Of his own free will, she again emphasized.

"Lady . . . what the fuck are you talking about?"

Her head turned slowly back toward him. Her expression was absolutely blank again. "Here it is. You can get up and walk away from here. You can choose to continue with your life as it was a few moments ago. You can marry that woman. If that is your choice, our paths will never cross again. This is my promise to you. And I always keep my promises, I assure you."

David laughed. "Why would I choose anything else?"

"If your devotion to Janine was as strong as you imagine, you would have stated your choice immediately rather than reply with a question."

He frowned. "Bullshit. It's simple human curiosity. Anyone would want to know the rest of it. The rest of . . . whatever the fuck you're talking about."

She stared at him without speaking for several moments. During the silence, he found himself entranced by her lips, which looked . . . delicious. He felt guilty for even thinking about it. It'd been a long time since he'd allowed himself to think of another woman in even a vaguely sexual way. It often wasn't easy, but until now he'd managed to still his roving eye, which had been so active prior to Janine. No other woman could ever seriously tempt him when he had her to come home to every day. But this woman's mouth changed that. He wondered if her lips were as soft as they looked. He wondered whether they would be as cold as the hand on his knee if he were to kiss them.

Her hand came away from his knee.

He drew in another big breath and expelled it. He only became aware of his physical reaction to her touch after she'd removed her hand. He was hard. *Achingly* hard.

A corner of her mouth subtly twitched, hinting at a hidden emotion. Was she smirking or smiling at him? Maybe a little bit of both. She was playing with him. Toying with him, like a spider prolonging the misery of a bug ensnared in its web. And it amused her to do so. This was her idea of entertainment. It should have bothered him, but he found he was oddly okay with it.

"Very well."

He shook his head. "Um . . . what?"

"Here's the rest of it, as you put it."

"Oh. Okay."

"Here is your other choice. Please listen carefully."

He shrugged, his brow furrowing again. "Okay."

"Excellent."

She clasped hands with him. He felt that bone-deep chill again, only now it was more intense, probably because of the direct skin-to-skin contact. The chill spread from his hands up the length of his arms. She leaned closer to him, peered into his eyes, her expression very intent. There was still no obvious emotion he could read, but she was studying him as closely as anyone ever had.

"You can come with me to my secret place."

"You mean . . . your home?"

"Yes. We can go there now, be there in a matter of moments if you accept my offer. I'll show you pleasures beyond anything you ever dreamed possible. You'll have power. You'll live forever." A hint of a smile. "In a manner of speaking."

David managed a nervous laugh. "You make it sound like an offer I can't refuse."

"I've already told you you can refuse it."

Obviously she'd never seen *The Godfather*.

"Wait. What do you mean . . . 'in a manner of speaking'?"

She ignored the question and leaned closer still, until their faces were separated by just inches. Her cold breath frosted his cheeks. "If you choose to come with me, you can never return to your former life. I will own you. Completely and forever. You will do my bidding as long as you exist."

Another nervous laugh. "Oh. Really?"

"Yes."

The cast of her features still conveyed an intense curiosity, but was that a hint of something predatory in her eyes he was seeing now? Her grip on his hands tightened by a very small—but perceptible—degree. The chill her touch conveyed now permeated his entire body. She licked her lips. His heart stuttered at the sight of that pink wedge of tongue. She tilted her head slightly and her face came closer. Their lips were no more than an inch apart now.

"Do you mind if I kiss you?" she asked.

He blinked moisture from his eyes.

Janine, he thought.

He knew he had to keep thinking of her. Understood suddenly that it was the only way to break this spell. More than anything else, he knew he couldn't allow this woman to kiss him. Because if that happened, what remained of his free will would evaporate in an instant.

Janine.

I can't do this.

I can't.

I CAN'T!

Her lips grazed his mouth. He felt her cold breath steal between his lips. Her voice dropped to a whisper. "I need your answer. Now."

He sniffled.

Janine . . . oh, God . . . I'm so sorry . . .

He swallowed thickly. "Yes."

For the first time, a fully formed smile spread across her pale-as-snow face. "*Yes.*" Her voice dropped to a slightly huskier register. "You're mine. All mine." She cupped his face in her ice-cold hands and kissed him fully on the mouth. He groaned. An arctic chill filled his lungs, took root deep inside him, making his whole body tremble uncontrollably.

She broke the kiss off and clasped hands with him again.

"Now we go to my secret place."

"And then what?"

She smiled for a second time. This time there was something secretive in it.

"You'll see."

"Okay."

It was strange. Now that she'd kissed him, thoughts of Janine seemed far away. He was betraying her, but it didn't seem to matter.

And yet, this woman scared him. No amount of mental trickery could disguise that. Or perhaps she was allowing him to remain in touch with his fear of her for obscure reasons.

He knew only one thing with absolute certainty.

She was right.

He belonged to her now.

Completely.

4

HER SECRET PLACE

SHE WAS NUZZLING HIS NECK now. Her cold lips raised goose bumps on his trembling flesh. Something . . . unnatural was happening. There was power in her kisses. Real, palpable power. Each application of her lips to his flesh was like a shot of anesthetic. He was becoming numb. He felt disconnected from his body. It was scary and fascinating at the same time. They were still sitting on the bench in the mall, but the mall was swathed in a shimmering white light. The shoppers walking past the bench were indistinct gray shapes moving in the light, nothing more than vague outlines. They didn't seem real at all now, more like suggestions of people, faint pencil sketches on an otherwise empty sheet of white paper. He felt sort of like a suggestion of a person himself, able to cling only to the faintest notion of who he was. *I'm . . . David?* But the matter of his identity seemed of little consequence. He felt lighter than air, like a balloon floating in the sky on a warm summer breeze, drifting ever higher and higher. It was the most wonderfully freeing sensation he'd ever experienced.

And then it was gone.

Total blackness displaced the tableau of shimmering white light.

The feeling of near weightlessness verging on non-existence ceased in the same abrupt instant. He was in his body again. He felt the ground beneath his feet. He heard sounds. A metallic clinking. Followed by someone moaning. Though he couldn't see anything, it was immediately clear this was not a sexual sound. It was the sound of someone in misery. The moan trailed off into a pitiable whine, followed by a deep inhalation of tortured breath.

A disturbing thought occurred to him. He was dead. This was Hell. He'd died on that bench in the mall. The nameless girl hadn't been a girl at all but was instead some kind of demon. He recalled the way her kisses had numbed him. Wasn't it possible that, with each kiss, she'd been draining the life out of him through some unfathomable supernatural means?

He'd been in a crowded shopping mall a few moments ago. Now he was in this dark place of misery and pain, transported here by some inexplicable method. In a world in which something that incredible could happen, of course it was possible.

He heard a thump, followed by a wet, squelching sound. A scream followed. High and piercing. Then another squelching sound. David didn't need to see what was happening to know what had occurred. What he'd heard was the sound of a blade, likely a rather large one, being thrust into living human flesh and then withdrawn. The victim screamed again. This time the sound was abruptly cut off after another loud thump, which David guessed was the big blade hacking into flesh again. Something hit the ground somewhere just ahead of him and came rolling toward him.

A head, he thought.

That's what I just heard. Some poor bastard just got his head chopped off and it came sailing in my direction. Shit.

The smart thing to do was obvious—get as far away from the invisible murderer as possible. He turned slowly in the perfect darkness, moving with utmost care as he searched in vain for some dim source of light. His whole body was trembling—and not just from the wintry chill in the air. There was nothing. Nowhere to go. Any possible escape route, in the unlikely event one even existed, was perfectly hidden.

The hair on the back of his neck prickled as he became aware of a presence somewhere behind him. A presence coming *toward* him— from the direction he'd been facing a moment ago.

Death is coming for me. This is the end of my life.

If this was truly the end, he could at least face it with some degree of dignity. Better that than to go stumbling blindly into the featureless darkness. He'd trip over something and go sprawling to the ground within moments, then wind up crawling and begging pitifully for his life as Death bore down on him. And probably pissing his pants in the bargain.

Screw that.

He turned slowly around again, willing the tremors to leave his body as the thing in the darkness came closer still. He could sense it out there, moving slowly, coming straight at him, able somehow to see him despite the unbroken blackness.

The voice, when it spoke, was what he expected to hear.

"You are mine."

Her.

He sighed. "Yeah. I suppose I am."

At the sound of his voice, a chorus of moans and entreaties arose from the darkness. It was the sound of the helpless begging for succor, for release from their bonds. Other voices urged him to run before it was too late. He ignored them all. Everyone here was beyond any hope of rescue, himself included.

"You know what amuses me, David?"

Her voice was as chilly and devoid of emotion as it had been during their strange conversation on that mall bench. It was impossible to imagine this creature being 'amused' by anything, but this was her game. Her rules. He was nothing but a pawn. A puppet. He had no choice but to play along.

"No. But I suppose you'll tell me."

She was very close now, perhaps only a few feet away. Her proximity triggered the same mixture of terror and arousal he remembered from before.

"Your notion of dying with dignity. You must know by now you'll only have as much dignity as I allow you. If I want you to beg for your life, you *will* beg. Understand?"

David took an involuntary step backward. "Stay out of my head, lady. This reading my thoughts thing is freaking me out."

Another step back.

And another.

He sensed her rushing toward him. There was no sound of footsteps. It was as if she were gliding above the ground.

Hell, she probably is. Maybe she's not a demon at all. Maybe she's some kind of fucking witch.

"Stay where you are!"

Her tone was stentorian, louder than usual and with a discernible tinge of anger. It was a terrible sound, more awful by far than the now silenced screams of the person she'd just killed. Her voice thrummed with power, conveying her will through streams of energy that effectively locked his feet to the ground. Further retreat was impossible. Disobedience was unthinkable. His head was hurting and his stomach was in knots. He hunched down, hiding his face with his shaking hands. Somewhere very nearby someone was whimpering. In a moment he realized the sound was coming from his own throat. He felt like something low, something less than a man. He was a worm beneath her boot, waiting to be stepped on and crushed out of existence.

"I'm sorry. I-I . . ."

"Shut up."

His mouth snapped shut.

"Drop your hands and stand up straight. And stop cringing."

He did as she said without hesitation—there was no other choice.

She said nothing further for a while, but she was even closer now. He felt her frosty breath on his cheeks. He was turned on again. It was insane. He was in a place of horror, a place that felt like a chamber of hell, a repository of damned souls. Her 'secret place', as she'd called it, was a nightmare land inhabited by people like himself, other flies she'd drawn effortlessly into her web, and here he would spend what remained of his life, probably being tortured without mercy until he was just another pitiful moaning husk lurking in the darkness. And yet, in this moment, the terror he felt at the prospect of this bleak future was not enough to suppress his desire for this creature. When he felt her cold fingertips caress his chin, the light touch was nearly enough to bring him to orgasm. The feeling was so intensely pleasurable that tears welled in his eyes when she pulled her hand away.

A cold exhalation of breath touched his cheeks. Accompanying it was a soft, almost inaudible sound, uncharacteristic for her—soft laughter. It should have angered him, but all he felt now was a deep sense of resignation. And regret. He knew he would never see Janine again, would never have a chance to apologize for his weakness.

"Stop thinking about her."

David shoved any further thoughts of Janine back down into his subconscious. It wasn't easy, but the primal terror evoked by the fierceness of her tone provided all the motivation necessary.

"Would you like a better look at your surroundings?"

Well, that was a strange way to phrase it. A *better* look implied he'd had some kind of actual glimpse of the place at some point. Such was not the case. And, listening again to the low moans and whimpers issuing from seemingly every direction, he wasn't sure that was a bad thing.

"Um . . ."

"I sense reluctance."

David scratched the back of his head and frowned. "Um . . . yeah. It's just all this screaming and so forth. The moans and the carrying on. I find it sort of disturbing."

To understate.

"I see." A brief, contemplative pause ensued. When she spoke again, there was a note of genuine curiosity in her voice. "Tell me something. Whom would you rather be—the person suffering, or the person inflicting the pain?"

"Neither."

"That isn't a choice."

"Oh. Well. Shit." There was no good answer to her question, but he wasn't stupid. He knew what she wanted to hear. "The latter, I guess."

"Smart boy. Too many of your kind are constricted by artificial notions of right and wrong. I sensed you were better than that from the moment I set eyes on you."

David's frown deepened. "What do you mean?"

"On the surface, you are like most other humans, a believer in morality and the concept of consequences for misdeeds. Beneath the surface, though, lurks a capacity for boundless cruelty. For infinite sadism. It was this quality that first drew me to you."

"Well, that's just crazy talk. I'm not a bad person. I'm not . . . cruel."

She laughed. "But you are, as you'll soon discover. I'll show you the truth about yourself. But before I can do that, I have to show you my truth."

Countless flickering pinpoints of light flared to life all around him, tall candles burning in thousands of sconces embedded in the high walls of a vast cavern. The moans of the suffering were suddenly louder, as was the metallic clanking of chain links as they cringed away from the glare of the dancing columns of flame. It was hard to tell how many people were imprisoned here, but the number had to be in the high hundreds, at least. Most of them were bound by chains bolted into the stone walls of the cavern. Iron manacles fastened about their wrists and ankles severely limited their range of motion, which meant they were forced to intermittently move their bowels and empty their bladders wherever they happened to be chained. They were forced to wallow in filth. The entire place reeked of piss and shit and vomit. How had he not noticed that until now? Dozens of other prisoners hung suspended from chains dangling from the roof of the cavern. A closer look revealed that a number of the chained men and women were dead. Some had been dead a long while, their bodies mere husks. Others were freshly dead, the scent of their ripe and rotting corpses battling for supremacy amongst all the other putrid odors. Those still alive were nude and emaciated, their flesh ghostly pale from the lack of sunlight.

In the cavern were several roughly constructed wooden tables, upon which were strapped other emaciated persons (some living, some decidedly not), as well as numerous devices of torture David recognized as being from the Middle Ages. He couldn't name them all, but he was able to identify an Iron Maiden, a Breaking Wheel, and a Spanish Tickler, which was used to tear skin from the bodies of its victims. He recalled being fascinated by descriptions of such devices when he read about them in a long-ago history class. Now, however, he only felt repulsion. These devices weren't museum-piece curiosities. Here, in this stinking section of Hell, they were all in active use.

"This isn't Hell," she said.

David choked back a tide of nausea and focused on the girl again. In the darkness, he'd thought of her only as a creature, as a thing, an . . . *it*. An evil *thing*. The Devil posing as a human female. But the notion was hard to hold on to now that he could see her again. She *was* evil. Of that he was certain. The evidence was all around him. Whatever manner of thing she was, though, human or not, he was certain she was female. A thing composed of flesh and blood rather than a demonic spirit. And he suspected much of her power was in some way rooted in her femininity.

"About that you're right. I am not the Devil." She smiled. "I'm something better."

David was close to losing the battle against the tide of nausea rising within him. The rich stink of the place was thick in his nostrils.

His throat felt constricted. He hunched down and braced his hands on his knees, struggling for breath.

He glanced up at her and managed to squeak out a few words. "Help . . . I'm . . . dying."

Her smile broadened. "About that, you are also right."

He went very still.

Something in her eyes told him she wasn't joking. His gaze went to the long sword she was holding. Dark red blood dripped from the tip of the curved blade. The blood, he realized, of the man he'd heard her decapitate only moments earlier. He tensed. Any second now she'd raise the sword again and the razor-sharp steel would chop through his neck and liberate his head from his body, which at least would have the benefit of putting him out of his goddamn misery.

The slender hand gripping the sword's handle opened.

The heavy blade fell to the ground.

David stared up at her again, confusion etched in his flushed features. "What—"

Whatever he'd been about to say was forgotten as her jaw dropped open, distending to an unnatural length. Rows of glistening sharp teeth flashed in the flickering candlelight as her plump lips peeled away from her mouth. Her nostrils flared and a hissing sound emanated from her throat.

David opened his mouth to scream.

She leaped upon him, clamping her teeth to his throat as she drove him to the ground. She growled and snarled like a wild animal, ripping at his flesh and drinking deep from the blood spurting from his jugular as a final scream died in his throat.

5

THE FIRST NIGHT OF DAVID RUCKER'S UNDEATH

EVERYTHING WENT BLACK.

Not this shit again.

He couldn't see anything, hear anything, or feel anything. He was a nowhere man in a nowhere place. Which reminded him of some fucking song he'd heard on an oldies radio station. It was similar to what he imagined purgatory might be like. The logical conclusion was obvious. He was dead. Or was he? The lack of any sensory input suggested he was no longer among the living, but the ability to form conscious thoughts contradicted the death theory. Or did it? Most major religions believed in a continuation of consciousness after the expiration of the physical body. He could be some kind of floating, disembodied remnant. A soul, he supposed, detached from the physical moorings of a no longer functioning flesh and blood shell.

Blood.

Something about that word excited him, inasmuch as a free-floating remnant or cloud of consciousness can feel such a thing. There was no spike of adrenaline to quicken his heart rate or make him breathe faster. But there was a detectably greater depth of clarity to his thoughts, a sense of discernible mental agitation. The impression was so distinct it was almost as if his thoughts were glowing, manifesting as words and sentences written in bright neon against the backdrop of blackness.

BLOOD.

The last thing he could remember prior to this black nothing was the incredible physical pain resulting from having his throat torn out. All those hideously sharp teeth shredding his flesh, sending shockwaves of the most excruciating agony imaginable coursing through his body. Being without physical substance, he now felt a curious disconnect from that pain, almost as if it had happened to someone else. He was glad for that. Being a disembodied whatever was pretty lame, but it was better than hurting.

Then he remembered something else. It had happened right after the infliction of the fatal wound to his throat. The creature, the whatever-the-hell-she-was, had opened her mouth even wider and had clamped it tight around the wound, her teeth puncturing his ravaged flesh again even as her lips formed a vacuum-tight seal around the wound. And as consciousness had faded, he'd heard a distinct gurgling sound.

The bitch drank my blood.

Every damn drop of it.

That state of mental agitation intensified.

Blood.

Blood.

BLOOD.

It was suddenly all he could think about. Blood was everything. Blood was life. There was no commodity more precious, not even gold. He found he could no longer hold a grudge against the creature that had taken his life. Of course she would want to drink his blood. Blood was food. Sustenance. Drinking it was as necessary as breathing.

It occurred to David his thoughts had taken a very strange turn indeed, but this was a distant realization, occurring at a level far below the important stuff. What *was* important was how very . . . *hungry* he was.

The word pulsed brighter against the blackness now, five block letters in blazing crimson neon:

BLOOD!

BLOOD!

BLOOD!

His eyes snapped open.

He was back in the creature's secret place. That hellish chamber. He heard the moans of the shackled prisoners and the clank of their shifting chains. He blinked and stared up at the high roof of the cavern. The bodies of dead men hung suspended from chains directly above him. Their limp forms filled him with a strange despair.

No blood to be had there.

He stared at the slowly twisting dead bodies some more.

Wait.

Dead?

Like me?

Or . . . not?

Well, surely he'd been wrong about that. He'd merely been unconscious. He was back in his body now. He could think. He could feel. He'd never actually been dead at all. Sure, it was a bit odd how lucid his thoughts had been back there in that formless darkness, but—

His eyes opened wider as he thought of something pretty damned important.

He slapped a hand to his neck and his fingers probed for evidence of the damaged flesh that had to be there. But the wound was gone, replaced by perfectly smooth, unblemished tissue. Had he imagined the whole thing? He didn't think so. He remembered the sensation of her teeth sinking into his flesh with exquisite clarity. And remembered just as clearly the subsequent mind-searing agony. Now he felt something altogether different. Hunger. Arousal. He kept rubbing at the place where the wound had been and realized how cool the flesh was to the touch.

It was like touching ice.

He sat up.

And gasped when he saw her. She was a dozen feet away, sitting in a chair fashioned from the blackened skulls and bones of dead human beings. Except "chair" wasn't quite the right terminology. It was a throne of sorts, a small-scale version of how Satan's infernal perch might look. She was nude now, her discarded goth-punk clothes nowhere in sight. He saw flecks of slowly coagulating blood smeared on her chin and around her mouth. Her naked body was distinctly feminine, her breasts larger than they'd seemed underneath that jacket and t-shirt. She looked like some kind of barbarian queen from an old pulp novel. "You . . . what have you done to me?"

She smiled. "I killed you."

"But . . ." He trailed off, realizing something. This place had felt too hot before, a sensation amplified by the press of too many filthy bodies in an enclosed space. But now he was cold. He held up his hands and stared at them, noting at once that they were paler than before, an almost pure shade of white tinged with blue. His gaze shifted back to the girl—no . . . *woman*; this creature was no mere girl—and he repeated his previous question. "What have you done to me?"

She smirked. "I already answered that one. Surely you have other questions."

He touched his forehead.

Cold. Jesus, why am I so fucking cold!?

"Why am I so fucking cold?"

Another of those chilly, soulless smiles. "Because you're a dead thing, David. You'll feel colder and colder until you feed. And if you don't feed . . . well, that'll be the real end of you."

David wrapped his arms around his torso and began to rock slowly back and forth. "By 'feed' do you mean . . ."

He couldn't bring himself to say it.

She nodded. "You'll have to drink blood."

David stared blankly at her for a long moment.

Then his mind made an intuitive leap.

"Holy shit, you've turned me into a vampire."

She shrugged and scratched flecks of dried blood—*his* blood—from a corner of her mouth with a thumbnail. "Obviously."

He abruptly stopped rocking. His terrified expression gave way to a glare. An urge to charge her and tear her head off her shoulders consumed him. He leaned forward a little, the muscles in his body tensing as a low growl emanated from deep within him. "You . . . *bitch.*"

She laughed. "I won't deny it. I'm the meanest bitch you'll ever meet. Of that let there be no doubt."

His hands curled into fists. He was surprised at how little fear he felt now. Despite the deep chill permeating his body, he realized how good he felt. How strong. How perfectly aware. He'd always kept himself in reasonably good shape, but he'd never been what you could call an athlete. He did a bit of exercising every day, just enough to feel like he wasn't getting sloppy, mostly cardio stuff, but he didn't lift weights or do any other kind of strength conditioning. And yet now he felt real power coiled in his muscles. He felt like he could go toe-to-toe with the toughest motherfuckers around and come out on top. His senses were heightened, too, particularly his sense of smell. Every scent was sharper now, crisper and bolder. The scents of human filth—shit, piss, and sweat—were now so pronounced they should have made his gut clench. He should be on his hands and knees puking his guts up. However, while the smells did disgust him, they produced no physical reaction. Instead, the disgust he felt was psychological. He felt contempt for the producers of the vile excretions.

For the fucking *humans*.

She ran a slender hand up and down the length of one of her porcelain-white thighs, licking her lips as she watched him. David felt his cock grow as he watched her caress herself. Her voice was huskier when she spoke: "You feel it now, don't you? The difference."

David couldn't help it. He smiled. "Yes."

He sprang to his feet and exploded toward her. Exploded, that was the only way to describe the physical sensation. He was upright and mobile in the blink of an eye, all before he was even remotely cognizant of what was happening. The newfound power buzzing through every tendon and nerve-ending in his body propelled him through the air like a rocket. Despite the speed of it, he was conscious of the movements of his body. The pumping of his arms. The pistoning of his legs and the flexing of his powerful thighs. He was running, a simple physical act in essence, but to the human eye he would be just a high-speed blur slashing across space.

Then he was on her.

His astoundingly strong hands wrapped tightly around her neck and began to squeeze. He snarled, eager to feel the surrender of her tender flesh to the crushing force of his hands. He stopped squeezing when he felt something strange inside his head. It was a crawling, insidious sense of something alien, some ethereal tendril, wending its way through the nooks and crannies of his brain.

He let go of her throat and staggered backward a few steps.

Maddeningly, she'd never stopped smiling. "You have a lot to learn about the new you. Many lessons. Here's the first."

He felt something flex inside his head.

Then he was on his back and convulsing violently. He remained conscious and perfectly aware as the tremors continued for an interminable time, his limbs twisting themselves into awkward and frightening configurations as he strove in vain to regain even the slightest measure of physical control. It was useless. She had him firmly in her grip. He was her slave. Her plaything. She could lock his body in a spastic state until he died, if she so desired. He feared his unthinking attack had pissed her off enough to make her do just that. Tears were leaking from his eyes by the time the convulsions abruptly ceased. The instant the shaking stopped he sucked in a massive breath and exhaled a cry of the deepest anguish. Then his body was shaking again, but this time it was from the force of his sobs. He turned onto his side and curled into a fetal ball, squeezing his eyes shut as tears dripped from his face to the damp earth beneath him, ground already stained with the blood of this creature's countless other victims.

His cries mingled with the sobs and moans of the chained men and women hanging from the walls and the cavern's ceiling. For a time he gave himself over to this expression of misery and grief, lost himself in it, and for a fleeting handful of moments it provided a kind of comfort. He wasn't David Rucker, newly minted dead man. He wasn't a man at all. There was no sense of self. He was just a part of a larger organism. A new thing forged from the flesh of all imprisoned in this awful place. It was good not to be David Rucker. Good to be just an unthinking, unfeeling *thing*.

Until the spell was abruptly broken.

"Enough of this pitiful mewling."

David drew in another big breath and forced his eyes open.

She stood over him now, her hands on her hips, primitively regal and majestic, a pose that again reminded him of old pulp novel covers. Something by Boris Vallejo or Frank Franzetta, maybe, from some long-ago sword and sorcery epic. Her body entranced him all over again from this perspective and for a long moment he forgot all about his terror of her. Her legs were perfect. Long and shapely. The sweet swell of her hips and the flat plane of her belly were equally mesmerizing. And those full breasts . . .

Then he looked at her face and saw her smirking.

He gave his head a hard shake and glared at her. "I hate you."

"No. You love me. I am everything to you."

David sneered. "Saying it won't make it so, you evil cunt." He surprised himself with a laugh. Even more surprising was the pronounced disdain in the sound. "Hell, I don't even know your goddamned name. I only love one woman and her name is—"

Her mouth opened in that unnaturally wide way again, her eyes bulging from their sockets as her jaw distended and a scream loud enough to shatter skyscraper windows filled the cavern. The sound went on and on, increasing in volume with seemingly each passing second as the black hole at the center of her face grew wider. David slapped his hands to his ears, but this did nothing to muffle the sound. The sound drilled into his ears and made his brain quiver like jelly until his eyes rolled back in their sockets and consciousness again deserted him.

6

DEPRIVATION

HIS HEAD WAS STILL THROBBING when he awoke an indeterminate time later. The ache extended from his frontal lobe to the back of his neck. It felt much like a hangover after a night of serious drinking. For those first few groggy moments after regaining consciousness, he allowed himself the hope that it *was* a hangover. He'd gone out for a night of boozing with buddies and things had gotten a little out of hand. At some vague point a few too many had turned into *a lot* too many, which accounted for his present state of misery and all the crazy dreams about gorgeous naked vampires and imprisonment in some remote, hellish cavern.

The delusion lasted until the moment he became aware of the heavy chain links encircling his wrists and ankles. His head tilted downward as his eyes fluttered open. His eyes widened and he sucked in a big breath as he realized how high above the ground he was. The vampire woman's throne of blackened skulls and bones looked like a piece of pretend furniture plucked from a dollhouse belonging to Satan's granddaughter. Ditto for all the rickety tables and torture devices. But this did nothing to distance him psychologically from the gruesomeness of the grisly tableau. If anything, this new perspective only enhanced the overall horror of the situation. For one thing, the cavern was much bigger than his original perception of it. You could fit a professional football stadium in this space with plenty of room to spare. He'd noted piles of bones and decaying body parts before, but now he understood how little he'd appreciated the scope of the human detritus. Many of the bone piles were simply *massive*. You'd need a fleet of bulldozers to clear them from the cavern. The ache in his head intensified again as he tried to comprehend how long it would take any single person, vampire or not, to kill this many people. He finally gave up trying to understand it. It was beyond understanding. She wasn't an old thing, she was *ancient*. The beautiful, youthful appearance was a façade, one she maintained through all these stolen lives.

He shifted slightly and winced as the rough cavern wall abraded his bare back. This caused him to shift again. The movement sent spikes of pain shooting up his arms, which were stretched straight up over his head. He turned his head up and peered at the thick length of chain wrapped around his wrists. The chain was secured to an iron bracket bolted to the rock wall. He jerked against the chain links, but they didn't budge. He tried again, putting all his amplified vampiric strength into the effort. One of the bracket's bolts seemed to give an infinitesimal amount. He gathered up his strength to try yanking at it again when something occurred to him. What if he *did* succeed in ripping the bracket from the wall?

His head tilted down and he stared again at the ground far below. *Shit*.

He was already dead. At least that was the case if the vampire had been telling the truth. He was certain, though, that she hadn't been lying about that. He was dead. Undead. Whatever. What was the worst that could happen to him if he fell? He couldn't die again. Could he?

No. Probably not.

But the impact when he hit the ground might shatter every bone in his body or reduce his flesh to pulp. It was what would happen to any normal human body dropping from a height this great. However, the vampire's bite had changed his physiology in some fundamental ways. He suspected the fall would hurt him tremendously, but that he would then heal, become as good as new in a short amount of time. It was a truth he felt in his bones, an essential part of his new reality.

Still . . . it would fucking hurt.

The best course of action could be just to hang out—he couldn't suppress a laugh at that thought—until the she-bitch decided she'd punished him enough. The bitch about that was she might decide to really teach him a lesson and leave him here for a seriously long time. He began to feel sick again as he thought about how a creature like his captor might perceive the concept of "a seriously long time."

Hell, he could be up here for *years*.

He thought about that for a while.

Man. Holy shit. That would really fucking suck. The horror of the situation would begin to abate after a while, after, say, the first six months. Boredom would set in at some point. And then what? He felt an intense queasiness that again ramped up the pain resonating in his skull. This passed quickly, but the sensations were intense enough to tell him he'd overlooked something critical. Another cramp made him wince and cry out. A fresh horror dawned inside him as he realized he was going to have a much larger concern than mere boredom if he was kept hanging here for any significant period of time. His teeth chattered and his whole body began to quiver. The sensation of cold permeating his body was intensifying, becoming all-encompassing, making him feel like some kind of mythological beast. *The Ice Man*. And, like the cramping ache in his belly, it was only going to get worse the longer he went without . . . feeding.

Damn that bitch.

He wanted it. Needed it more than ever. The compulsion to drink blood filled his brain like a fever, as it had in those first frenzied moments of his undeath. The gnawing, churning ache of the need was already nearly intense enough to drive him mad should he be unable to slake the thirst.

He wanted to scream.

He opened his mouth to do just that.

But before he could give voice to the howling need consuming him, a weak sound from somewhere to his left stilled his rage, if only for a moment. He willed his body to stop shaking and turned his head toward the source of the sound. The sound came again as he got his first glimpse of his nearest comrade in torment. An emaciated middle-aged woman was chained and bolted to the stone wall less than six feet away from him. Well, he assumed she was middle-aged, but her actual chronological age was difficult to gauge, so advanced was her state of physical deterioration. She was little more than paper-thin gray skin and bones. David knew at once she'd been hanging there a long time. The muscles in her legs and arms had atrophied. Her breasts were saggy little nubs. Never in his life had he set eyes on a less physically attractive female. He was nevertheless enthralled by the sight of her. Droplets of drool welled at the corners of his mouth as his gaze locked on the weak throb of her pulse visible at the side of her neck, the place where her jugular lurked beneath that fragile gray skin. He pictured himself tearing the vein open and drinking deeply from it. His penis stiffened at the thought. He could even feel a bit of warmth pushing against the awful cold gripping him.

Her eyes fluttered open as she began to perceive his scrutiny. Her head lolled toward him and her mouth dropped open to emit a single hoarse word: "... *helllppp* ..."

David didn't bother responding. She was beyond help. He made a snorting sound deep in his throat as he continued to stare at her neck. He licked his lips and yanked at the chains binding his wrists. There was a scrape of iron against stone as one of the bracket bolts gave way to another infinitesimal amount. He could feel her heart beating and savored the way it sped up as she sensed his hunger.

She shook her head weakly. "*Nooooooo* ..."

The part of him that was still human, some withering remnant of his conscience, was repulsed by the thoughts swirling in his head. But this voice of dissent was no match for his deepening hunger. If he could get to this woman, he would kill her without hesitation and drink every last sweet drop of her blood. He yanked at the chains again, this time putting more strength into the effort than ever. Shiny tears were spilling down the woman's gaunt cheeks. Her terror excited him, added fuel to his exertions. He bellowed his rage and yanked mightily at the chains again and again. But he soon realized there was a limit to how far he could pull the bolts out of the stone. They were anchored pretty effectively, despite the slight amount of give he'd initially experienced.

He opened his mouth wide and screamed out his frustration until his lungs were burning.

And then he screamed some more.

He only stopped screaming when he sensed something rushing toward him from below. He glanced down and saw a sleek, pale shape coming straight at him. It was her. It could only be her. She was coming to punish him in some new way, to maybe rip out his throat to silence his screams. He realized he was wrong an instant later. The sleek white blur solidified as it alighted upon the emaciated woman to his left, hanging onto the bound hag as easily as a bird grips a tree branch. He had been right. It was the vampire. She held his gaze for a moment, a ghoulish grin etched across the pale, angular planes of her beautiful face.

David shook his head. "No. No. She's mine."

The vampire laughed, but said nothing.

She raked the nails of her left hand down the front of the gray-skinned woman's torso, opening five angled horizontal gashes from just above her right breast down to her waist. Dark blood leaked from the rents in her flesh. The vampire dipped her fingers in the blood. Thick globs of crimson dripped from her fingertips as she raised her hand to her mouth. David's heart shot into overdrive as he watched her slowly lick the blood from her fingers. He was already painfully aroused, so there was no need to overtly sexualize the blood-drinking, but she did so anyway, drawing the full length of each finger slowly in and out of her mouth, groaning and curling her lips in a parody of fellatio. David moaned and bucked against the chains binding him to the wall. He cried out and strained toward her with all his might, but both the vampire and the bleeding woman remained frustratingly out of reach.

The vampire laughed.

Then she let go of the gray-skinned woman and fell away from her, speeding back to the blood-stained ground far below. David watched her sleek form slice through the air, knowing she'd land as lightly and easily as she'd alighted upon the bound woman. He wondered if he could do the same thing. It wasn't something he sensed innately, the way he knew he'd recover from most any grievous injury. His brow furrowed as he gave it deeper consideration. He was a new vampire, but she'd been this way a very long time, centuries, perhaps even longer. Maybe the flying thing was an ability he could develop over time. Being bound, however, flight experimentation wasn't an option anyway, so his attention soon shifted back to the bleeding woman.

Her glassy eyes stared at him, bespeaking a silent, anguished plea. *Help me . . . help me . . .*

He didn't care about helping her. The realization should have disturbed him, but it did not. He understood now the true reason for his current shackled state. He was being forced to accept the truth of what he had become. Well, the lesson had been driven home with insidious effectiveness. He no longer cared about right or wrong. Any sense of repulsion had vanished. There was only . . . attraction. Need. All-consuming thirst. The angled slashes across the woman's torso were deep and blood continued to spill out of them. He watched as a thick stream of crimson slid down her inner thigh, then into the crook behind her knee and down the back of her atrophied calf. He kept watching in helpless fascination as the life continued to leak out of her, his frustration growing with each wasted droplet of precious blood. This was torture of a most exquisitely cruel variety. The thing he desired most—*needed* most—was so tantalizingly close . . . and yet so completely beyond his reach.

He began another furious, flailing assault on the chains. Maddeningly, they gave no more than they had before. But this failure only further inflamed him. He screamed and flailed and raged until both his wrists snapped and his voice was reduced to an inaudible rasp. His broken bones knitted back together within minutes, but he was unable to maintain the intensity of the struggle.

The bleeding woman's head drooped forward. The blood had ceased spilling from the wounds because her heart was no longer pumping. She was dead.

David sobbed quietly for hours.

He was so hungry.

So thirsty.

Would there ever be any relief?

The answer came a few long hours later. He sensed something rushing up at him again and knew the vampire was returning. She unlocked the chains, cradled him in her arms, and swooped back toward the ground. David felt dazed as she landed smoothly and set him down on his feet.

On the ground in front of him was another bound woman. This one was much younger and infinitely more attractive than the pitiful, gray-skinned thing the vampire had used to taunt him. She'd been stripped naked. Unlike most of the pitiful things chained to the walls here, she retained most of her vitality, so much so David suspected she'd been freshly captured. She had long, midnight-black hair that fell lushly about her narrow shoulders. She was slender but curvy, with long, exquisitely toned legs.

She looked . . . *delicious*.

That screaming, agonizing, overwhelming hunger returned with a vengeance and he strained toward her, but the vampire kept a firm lock on his wrist, holding him easily in place. "Look at me."

David looked at her.

She smiled. "Yes. You are much more compliant now. Good. Do you want her?"

He groaned. "Yes. More than anything."

"More than you want me?"

David hesitated. He didn't know how to answer that one. He only knew he didn't want to piss her off again. "I . . ."

"You said something about not knowing my name before. Would you like to know it?"

David blinked at the abrupt shift of topic. He wanted the focus to remain on the apparent sacrificial offering chained up on the ground in front of him, but this was a tricky mental game the vampire was playing. He didn't want to make any more missteps. "Um . . . sure. I'd like that."

"My name is Narcisa Vulpes."

She watched him with a strange glitter of expectation in her eyes.

David coughed. "Okay. Cool."

"Do you like?"

David summoned a smile. "It's a fucking awesome name. Maybe the coolest ever."

"It's Romanian."

David nodded eagerly, as if no one had ever said anything so astonishing. "Wow. Romanian. That's super fantastic."

She relinquished her grip on his wrist. "Look at her. I selected her for you. Are you pleased with my choice?"

David nodded again. "Pleased. Yeah. That's one word for it."

"Then take her. Drain the life from her. Complete your transformation."

David didn't need to be told twice, even as her choice of words carved a niggling slice of doubt in what little remained of his conscience. Was she saying he wouldn't fully be a vampire until he consumed the blood of an innocent? It seemed an obvious conclusion, but the fierceness of the ache churning in his belly rendered the question irrelevant. He was no longer capable of holding back.

He snarled and leapt upon the bound woman. Her eyes fluttered open as he shoved her legs apart and shoved his rigid cock deep inside her. She moaned as he moved inside her, becoming helplessly aroused by the invasion. David knew she'd be screaming and flailing at him if he was still a normal man. But he wasn't normal. He wasn't even really a man anymore. She sighed and strained toward him. He leered at her and opened his mouth wide. He felt a popping of his jawbones as his mouth distended, his gums bulged and his teeth grew sharper and longer. His cheeks felt strangely elastic as his jaw dropped lower than humanly possible. He kept staring into the woman's eyes, expecting to see terror bloom there any moment. But she seemed numb to the reality of what was happening to her. She looked drugged. Perhaps the effect of some vampiric pheromone. He had no way of knowing.

He slapped her. Hard. "Look at me."

Her pupils remained dilated. Her smile was beatific. She moaned. "Yes. Yes. I see you."

He slapped her again, much harder than before. Her eyes began to focus more sharply on him. Good. That was what he wanted. "I'm going to kill you."

There it was. The terror.

It was the most beautiful thing he'd ever seen.

He ejaculated deep inside her as he snarled again and ripped out her throat. A jet of hot blood hit his face. The feel of it against his flesh was wonderfully warm. The bone-deep cold began to leach from his body. He clamped his mouth around the ragged wound, perfectly sealing it, and drank deeply from her. She moaned and writhed slowly against him, still aroused despite what was happening to her. He drank greedily, his throat bulging as he quickly suctioned every drop of blood from her body.

He rolled away from the corpse and sat up, grinning at Narcisa, who stood nearby with her arms folded beneath her breasts. She wasn't smiling now. The coldly appraising expression he remembered from the shopping mall was back.

"Enjoy yourself?"

The grin wouldn't leave his face. "Yes. God, yes."

"Feel any guilt for the life you've taken?"

"None."

She nodded. "Good. It's finished then. There's nothing human left in you."

"Good fucking riddance."

Another nod. "Do you feel satisfied, as if you couldn't possibly drink another drop?"

He shook his head again. "Not even close."

Now she allowed herself a smile, a small one that slightly dimpled the corners of her mouth. "Care to join me in a hunting expedition?"

BLOODRUSH

He surged to his feet and approached to within inches of her. He felt her cool breath on his cheeks, an indicator she hadn't imbibed since partaking of the gray-skinned woman. And that had only been a taste. She was ravenous. He could smell the need on her. Sniffing it reignited his own thirst.

"I'll follow you anywhere."

Her smile broadened. "Good."

She clasped hands with him. A white radiance began to fill the cavern as the tactile world started to fade. This he remembered from those last moments on the bench at the shopping mall. He felt a little twinge of nervous anticipation as he realized what would happen next. The moments of fading consciousness, that strange sensation of ceasing to exist. He experienced a moment of starkest terror as the process began, then relaxed as it continued, a numbness overtaking him as the world and consciousness itself faded . . .

7

INITIATION

HE CAME OUT OF THE light and into the dark. There was a jarring sense of displacement, followed by a wave of disorientation. For a long, heart-pounding moment, he wasn't sure who he was or what he was. He was a thing in the darkness, possessed of a rudimentary consciousness but no deeper sense of self. There was something oddly comforting in that. Then it came to him. His name was David Rucker. He was a man. Or formerly a man. He was something else now. Something stronger. Something better.

Something hungry.

Always fucking hungry.

The darkness puzzled him. It was dark and someone was screaming. There was an obvious conclusion. She had been toying with him. There would be no hunt. No rampaging exercise in wanton, unrestrained slaughter. He was still in Narcisa's secret place. He'd wind up chained to that cold cavern wall again, where he'd spend the rest of his miserable existence, gasping and starving from lack of—

The paranoia deserted him as his newly sharpened senses began to detect distinct differences between this place and that filthy cavern.

95

They were in a house. A bedroom. Two figures writhed atop a dimly visible bed, covered by a single silk sheet. One of the figures, a woman, was screaming, but it was a sound of intense pleasure rather than pain. The air in the room was rich with an array of pungent odors, chiefly sweat and the musky scent of sex. He listened for a while as the couple on the bed fucked with admirable enthusiasm, both of them perfectly oblivious to his presence here, at least for the moment.

He felt something touch his elbow.

Narcisa.

She smiled. "Kill them."

The woman on the bed made another high-pitched sound, but this time there was a note of surprise mingled with the passion. The man atop her grunted and chuckled softly, the smugly satisfied sound of a man who believes he has just taken his woman to previously unattained erotic heights.

David took a step toward the bed. He could see better in the dark now. There was no artificial light in the room and only the dimmest diffused moonlight filtered through the closed window shades. Seeing anything should have been next to impossible. Yet the shape of the bed was now crisply defined within the gloom, as were the shapes writhing on the bed. The man and woman were both young and athletic. The man's upper torso was heavily muscled, yet lean, likely the result of a balanced mix of cardio and strength training. The knowledge should have given him pause, but he felt no fear. Not the slightest flicker. This man would be a formidable opponent for any human assailant. But because David was no longer human, all he felt was a sense of heightened anticipation. In life, he would have been no match at all for this man. Now, though . . . now he would revel in tearing the smug son of a bitch to pieces.

The woman made a sharper, even higher-pitched sound of surprise. She was staring straight at him now, straining to make out the shape moving toward her in the darkness. David kept coming closer. The woman started pounding on her man's back when he reached the edge of the bed.

"STOP! STOP!"

She was screaming yet again, but this time in sheer terror. Her lover stopped in mid-thrust and craned his head around to squint at the darkness. He let out a startled gasp that made David smile. The shape of his body would be visible now against the faint backdrop of the moonglow seeping in at the edges of the large window directly behind him. The man disengaged himself from his woman and spun around on the bed, priming his body for attack. The woman scrambled away from him, going for a nightstand next to the bed.

A light snapped on. A lamp with a heavy brass base. The woman was still in motion. She was a tall blonde, maybe an inch or two shy of six feet, lean and muscled like her lover. She also had enormous tits. Real ones, too. He could tell from the way they moved and jiggled as she strained and reached for the handle of a nightstand drawer. The drawer came open and out came a handgun. Some kind of automatic. David didn't know much about guns, but he knew that.

The man was sneering at them. "Who the hell are you freaks and what are you doing in my house?"

David's smile broadened. "My name's David Rucker and I'll be your murderer tonight." He shot a glance over his shoulder at Narcisa and chuckled. "That was a wicked badass line, wasn't it? I'll have to remember that one so I can use it every fucking time I do this."

The man glared at him. "What!? You people need to get out of here before we call the police."

Narcisa approached the bed, propped a bare knee on the edge of the mattress. "No one's calling the police tonight, dear."

The blonde waved the automatic at her. "Off the bed or I'll fucking shoot you both." Her lithe, toned body glimmered in a sheen of sweat, a result of the interrupted erotic exertions with her husband, boyfriend, whoever the fuck he was. The sight of her glistening skin stirred something in David, almost to the point of distraction. His eyes narrowed to slits as they traced the lines of her luscious curves. Drool collected at the corners of his mouth.

And now the woman was scowling at him, a mixture of alarm, disgust, and disdain flashing in her eyes. "Oh my god, he's getting a hard-on."

The man's face twisted in disgust. "Ugh. You fucking creep. One last chance. Find your clothes, wherever the fuck they are, put them on, and get the hell out of my house. Otherwise I am definitely calling the cops. You've got ten seconds to get gone. Ten, nine—"

David ignored the countdown. He stroked his chin and continued to ogle the blonde woman. All he could think of was how much he'd love to feel those giant tits crushed against his chest. Only thing better would be the subsequent feel of her mangled neck flesh sliding down his gullet, followed by the warm rush of her blood.

The woman's scowl became more pronounced. "Oh, Jesus. He's touching himself." She aimed the barrel of the gun straight at his face. "Fuck this. I'm shooting the fucking pervert. Then I'm shooting his bitch. They're intruders. Naked, perverted home invaders."

A blur passed before David's eyes. Narcisa, of course, doing that super-fast thing again. He heard a loud snap, followed by an agonized cry. The gun went spinning across the room. It banged against a closet door and dropped to the carpeted floor with a quiet thump. And now the blonde woman's right wrist was broken and hanging at an obscenely unnatural angle. She scooted backward in the bed, cradled her mangled limb against her chest, and screamed. The man tumbled sideways, falling prone on the far side of the bed. He gaped at the sight of his woman's broken wrist. His gaze jumped from Narcisa to David and back again, his face a study in wide-eyed, uncomprehending horror. He was a classically handsome type, with a chiseled jaw, piercing blue eyes, and short, spiky hair. The good looks and the athletic physique made him the kind of guy David would normally envy and even kind of hate. David knew he was okay-looking enough in his own right, but nowhere near this dude's league. This was the kind of guy who would always have whatever he wanted. Nice clothes, nice house, nice car, good job, and, of course, the hottest girl around. And he would certainly have more than enough scratch to buy that girl the flashiest, most expensive engagement ring possible, the kind David had been so desperate to give Janine.

Janine. Jesus.

It was the first he'd thought of her since being released from the chains. Thinking of her was like a slap in the face. A hard one. The terrified man's expression changed, became almost hopeful. Which was ridiculous. He was going to die. How could he not know that? But Janine's abrupt intrusion into David's thoughts must have caused his face to convey doubt about what he was doing. And, in fact, it did stir a mild flicker of conscience. He experienced a dizzying moment of surreality, during which it struck him as insanely absurd he was a participant in an apparent torture-murder scenario. The sensation deepened as he imagined what Janine would think if she could see him now.

Mr. GQ slithered off the bed, stood erect, and backed up until he was against the wall. He glanced nervously to his left, where the bedroom door stood open. Any moment now he'd be making a dash for it.

David gave his head a hard shake, clearing it—at least temporarily—of thoughts of Janine. A nasty, smirking half-smile twisted one side of his face. "Not thinking of making a run for it, are you?"

The man was shaking. Tears leaked from his eyes. "Please. You don't want to do this. I know it . . . I—"

"You don't know shit."

The man must have read something else in his expression now, because he dropped any further pleas for mercy and made an abrupt break for the door. David hurried after him, tackling him in the hallway. He was laughing as he took the man down, an evil, nasty madman's cackle. He'd never moved so fast when he was alive. Apparently that vampire fast-running thing happened instinctively. The man was screaming and thrashing, but David held him down easily, savoring the feel of the struggling thing beneath him. That's what humans were to him now. Things. And this son of a bitch certainly wasn't his superior in any way that counted at this point. His charmed life was over. No amount of money or charisma could save him from his fate.

David dragged the guy back through the open doorway and flung him across the bedroom. One problem. He'd held onto the guy's wrist too tightly and his arm came off at the socket. A bright arc of blood spattered the bed, the ceiling, Narcisa, and the woman with the broken wrist as the man's body flew through the air and smashed against the far wall. Narcisa was off the bed in an instant, eager to drink deeply from the man's severed arteries before he could bleed out. Her mouth opened and elongated before clamping over the wound. The man's head thumped back against the wall and his eyes glazed over as Narcisa fed, quickly draining the life from him.

The woman's screaming was getting louder and shriller. She sounded like a goddamned air raid siren. Time to put a stop to that. David didn't know where this house was or how close it was to its nearest neighbor, but it couldn't be a good idea to let that continue. He jumped on the bed and pounced on her, slapping a hand over her mouth. Her eyes bulged from their sockets as she continued to scream against his palm, which effectively muffled the shrill sounds. He positioned himself comfortably atop her, utilizing his vampire's strength to pin her in place, then he used his free hand to grip her broken wrist and twist it even further out of shape. He heard a grinding sound. Bones twisting and cracking. But he was careful not to use too much force. He wanted to hurt her, but he didn't want her hand to snap off. He wasn't ready to make her bleed out yet. He wanted this to last.

An image of Janine's face abruptly appeared in his head.

His body abruptly went rigid.

I'm a monster. Oh, Jesus, I've become a fucking monster.

For a single flashing second, he felt like crying. But the pang of conscience was even shorter-lived this time. He made a mental note to quiz Narcisa later regarding how long he could expect to deal with these lingering traces of departed humanity. They were a serious drag as they were happening and were getting in the way of his fun. Just as her man had done, the woman detected the brief flicker of doubt by looking into his eyes. She stopped struggling.

Which was awfully considerate of her.

David's mouth snapped open, jaw unhinging as his teeth sharpened and lengthened. The woman's eyes went wide again. David tore a side of her slender throat open and clamped his mouth over the ragged hole. A hot gush of blood filled his mouth and he drank deeply of it, greedily, as if he could never get enough. Which, come to think of it, was probably true. He drank and drank, keeping at it as the woman's body went still beneath him, until after she was dead and he'd suctioned out the very last drop. Sated, he pushed himself away from her and sat back on the bed, resting his head against the headboard. He felt warmer than he'd felt since the change. There wasn't the slightest trace of a chill. He smiled and savored the feeling, knowing it wouldn't last nearly long enough.

Narcisa crawled onto the bed, slithered over to him and straddled him. Her voice was a husky, hot whisper against his ear as she leaned into him, brushing his chest with her erect nipples.

"Fuck me."

David smiled. "Mmm . . . okay."

She mounted him, guiding his rigid cock up inside her wet center. Within a few moments, there was screaming in the room again. More than once as their lovemaking continued, David snuck glances at the dead woman next to him.

Stared at her unmoving eyes.

It made it better.

~

They fucked another time before leaving the house, this time in the shower with the water cranked to its hottest temperature. The scalding water sluiced the blood from their bodies as they writhed against each other and hungrily clawed at one another. Sharpened nails opened gouges in their flesh that wept blood but healed instantly. It was the most intense sex David had ever experienced and as it was happening he wished it would never end. While it was happening, Janine didn't exist. Nothing mattered but Narcisa and this incredible experience they were sharing.

But it did end and, inevitably, thoughts of Janine returned.

And this time they didn't abate instantly.

They were back in the bedroom now, sifting through the dead couple's respective wardrobes in search of suitable clothing. The blonde's clothes were a little big for Narcisa, who was shorter and slightly built, but the difference wasn't so pronounced she couldn't wear them. David and the dead man were the same approximate height, but Mr. One Arm had been thinner and his clothes were a snug fit. However, they would do until he found more appropriate attire.

Narcisa watched him as he sat on the edge of the bed and tried on a selection of the dead man's shoes. "You're thinking about her."

David grunted. "Huh. You can still read my thoughts, even though I'm like you now, but I can't read yours."

"I'm many hundreds of years older than you. It will be a long while before you can read anyone's thoughts, let alone mine." She pursed her lips. "And you're evading the question."

Another grunt. "I wasn't aware there was a question. Sounded like a statement to me." The athletic shoes he'd slipped on were too small. He tossed them aside and tried on a pair of hiking shoes, brown Timberlands. "But, yeah, you're right. I can't seem to keep her out of my head. She keeps popping back in. It bugs the shit out of me."

"Oh?"

Narcisa's tone was neutral, but David knew he had to tread carefully here. She'd already made it abundantly clear there could be no room in his life for anyone other than her. Which, now that he was able to think about it with a clearer head, was sort of strange, considering she'd only set eyes on him for the first time less than a day ago.

Unless—

He frowned.

Unless that wasn't the case at all. It didn't make sense that she'd focused on him so intently after chancing upon him randomly. Otherwise, he'd be another dead body piled atop a towering mountain of moldering carcasses in her secret place.

"I've been watching you for months."

Oops.

Mind reader. Right. He was going to have to stay cognizant of that. "Um . . ."

She shook her head. "Never mind that now. You were saying how it bothers you that you keep thinking of the cunt you'd been wasting your time with."

"Well . . . I don't think I phrased it quite that way, but . . . yeah."

She was staring at him very intently now. It was hard not to squirm under the power of that gaze. It took every shred of nerve he possessed not to look away. "There is a solution to this problem."

The Timberlands were a more acceptable fit. Still loose around the toes, but better. He stood up. "And what would that be?"

She smiled. "We cut out the problem at its root. We go see this cunt and . . ." The smile broadened. "We tear her to pieces and drink her blood together."

"I see."

"Do you have a problem with that?"

"I . . ." David fidgeted, shifted his weight from one leg to another. She would know if he lied. That was the problem. He sighed. "I honestly don't know."

Narcisa moved a few steps closer to him. "This does not make me happy. You may require further discipline. Would you care to spend more time in chains?"

He was trembling now. As much as the thought of killing Janine troubled him—and he was surprised to discover it troubled him immensely—the thought of being deprived of blood again bothered him more. "No. I'll do whatever you say. Whatever's . . . necessary. I trust you. If you think this is how I'll get past this problem, then that's what we'll do."

She laughed. "Of course we'll kill her. I wasn't seeking your approval. Killing the cunt has been on the agenda from the beginning. Of course, I could've done it already, but it's important to me that we kill her together. It's the only way we can bond in the way I want. And it's the only way I could come to truly trust you."

David nodded. "I understand."

The fucked up thing was that he did understand.

Completely.

8

OLD TIMES THERE ARE NOT FORGOTTEN

ON THE FREEWAY NOW, HEADING into the suburbs of Atlanta. It was past midnight and the traffic heading out of the city wasn't too heavy. Narcisa sat behind the wheel of the BMW Z4 convertible, one hand on the wheel with the stiff wind blowing her midnight-black hair straight back. The car belonged to the blonde woman they had killed. The blonde woman *he* had killed, David reminded himself. That one was solely on him. It was still hard to think of himself that way. As a killer. But the oddness of it didn't make it any less true. He'd spent a few moments riffling through the dead woman's purse before they departed from the house. Her name had been Anna Cooper. According to her Georgia driver's license, she'd been barely twenty-six-years-old at the time of her death, having had a birthday a week earlier.

Her license photo showed a young woman with a radiant smile. A winning smile. He'd never seen anyone look so good in their driver's license photo. It was almost kind of nauseating. Not enough so to confirm her as deserving of a horrible death, of course, but it did make him feel somewhat better about it, albeit in a twisted way.

"Humans don't deserve your sympathy."

David flinched. He'd been lost in his own thoughts. He glanced over at Narcisa. She was staring straight ahead, her eyes locked on the road.

"It's not sympathy. Not exactly."

"Oh?"

He shrugged. "What do you expect? I'm new to this whole killing thing." He recalled the sense of sick exhilaration he'd felt as he'd played with the dying woman's broken wrist. "It's not sympathy, at least not more than a mild echo of it. I enjoyed killing her. I can't deny that. And yet there's this nagging little trace of a conscience now and then. It's that remnant of humanity that makes me curious, that makes me need to understand what I've taken out of the world."

Narcisa's head inclined slightly forward, a noncommittal half-nod. "I vaguely recall similar feelings when I was turned, but that's been so long ago now."

He stared at her for a long, silent moment, "So . . . how long ago, exactly, was that?"

"Too long ago to make sense to you. So long ago we are almost literally from different worlds."

David frowned. "Then why—"

She eased the BMW into the right lane and hit the blinker switch. David glanced to his right and saw a green exit sign looming ahead.

"Um . . . what are we doing?"

"Stopping. Obviously."

He watched the green exit sign whiz by, his brow furrowing as the BMW's speed decreased. "Reason?"

She smiled without looking at him. "There's an all-night diner near here. Quaint little place. I . . ." She chuckled. ". . . dined there some time ago."

The car slowed more, leaving the highway as its tires kissed the exit ramp, a gray loop that curled around behind a stand of tall trees. David saw bright neon through the trees. The diner, he assumed. "When you say you 'dined' there . . ."

"I slaughtered a half-dozen so-called innocents. This was before your time, back in the 1970s. I haven't been back since."

"And you're returning now . . . why?"

She smiled and shrugged. "Nostalgia. A wistful desire to revisit the site of fond memories. We're in a little suburb called Alpharetta. Unimaginative press types dubbed my previous visit here 'The

Alpharetta Diner Massacre'."

David grunted. "I suppose you're planning a belated encore performance."

"Of course."

"How many people are we gonna kill tonight?"

"Many. Very, very many." She glanced at him. "Does that trouble you?"

"Killing doesn't trouble me. Possibly getting caught does. Surely we've each had enough blood tonight to last us a while. Doesn't it make sense to strike fast one time, like we did back there at that house, then lie low for a while?"

A broad smile spread across Narcisa's face as she tossed her head back and laughed without any of her usual reservation. Then she looked at David, a big smile still stretched across her face (though he noticed there was no hint of mirth in her pitiless eyes). "You're still thinking like a human. Getting caught isn't a concern." She reached out and touched his face, her fingertips tracking a cool path along his jawline. "New vampires are so adorable."

David frowned. "Do you make new ones often?"

"Depends on your definition of 'often'. I am surpassingly old. I last turned a human a decade ago. She was a disaster. An unruly, rebellious, insolent child."

"What happened to her?"

"I destroyed her."

David drew in a slow, shuddery breath and carefully released it. "Oh. I see."

The BMW pulled into the diner's mostly empty lot. Narcisa parked the car behind a big Ford F-150. She turned the engine off, twirled the keyring around a finger, and patted him once on the cheek. "Oh, don't worry. You're nothing like her. You're far more mature, for one thing. That's why I watched you for so long before drawing you in. I needed to be certain you were the one for me."

David felt uncomfortable again. He shifted in his seat, stealing glances at the brightly lit diner as he fidgeted beneath Narcisa's steady gaze. "How did you . . ."

"Choose you?"

"Yeah."

"Fate. You caught my eye one day several months ago while I was out people-hunting in the same mall where you were shopping for the cunt's engagement ring. That day you were engaged in something marginally more sensible."

David frowned and scratched his chin. "I was?"

She nodded. "You purchased a large television from an electronics store."

"Huh. Funny. I remember having the strangest feeling that day, as if someone was watching me. I kept looking around, trying to figure out who was eyeballing me." He laughed once, a humorless sound. "I chalked it up to paranoia. I guess I should've trusted my instincts."

Narcisa shrugged. "Sometimes they *are* out to get you, as the saying goes. The people I track only see me if I wish them to. That day I elected to stay invisible. So I could study you. And that's what I did. I followed you everywhere. Saw how you lived your life. Came to know all the things you cared about. By the time I decided to draw you in, I knew you inside and out. And I liked what I'd discovered. I knew I had to have you, had to make you mine. Forever."

Hearing all this was more than a little creepy. It wasn't every day you learned a mysterious supernatural creature had been stalking you for the better part of a year. He supposed it didn't matter much anymore. She'd drawn him in, as she put it. She had turned him. It was done and there was no going back. It was best to accept it and let her show him the way from this moment forward.

After all, he didn't want to wind up like that "insolent child".

She patted him on the cheek again. "Smart boy."

This time David didn't even cringe. The thoughts she'd read would reassure her she'd made a good choice. And that felt really, really important at the moment. Right now he was her prized new pet, but she had him on a short leash. He sensed it wouldn't take too many mistakes to cause her to reassess her choice.

So don't make any mistakes, motherfucker.

And yet . . .

There was one more thing he had to know. "You remember at the mall, when you told me it was my choice, whether to go with you or not?"

Her eyes glittered with amusement. "Yes."

He forced himself to say it. "That was a lie. Wasn't it?"

"Yes."

Well, that pretty much said it all. It was what he'd suspected. And given the circumstances, pursuing it was less than useless.

She elaborated a bit anyway. "It's fun to play with helpless things."

"Okay."

"You learned that for yourself tonight, didn't you?"

He grimaced. "Right. Yeah. I guess I did."

"Good. Now then—let's eat."

They got out of the car and started across the parking lot toward the bright lights of the diner. It was a cool night, a fact emphasized by the stiff breeze that roughly brushed his face before shifting direction. He shivered and noted a chill was beginning to prickle his flesh again. It was disconcerting to realize how short-lived the warmth provided by draining out a human body was. Narcisa was "surpassingly" old. It was little wonder her secret place doubled as a mass grave that could rival any other in history.

Thinking of that wretched place prompted another question. "Why are we driving anywhere? Couldn't you just magic us to wherever we need to be?"

"I find driving soothing. I like the feel of the wind in my face. And I like the throb of the engine vibrating through my body. I like the sound of tires on the open highway. It's all so very . . . mmm . . . *sexy*. Few things are more sensually satisfying than driving a finely tuned automobile."

David said, "Huh."

A bell jingled as Narcisa banged through the diner's front entrance. Heads turned at the counter as they came strutting inside. Well, Narcisa strutted. David followed stiffly in her wake, his eyes darting in every direction, his nerves buzzing even though he knew there was virtually no chance anyone here could harm him. On the plus side, there weren't many people in the diner at this hour. A pudgy, gray-haired woman sat on a stool behind the counter near the cash register. She was reading a paperback romance novel and didn't look up as they entered. David guessed she was in her fifties. A younger man dressed in white was visible in the open kitchen area behind the counter. The cook, presumably. A skinny Mexican janitor moved a wet mop in slow circles over the tiled floor at the far end of the dining space. A waitress in a short skirt was bussing tables as they came in, loading dishes onto a black tray. The waitress was a slender woman with tired, red-rimmed eyes and the kind of blonde hair that came from a bottle, age probably a shade south of forty. The only customers present were the three at the counter, all of whom were grossly overweight. Their massive bottoms overlapped both sides of the stools upon which they were sitting. Their bulging bodies strained the cheap Wal-Mart clothes they wore. Two were jowly, red-faced men, and the other was perhaps the single least attractive woman David had ever had the displeasure of setting eyes on. It was obvious the trio were all related somehow.

He couldn't suppress a smirk.

The family that dines together, dies together.

The gray-haired woman behind the register glanced up from the romance paperback as they approached the counter. She squinted at Narcisa for a moment, then her eyes went wide with shock. She dropped the book and hopped off the stool, instinct propelling her backward until her back met the partition separating the counter area from the kitchen. The stool toppled over and struck the floor with a clatter.

Narcisa beamed at the terrified woman. "Well, hello. We meet again. Long time, no see."

The woman opened her mouth wide and screamed with everything she had.

David cringed.

Murder and the joys of sadism were things he'd come to appreciate, but all the screaming that went along with those simple pleasures was a thing he could see tiring of in a hurry.

Narcisa glanced at him. "I didn't kill them all that night back in the '70s. This caterwauling hag was barely out of her teens then. Back then she was a hard-working young waitress. But now, apparently, she's paid her dues and gets to sit on her fat ass all night. It warms my heart to know she made the most out of the second chance I gave her back then. And all she had to do to earn that chance was slit her manager's throat." She smiled at the gray-haired woman again. "I suppose you left that part out of your account of the incident to the police, eh?"

The woman screamed throughout this speech.

David glanced around, becoming decidedly nervous again. Everyone in the place was watching them warily now, eyes shaded with confusion and heaping helpings of mistrust. One of the obese trio, the woman, shoved another thick strip of bacon into her mouth as she watched them. David had a sudden urge to seize her and fill her throat with every scrap of food in the place, just keep shoving it all in until she choked on it.

The waitress shot glares at each of them as she hurried to the counter and tried to engage the screaming woman. "Martha! Martha! What's wrong? Who are these people?"

Martha pointed a shaky finger at Narcisa. "It's her. The murdering bitch who killed all my friends in the '70s."

The waitress's eyes narrowed with obvious skepticism as she appraised Narcisa again. "Martha . . . this girl's barely more than twenty. She can't be the—"

Martha resumed her screeching: "*IT'S HER!*"

The two fat men at the counter glanced at each other. One of them wiped the grease from his fingers with a well-soiled napkin and said, "Somethin' funny's happening here."

The other one answered, "Uh-huh."

David guessed the trio's combined IQ *might* reach the triple digits.

The waitress managed a strained smile as she addressed Narcisa. "Ma'am, maybe you and your friend should just go. Martha's overworked and tired and needs to calm down. We're awfully sorry for the inconvenience."

Narcisa giggled. "Oh no, we're not leaving. You see, she's one hundred percent right. I killed Martha's friends way back when, with a little assistance from her, and now I'm back to further reduce the moron population."

The cook emerged from behind the partition. He clutched a large caliber revolver in a meaty hand. "Get out before I call the police."

Narcisa rolled her eyes. "Again with the calling the police threats. I've had about enough of that nonsense for one evening."

She leapt cat-like onto the counter, then dropped down on the floor behind it. This happened faster than anyone could blink. She pried the pistol from the cook's big hand, pointed the barrel at his face, and squeezed the trigger.

BAM!

The bullet blew a big hole through the center of the man's face and a bigger one out the back of his head. A spray of blood and bone fragments sailed over the partition and splashed on the sizzling oven on the other side. His big body dropped like a rock, toppling backward against a sink and knocking over stacks of just-cleaned glasses, which rolled off and shattered on the floor. Suddenly everything was chaos and noise. The Mexican janitor dropped his mop and made a run for the door. David intercepted him before he could get there. The man fought hard at first, landing a solid, hammering punch to the side of David's head that would have turned his lights out if he'd still been human. But David the vampire was unfazed. He grabbed the man's wrist and spun him around. The man continued to struggle as David drove him down to the floor. He took the feisty janitor out of the equation by breaking his legs. The loud snapping of bones was very satisfying. He left the broken man squalling on the floor to deal with the waitress, who was the next to try for the door.

He got there well ahead of her, leering lasciviously as he blocked the door. "Sorry, not happening. We're just getting started."

Her eyes filled with tears and looked even redder than before. "Please . . . I have a kid."

David smirked. "Your kid had a mom." He chuckled. "Notice the tense I used?"

She fell to her knees before him, hands clasped together and held toward him. She looked like a penitent in church begging God for forgiveness for some transgression. "Please . . . please . . ." She shuffled closer toward him on her knees, tears etching lurid tracks in her mascara. "My baby . . ."

"You're pathetic."

David seized a handful of her hair and wound it around his right hand. She clutched at him and buried her face against his leg, her tears quickly soaking the fabric of his jeans. David tightened his grip on her hair, flexed his fingers, preparing to rip a hunk of it from her scalp. In the last instant before he would have done it, he felt one of her hands slide up his inner thigh and grip him by the crotch.

He smiled at her. "Ooh, now you're speaking my language."

She gave his balls a gentle squeeze and looked up at him with hope shining in her eyes. "Please . . . I'll do whatever you want. I'll make it nice. I promise."

He kept smiling. "I bet you would. You look like you know what you're doing down there. Then again, most shitty dive waitresses double as whores, don't they?"

She didn't let the abuse sway her, just kept stroking him through his jeans. She made sounds that mimicked sexual arousal. It was irritating. He'd never heard anything so transparently fake.

He snarled and yanked his arm up with sudden, devastating force, ripping fake blonde hair from her head along with a large chunk of ragged, bloody scalp meat. He had an instant to savor her wails of agony before something started hitting him. It felt like getting punched repeatedly. Hard. He heard the reports of the gun an instant later.

Holy shit, I'm being shot.

The blasts propelled him backward against the door. His knees buckled slightly but he didn't fall. He glanced down. His chest and stomach were riddled with oozing holes. Another shot whizzed by his head and ricocheted off the doorframe. He looked up and saw the obese, bacon-gobbling woman he'd regarded with such disdain aiming an automatic handgun at him. An open handbag sat on the counter near her almost empty plate. There was a look of smug satisfaction on her jowly face as he gaped in disbelief at her. Of everyone here, she was the last one he would have expected to offer any serious resistance. She squeezed the automatic's trigger again and another hole punched through his chest and exited through his back. He felt unsteady on his feet and realized the bullets had blown the glass out of the doorframe. The fat woman squeezed the trigger one more time, but this time the only result was an empty click.

David summoned a shaky smile.

The woman's smug look began to crack as she realized he didn't seem to be dying. To her credit, she didn't immediately lose her cool. She ejected the gun's empty magazine and reached into her purse. David frowned. How much ammunition could this woman possibly be carrying around?

He didn't get to find out.

Narcisa leapt over the counter again and landed agilely next to her. She seized the big woman from behind in a chokehold and gave her neck a powerful twist. There was a loud *snap* and she released the woman's now dead body, which toppled forward and crashed into a table, sending chairs, condiment bottles, and salt and pepper shakers flying. The dead woman's male relations remained glued to their stools, their mouths hanging open in shock, their eyes shiny with grief and disbelief.

Narcisa looked at them. "You two won't be trying anything stupid, will you?"

They looked at each other.

One of them licked his lips and said, "No, ma'am."

The other one said, "Nuh-uh."

Narcisa smiled. "Good. Stay where you are."

She moved past them, reached over the counter, and seized the still-cringing gray-haired woman by the front of her blouse. Martha started screaming again as Narcisa hauled her over the counter and began dragging her toward David.

David's head tipped backward as he watched them draw nearer. He felt achy all over, throbbing twinges in his joints and at the back of his head. It felt sort of like having a bad case of the flu, minus the fever. He would've welcomed a fever right now. His bones felt like they were turning to ice. His heart began to slow as a crippling lethargy overtook him. It felt like he was dying.

Narcisa said, "You're not dying. Not yet."

She was a few yards away now. Martha was still struggling, but Narcisa controlled her with impressive ease, propelling her forward with one arm bent behind her back. David's head lolled forward as the two women came to a stop within a few feet of him. Martha changed tactics, lashing out at him with her free hand. Sharp fingernails raked across his face, opening gashes in his flesh that only dribbled a small amount of blood. David blinked slowly and dragged numb fingers over his shredded cheek, frowning at the minuscule flecks of crimson visible on his fingertips.

He blinked again and squinted at Narcisa.

She looked . . . fuzzy. Like something from a fading dream. Yet the intensity of her ice-blue eyes allowed him to maintain some semblance of focus, penetrating the cloud descending over him like a halogen lamp penetrating dense fog.

"You're hurt. You need to drink. Now."

The fingernails of Narcisa's right hand lengthened and became talons, then ripped open the captive woman's neck. Blood jumped from the ragged wound, splashing the front of David's stolen shirt. Narcisa's nostrils flared as she glared at him over one of the dying woman's shoulders.

"Drink. Take her. Now."

David didn't need to be told again. The smell of the blood was powerfully intoxicating. The heady aroma made his eyes open wide as it filled his nostrils. He grabbed Martha by the front of her shirt and yanked her toward him. She managed one more gurgling scream before he snapped his mouth open and clamped it over the still-gushing wound. He lapped up blood with an eagerness and greed that far exceeded even the horrible, aching need he'd experienced after being released from the chains. He made hungry sounds deep in his throat as he drained the blood from her in barely more than a minute. Martha's corpse fell away from him and dropped to the floor with a heavy thud. He wobbled a little as he pushed away from the ruined door, grinning broadly as the infusion of hot blood woke up every nerve-ending in his system. He felt instantly wired and eager for more, as if he'd snorted up several lines of really high-quality cocaine. It felt like he had lightning in his veins. The rush was incredible. Mind-blowing. He had to have more, more, more, now, now, *now*.

He touched his face, felt thin scars where fresh gashes had been mere moments ago. He ripped his shirt open and examined his belly and chest. There were puckers of raw, healing flesh where once there'd been holes. The wounds continued to heal as he stared at them, the puckers fading and giving way to unblemished, healthy skin. It was a miracle. He frowned. No. That was the wrong word. It was a *religious* word, purely the province of the holy. And he was *unholy*. He should be dead, but he wasn't. No, wait, he *was* dead. He started laughing. It was so confusing. And yet liberating. The most glorious thing about it was that he didn't much care. Life and death? Those were mortal concerns. He was like Narcisa now. A vampire. He was going to live—well, *exist*—forever. And he could do whatever he wanted. That kind of made him a god, didn't it? He laughed harder. So maybe it was a miracle after all.

Narcisa was laughing, too. Giggling. She sounded more like a naughty schoolgirl than an ages-old mass-killing supernatural creature. She was staring at him, very intently, and he realized she seemed to be reacting to the mad gleam in his eyes. One thing was obvious— she liked what she was seeing.

She abruptly spun away from him and fell atop the wailing janitor. Her mouth opened and her head snapped toward his neck. There was a sound of ripping flesh and soon bright red blood was flowing all across the white floor tiles. He watched her slurp blood from the twitching Mexican for a moment, feeling the hunger grow inside him again.

Then something caught his eye.

He grinned.

The waitress.

He'd almost forgotten about her in the wake of the fat woman's assault, but now he was pleased to see she was still in play. A bullet had winged her in the shoulder—*nice aim, you stupid dead cow*—but she was still alive. And still possessed with enough fighting spirit to make another go at escaping. That also pleased him. It would make things more fun. He remembered the feel of her hand caressing his crotch through his jeans and decided he'd make her finish what she'd started. Then he'd kill her. Maybe he'd kill her first and then violate her. He grew even more excited at the thought, thrilled by how wickedly decadent and powerfully evil it made him feel. There was no reason he couldn't do that. He wasn't human. He was beyond morals. He could do anything at all and it wouldn't matter one fucking bit.

She was crawling across the floor, making slow but steady progress and leaving a trail of blood behind her. She was nearly to the counter. Poor thing. He imagined the tentative beginnings of hope she must be feeling now, how it must be burgeoning inside her, becoming more real with each passing second, with each hard-gained inch of ground. Her likely escape route wasn't difficult to deduce. She would stay on the floor once she got behind the counter, then make her way into the kitchen and flee via a rear exit. She might even have made it if she'd been a little bit faster while he was distracted. He trailed after her, treading quietly, not wanting to draw her attention just yet. He wanted that hope to grow inside her a little more, until it was a fire consuming her—right up to the moment when she was certain freedom was in her grasp. He tingled with anticipation at the thought of crushing that hope.

He kept hanging back, watching as she reached the counter and began to drag herself behind it. In a moment only the cheap black pumps on her feet were visible. David winked at the two piles of greasy blubber masquerading as men still ensconced atop their stools at the counter. They were nearly indistinguishable, with their grimy blue-collar clothes and blunted physical characteristics that marked them as products of the same tainted gene pool. They differed in only one significant way. Both were clearly terrified, but one's scowling expression indicated a deep loathing for David. His contempt was obvious in the defiant gleam in his eyes and the sneering twist of his lips. David frowned. It was irksome.

He decided to stop fucking around. He stepped behind the counter and stopped the waitress's progress with a foot planted solidly in the small of her back. She squealed in frustrated terror and clawed at the floor tiles, shredding her nails in the process. Her escape attempt effectively interrupted, David shifted his attention to the sneering fat man.

"What's your problem, fatty?"

A corner of the man's mouth twitched. "I ain't got shit to say to you, scumbag."

David's annoyance deepened. "Scumbag? Do you really think you're better than me? You're a giant bag of lard. You're not fit to judge a turd-throwing contest, much less your betters."

"You and that whore of yours ain't my betters, asshole."

David glared at the man, willing him to wilt beneath the supernatural fierceness of his stare. It was a thing Narcisa would have done with ease. With barely any effort at all, really. But, as with so many other aspects of vampirism, David didn't have her level of ability, at least not yet. The scowling big man barely flinched.

David seethed.

You fat motherfucker. I'll show you.

David surged toward the counter, reaching for the big man's accusing eyes, intending to claw them from their sockets with the black talons popping from the ends of his fingers. One hand curled around the collar of the man's work shirt and dragged his upper bulk up onto the counter. The other hand reared back, ready to strike. Maddeningly, the man's expression didn't change. He looked resigned to his death and determined to remain defiant until the end. David had an idea. A good one. He smiled. He'd pluck the man's eyes out of his skull and force the fat fuck to swallow them one at a time.

Yeah, let's see how stoic you are then, cocksucker. I'll break you yet. I'll—

David screamed and arched his back as something sharp and cold slammed into him from behind.

That goddamn waitress! Fucking bitch!

His foot had come away from her back in the now aborted assault on the lippy fat man. She'd seized the opportunity, knowing she'd almost certainly never have another one. There'd been a knife around. A big one. It made sense. This was a diner, after all. It was probably some kind of carving knife. She was leaning into it with all her might, driving the big blade deeper inside him. He felt it slice into one of his lungs and screamed again at the pain. She might not be able to kill him with the knife, but that didn't make the physical agony any less real. Luckily, as a vampire, there was a way to deal with that.

Blood.

Narcisa loomed up behind the fat men. Her blazing blue eyes pulsed with malevolence. She opened her mouth wide, flashing long teeth stained crimson from freshly imbibed blood. She moved with deadly quickness and silence, reaching for the fat men and tearing both men's throats out simultaneously. As always, the sight of thick streams of blood gurgling from newly severed veins sent David into a frenzy. He propelled himself backward and slammed the waitress into the partition. This caused her to cry out, but also had the effect of driving the blade even deeper inside him. But David didn't care about the pain now. Yet again, all that mattered was blood.

He pushed away from the waitress and turned around to face her, savoring the fear in her tear-laden eyes. He reached an arm behind his back, tendons popping as the limb twisted and contorted in ways a normal human arm could not, and began to pull the big blade out. It emerged with a moist sound that would have made his stomach turn over before he became a vampire. He licked blood from the blade and shuddered at the sweet, intoxicating taste. His blood intermingled with the blood of those he'd killed. There was something so satanically beautiful about that.

He sighed, an almost peaceful smile pulling at the corners of his mouth. "You almost made it, didn't you? Almost got away."

She sniffled. Fat tears rolled down her cheeks. "Please. I'm begging you. I want to live. You can do anything you want to me, just please let me live. Please don't orphan my kid. Please . . ."

David's smile was almost a sad one now. "I'm sorry. I think you know that can't happen."

Her eyes went wide as he dragged the blade across her slender throat. Beautiful blood burbled from the opening he'd sliced in her jugular vein. This wound wasn't like the ragged holes he'd created with his teeth. It was clean. Neat. Surgical. Something was entrancing about the way the woman's blood pumped from the thin line of the incision. The holes he made with his teeth were just as effective, but this had its own special allure. Staring at the wound was making his cock painfully stiff. He watched the blood issue forth a moment longer, then snapped his teeth around her tender throat. She gasped and went stiff at first, then relaxed as he began to drain her blood, eventually sagging against him. Her chin settled against his shoulder and her arms encircled his waist in a weak embrace. It was almost like being held by a lover.

It was this impression more than anything else that made him act on his earlier impulse. Once she'd been drained, he lowered her corpse gently to the floor and carefully undressed her. Her nude body was lovelier than he'd imagined, with fuller breasts and slightly wider hips. He removed his clothes, repositioned her legs, and let out a snort of animal satisfaction as he entered her.

When it was over, he put his bloody clothes back on and returned to the dining area, where Narcisa was sitting at a table with her legs crossed. The head of the insolent fat man was cradled in her lap.

She smiled at him. "Enjoy yourself?"

"Yes."

"Feeling any pangs of conscience this time? Any thoughts of you-know-who?"

He shook his head and answered honestly. "No. Not this time."

"Good." She tossed the head to him and he reflexively caught it. "That's for you."

David turned the head over and stared into the man's glassy, unmoving eyes.

Not so mouthy anymore, are you?

Narcisa stood and started toward the door. "We should go."

David looked at her. Then his head swiveled side to side as he surveyed the carnage. Everywhere he looked he saw blood and mutilated corpses. His smile widened as he thought of the field day the press would have with this story once a bit of research linked it to the earlier diner massacre. The scene was so spectacularly grisly it might even make the national news, though he doubted the authorities would ever mention the word "vampires" in their accounts of the incident to the press

He looked at Narcisa, who stared back at him with obvious impatience from the door. "Do people know about us? Law people, I mean."

She pushed the door open, taking care to avoid slicing her fingers open on broken glass. She paused there, staring evenly at him. "About me in particular or vampires in general?"

"Um . . . both, I guess."

She shrugged. "I'm a legend in some circles, but mostly they think I died a long time ago. Some have pursued me before, but they always give up the chase in the end. I'm a perpetually elusive shadow to them, impossible to catch or kill. Others of our kind aren't so skilled. And, yes, the law does know about us. Most governments have secret units dedicated to pursuing vampires and . . . other things."

"Other things?"

Narcisa's expression indicated she'd said all she intended to say on the subject. "We should go."

She left then and David watched the door bang shut, the impact with the frame rattling more glass fragments loose. He looked at the head in his hands again, smiling as he stroked the blood-stained hair.

He took it with him as he followed Narcisa back outside.

9

ACCEPTANCE

ON THE FREEWAY AGAIN, THE BMW speeding north out of Alpharetta. David stared at the head of the dead man as the cold wind brushed his face and whipped his hair about. The head was on the dashboard, wedged up tight against the windshield. Something was pleasing about the way it looked there. He'd heard stories about serial killers saving trophies from their kills, but he'd never understood the phenomenon until now. He liked having this physical reminder of what he and Narcisa had done. There was just one problem—it was a piece of organic matter, subject to decay. The flesh would rot and the fat man's face would melt away over time. He made a note to save something more permanent next time. A wallet or article of clothing. He supposed he could save the fat man's skull, but . . . hmm, where would he store it?

He glanced at Narcisa. "Your secret place . . . will I be living there with you?"

She kept her gaze on the road. "Of course you'll live there. What part of 'you belong to me' do you not understand?"

David didn't respond to that. When she'd said that before, it'd been an abstract kind of thing. He'd understood what she meant, sort of, but at the time he'd thought she would likely kill him after a period of imprisonment and torture. Now it seemed the role she had in mind for David was a kind of kept man. A companion and plaything, but by no means an equal. A part of him bristled at the thought. The smarter part of him realized he was lucky he wasn't another emaciated bag of bones hanging from chains until he bled out or starved to death. The realization didn't entirely erase his resentment, but it prevented him from saying anything stupid.

He frowned.

Except that—

Narcisa laughed.

Shit.

He'd forgotten about the mind-reading thing. Again. Damn.

Narcisa laughed some more. "Relax. It's natural to have thoughts like that. You'd be an unthinking dullard otherwise and therefore uninteresting to me. But you're a smart boy. You know your limitations."

"I'm no match for you and never will be."

She nodded. "Correct."

"You'd kill me if you ever suspected I had any serious intention of getting away from you."

"Also correct."

He sighed. "And there'd be nothing I could do about it."

She patted his knee. "See? I knew you were smart."

They drove in a surprisingly comfortable silence for several minutes after that. David's mind kept flashing back to all the incredible things he'd done over the last few hours. Multiple murders. Rapes. Torture. Necrophilia. All things that would have disgusted his former self. He was happy to find he was still feeling no lingering flickers of conscience. The only things he did feel were a new surge of arousal and a reawakened hunger.

He couldn't wait to kill again.

And to do . . . other things.

David winced at a sudden high-pitched burst of sound behind the BMW. It was followed by a pulsing strobe of blue light. He stretched his neck to peer at the rearview mirror. A police cruiser was hanging tight on their tail.

He glanced at Narcisa. "What do we do?"

"Pull over, of course."

She eased her foot off the BMW's accelerator and applied pressure to the brake, slowing quickly and smoothly as she guided the car to a stop at the road's shoulder. The police cruiser pulled to a stop behind them, but the cop didn't get out of the car right away. Several long moments passed. After everything he'd experienced tonight, David knew he shouldn't fear any human, but he was anxious nonetheless. He recognized it as an echo of how he'd felt any time he'd been stopped by a cop as a living man, but knowing that didn't entirely soothe his nerves. He reached for the head on the dash, figuring he should stash it somewhere. It reminded him of how he and some friends from his youth had frantically shoved beer cans under their seats during another stop a lifetime ago.

"Don't do that."

A hand on his arm. Narcisa, squeezing him. Hard.

"Leave it."

David let out a big breath and settled back in his seat. "Okay."

Finally, someone stepped out of the police cruiser. David heard a crunch of booted feet on gravel. Another glance at the rearview mirror showed a heavily muscled white man dressed in standard cop blue and equipped with the usual gear. His sidearm was holstered, but a big hand rested on its butt. David flinched at the memory of the fat woman's bullets slamming through his body. Bullets might not kill him, but he really, really, really didn't want to get shot again.

The cop reached the BMW's driver's side door and bent slightly at the waist to peer at them. "Evening, folks. License and—"

David watched the man's face, saw it go slack.

He'd seen the head on the dash, just as Narcisa had obviously intended. The cop's fingers curled around the butt of his gun and the weapon began to slide out of its holster. David was in motion before he even realized what he was doing, twisting and surging up out of his seat in the last moment before the gun could clear the holster, moving so fast he would only appear as a dark blur to the cop's eyes. He launched himself at the startled, backpedaling man, hitting him with tremendous force at center mass, exploding the air from his lungs as he drove him further backward. The cop staggered out onto the freeway and toppled backward, landing hard on asphalt. The gun flew from his hand, skittered across the road and disappeared into a grass median. David pounced on the man again before he had a chance to recover, tearing so much of his throat out it nearly decapitated him. Blood burbled and flowed like an intoxicating wine, filling

David's nostrils with its lovely aroma as it stained the road beneath them. There was a blare of horns as cars swerved to avoid the twisting figures in the road. One driver of a Lexus SUV was so startled she swerved too hard and went speeding into the median, where her luxury utility vehicle proceeded to flip several times before stopping in a grinding crash on the opposite side of the freeway. David laughed and drank deeply of the dying man's blood.

Then he felt hands on his shoulders, pulling him away. He snarled and fought for an instant, but the hands would not budge. He relaxed. *Narcisa.* He wanted more of the man's blood, but not at the risk of displeasing her. She steered him away from the road and he lurched toward the BMW. She tightened her grip on him and steered him away from the car, guiding him toward a stand of trees beyond the road's shoulder. David was still wired from the fresh infusion of blood and laughed with wild abandon as he allowed her to lead him into the darkness of the woods.

The laughing stopped as white light began to displace the darkness.

"Oh," he said, sobering almost at once. "Magic again. Where are we going?"

She didn't answer. There was no chance as the white light glowed brighter and the fuzzy feeling he recalled from before of disembodied near non-existence wiped out conscious thought. He relaxed and knew a few moments of seemingly timeless bliss. Then the world began to coalesce around him again, darkening and solidifying. He felt the ground beneath his feet and remembered his name as the last of the white radiance fizzled away. They were on a suburban sidewalk somewhere. He heard a snatch of conversation in the distance, saw rows of respectable houses on either side of an immaculate street.

Narcisa stood in front of him, smiling. "Recognize anything?"

David frowned.

He glanced to his left and then to his right—and froze.

Narcisa laid a hand gently on his shoulder. "It's time."

He turned to fully face the house that was obviously their destination.

Janine's house. Her parents' house, actually.

Narcisa leaned into him, whispering fiercely in his ear. "Are you ready to do it? Are you ready to rip that cunt to pieces for me?"

David shuddered.

Then he smiled and squeezed Narcisa's hand. "Yes. Yes, I am."

"Good. Who do you belong to?"

"You. Only to you."

"Let's do it, then."

Still holding hands, they started across the manicured lawn toward the house where he'd once shared warm meals and laughter with his beloved's family. The house where he and Janine had spent many late nights plotting their bright future together.

David and Narcisa climbed the steps to the front porch.

Narcisa rang the doorbell.

10

AND IN THE END . . .

DAVID SAT SHAKING ON HIS knees in the middle of the blood-spattered living room, squinting against the bright sunlight shining through the large bay window behind the Martins' plush leather sofa. He remembered almost everything now—everything up until the moment after he and Narcisa climbed the steps to the Martins' front porch. What happened after that was an enigma. It wasn't that the memories were hazy. They were just gone, like a file permanently deleted from a hard drive. No matter how hard he strained to remember, he came up empty.

Obviously something had gone wrong. Not because the Martins were all dead. That had been according to plan, after all. The sense of something wrong derived from the array of emotions raging inside him. Guilt. Anguish. Grief. Regret. A sense of loss so profound he felt utterly hollow inside. All things he should be incapable of feeling. These were human emotions, and he was no longer human.

Or . . . was he?

Perhaps yesterday's absence of those emotions was part of some trick Narcisa had played on him, a demented mind game designed to degrade him and forever taint his soul. She was powerful almost beyond comprehension. Wasn't it possible she'd manipulated his thoughts and impressions, had somehow immersed him in a convincing illusion or delusion? Which would mean he wasn't a vampire after all, just some gullible sucker she'd subtly coerced into participating in a slew of appalling homicides. It sounded like a plausible scenario and yet . . . it didn't feel right. Because even amid his grief and confusion, the scent of blood was driving him half-mad.

He lifted a shaking hand to his mouth and tasted dried blood with the tip of his tongue. It wasn't as electrifyingly potent as the fresh stuff, but it did light up his senses, stilling his tremors and bringing everything into a crystalline focus. The problem was it wouldn't last long. He needed more than a taste. He licked more dried blood from his fingers and rose smoothly to his feet.

A closer examination of the scattered body parts revealed enough information to confirm that virtually every member of the Martin family residing in the area had been present for the slaughter. Janine's parents, Ed and Margaret Martin, sat on the sofa, their heads lolling, facial features hanging slack. Ed's belly had been ripped open, his abdominal cavity scooped out and its contents flung across the room. Loops of intestine hung from a slowly twirling overhead ceiling fan. One of the man's kidneys was wedged in his mouth. Margaret's blouse was in shreds. Her breasts had been torn from her body. David began to feel slightly sick again as he cataloged the atrocities. He licked more blood from his fingers to quell the nausea.

More of Janine's relatives were quickly accounted for. Her uncle, Bob Martin, had been reduced to a limbless torso before finally being killed. His stumps had been cauterized and his face was frozen in a mask of eternal agony. A stench of burned flesh hung heavy in the air. The torso was propped in a corner by the front door. Carol, Bob's wife, was dead, too. Her head sat atop one of Bob's shoulders. The rest of Carol's distinctively plump body seemed to be missing, which was strange. Janine's brother, Michael, was also among the dead. Except for the ragged hole in his throat, his body was mostly intact. David squinted. Or was it?

David crossed the room to where Michael's body lay sprawled in front of the large entertainment center. The corpse was on its side, limbs splayed in a way that made it look as if he'd been reaching for something behind him when he died. David stepped over the body for a closer look and immediately gagged. Michael's lungs lay on the hardwood floor behind him, where they'd been left after being pulled out through the enormous, ragged wound in his back.

It was all suddenly too much. David staggered out of the living room, stomach heaving as he made his way by feel to the kitchen. The first thing he saw when he got there was the open oven, which provided the answer to the mystery of Margaret's missing body parts. Her charred remains were stacked on the oven racks. The stench of burned flesh was heavier in here and David gagged again. He started shaking again, almost uncontrollably this time, and desperately tongued the remaining traces of blood from his fingers. It helped only a little. His teeth chattered. He was freezing. He needed fresh blood and he needed it yesterday. As soon as fucking possible.

He staggered through the kitchen until he bumped up against a wall by the counter. He turned and pressed his back flat against it. There was something else he was forgetting. It seemed critically important that he remember it, more important than anything else by far.

What the hell was it?

Oh, yeah.

He almost laughed when it came to him, it was so obvious.

"Narcisa!"

Where was she?

He had to assume she was still alive. Still *undead*, he reminded himself. Nothing short of a thermonuclear strike could kill her (and he had his doubts about the viability of that or any other apocalyptic method). So either she was still here, lurking somewhere, playing with him, or . . . she'd deserted him. He didn't know which possibility terrified him more.

"NARCISA!"

He screamed her name over and over until his lungs were burning, but no answer came. The silence taunted him and ignited fires of paranoia. Something inexplicable had happened during the night, somewhere in that gap formerly occupied by his missing memories. He recalled what she'd said at the diner about secret government units that hunted things like her. Had some shadowy *X-Files*-type operatives caught up with her and killed her? It didn't seem likely, but he supposed it was at least theoretically possible. And if she'd died, was that somehow connected to the apparent resurgence of his conscience? Had the severing of their mental connection brought it screaming back to life?

Or was that another psychological hiccup, a very strong echo of his former humanity? He certainly hoped so. Because one thing was absolutely certain. He'd done many abominable things since falling under Narcisa's spell. All those murders . . . they were all real. As were the other things. The rapes and the . . . corpse violations. He couldn't bear the thought of enduring existence with a functioning conscience with those blood-soaked memories swirling endlessly in his head.

He pushed himself away from the wall and returned to the living room, pausing only a moment to shudder again at the carnage all around. Then he continued to the front door, hauling it open and knocking over Bob's mutilated torso in the process. He stepped outside, squinting his eyes against the bright sunlight. He knew it should be hot. It was a cloudless, sunny summer day in Georgia. But he felt colder than ever. At least he wasn't melting in the sun like a vampire in some cheesy movie. It wasn't much, but it was something. He shivered and hobbled to the edge of the porch, where he craned his head side to side in a desperate search for Narcisa. She was nowhere in sight, but an old lady out for a morning stroll was headed in his direction, flabby old arms pumping as she power-walked down the sidewalk.

David ducked back inside, slamming the door shut and turning the lock. He couldn't risk being seen by any neighbors, at least not until he'd devised some kind of viable strategy for dealing with his situation.

He frowned.

Wait a minute . . .

He opened the door a crack and peered outside again. The power-walking old lady had reached the Martins' block. She was one house away. David opened the door wider and stuck his head outside, taking a longer look around. There didn't seem to be anyone else in the vicinity. He stepped out onto the porch again and waited until the old lady was directly in front of the house. Then he used his vampire speed to zip out to the sidewalk, slap a hand over her mouth, and whisk her back inside. A kick to the door slammed it shut again. The force of the kick sent the brass door knocker up and down a couple of times. David's teeth were in the old woman's throat before the knocker was still again. She flailed against him with her weak little fists for a moment, but she stopped when he wrenched his head hard to one side and tore a huge chunk of flesh loose from her neck. He closed his mouth over the wound and drained her fast. When she was bone dry, he let her body drop to the floor. He felt better instantly. Everything was in perfect focus now. His conscience was quiet again. Thank fuck for that. Maybe the blood kept that at bay, too.

He smiled.

It was so good to see clearly again. So good to—

Something at the edge of perception was nagging at him. It took him a moment to process it. Then he tilted his head as he turned toward the coffee table and peered at the basket of magazines, where Janine's head was wedged in beneath the basket handle atop a copy of that month's *Vanity Fair.*

He moved closer to the coffee table.

Suddenly his heart was beating faster—and it wasn't from the recent infusion of fresh blood. He hadn't been thinking straight when he first regained consciousness. His perceptions had been off. Everything was out of whack. It was hardly a surprise he'd jumped to the wrong conclusion.

He lifted the head out of the basket of magazines and held it up for a closer inspection. It looked almost exactly like her. Same long blonde hair, a shade so bright it almost looked white. Same delicate facial structure, including those striking cheekbones. The eyes were the same color, too, a blue as pure and breathtaking as the sky on a cloudless summer day. A day like today, in fact. It was easy to understand why he'd mistaken Lisa Martin for her older sister. Lisa was only a year younger than Janine, and the sisters' resemblance to each other was so pronounced many assumed they were twins. A casual observer would never be able to tell them apart. But David knew Janine's face very well. Now that his initial shock at waking up in this slaughterhouse had waned, he could see clearly that this was Lisa's head. A tiny, almost invisible mole by her left ear gave it away. There were other telltale factors, including a subtle difference in the size of the head, but it was that mole that really sealed the deal.

David set Lisa Martin's head on the coffee table and did another careful survey of the living room. If he'd missed something that important, maybe there were other things he was missing. He began to tremble as he concluded this fresh inspection and was left with a single, inescapable conclusion—Janine wasn't here. And he was just as certain she hadn't been in the kitchen. Those had been Margaret's remains stuffed into the oven. The body shape was all wrong to be Janine.

So where the hell was she?

"Janine!"

No answer.

He screamed her name another time or two to the same result. Maybe she wasn't here. It was possible she hadn't been present for the slaughter. She did live here, but on occasion she would spend the night at a friend's place.

Or, more often, at his apartment, to which she had her own key. That was it. It had to be. It made perfect sense. She hadn't seen him in more than a day, nor would she have heard from him. Janine loved him. She would've been frantic over not being able to locate or contact him. She almost certainly would've gone to his place in a search for answers, perhaps would even have spent the night there.

There was an easy way to confirm this.

He circled the coffee table, bent over the corpses on the sofa, and fished Ed Martin's iPhone out of a trouser pocket. He tapped in Janine's cell number and put the phone to his ear. It rang once. Then he jumped as a familiar noise began to emanate from somewhere inside the house. He moved away from the sofa, straining to locate the sound. He passed out of the living room and stood at the bottom of the staircase to the second floor. The sound was louder here. It was coming from upstairs. The dial tone continued to buzz in his ear as he began to ascend the stairs. By the time he was halfway to the second floor, the sound was identifiable as Janine's ringtone, which was a snippet of "Telephone" by Lady Gaga.

He reached the second-floor landing and rounded a corner, heading fast down a hallway. There were two open doors, one to the left and one to the right. A quick toss of each room turned up nothing. He hadn't expected to find her in either one, but he needed to be thorough. A closed door stood at the far end of the hallway. Janine's cell had gone to voicemail and the ringtone had stopped playing, but he didn't need to hear it anymore to know the sound had been coming from behind that last door.

David shoved Ed Martin's phone in a hip pocket and cautiously approached the door. He curled his fingers around the doorknob and placed an ear against the thin wood. Moments passed. There was no sound. Then he heard something. A muffled whimper. Heart hammering again, he tested the doorknob. It wasn't locked and turned smoothly in his hand. He pushed the door open and saw Janine sprawled across a bed, arms splayed behind her and tied to the wrought iron headboard.

He experienced a moment of vast relief.

"Janine—"

Her eyes went wide as she saw him come into the room and she began to jerk against the lengths of rope binding her to the headboard. The gag in her mouth muffled a scream. David felt something twist deep inside his guts. The truth was unavoidable. She was afraid of him. No, more than that. Scared to fucking death was closer to it. Terror mixed with disgust. Which could only mean she'd been here the whole time, had probably witnessed his participation in the torture and slaughter of her family. There was nothing he could say to her to vanquish her terror, so he kept his mouth shut. An "I'm sorry," regardless of how sincere, wouldn't cut it either. That twist in his guts became more pronounced as he imagined how she saw him now— as a monster.

As a horror show freak covered in the blood of her loved ones.

David moved further into the room, leaving the door open behind him. He peered closely at Janine's nude form. Someone had stripped her. Narcisa? Another frustrating puzzle to which he didn't have an answer. A white envelope with his name written across the front was attached to her stomach with a strip of duct tape. Janine squealed and jerked against her bonds again as he bent over her and peeled the envelope from her flesh.

He ripped the envelope open and read the brief note.

David,

Last night was wonderful. Truly the most enjoyable evening I've spent with another person in many years. I'm afraid we overdid it, though. I should have told you earlier—overindulgence sometimes results in a morning-after state much resembling an alcoholic hangover. I have returned to my secret place to sleep, but I have left you with a final test. I have also left a way back for you in the basement of this house. But you must hurry as it will close by nightfall.

Bring the cunt's head with you.

Love,
Narcisa

David let the envelope and letter flutter from his fingers and drift to the floor. He had some answers now. A kind of blackout likely accounted for the gaps in his memory. He had no reason to doubt Narcisa. "Overindulgence" was a more than accurate description of last night's dark work.

He made eye contact with Janine and smiled. "I'll be right back. Just have to check on something."

He left the room and vaulted down the stairs, then hurried into the kitchen and tore open the door by the pantry that led down to the basement. Ordinarily it was very dark down here and you had to tread carefully down the rickety wooden stairs. But the radiant white light made it easier than usual. He descended the stairs to the bottom and stared at the source of the light for several moments. The light was beautiful. Entrancing. It took every ounce of willpower he possessed not to go toward it. The light subsumed an entire corner of the basement. It danced and flickered, beckoning to him. He longed to step inside its radiance.

But he couldn't.

Not yet.

He forced himself to retreat from the basement and hurried back to Janine's bedroom. She squealed again when she saw him. He went to the bed and sat beside her. He put a hand on her stomach and rubbed at the sticky residue left behind by the duct tape with the ball of his thumb. She tried to twist away from him, but he pressed his hand down flat.

"You're not going anywhere."

She threw her head back, stared straight up at the ceiling. Tears began to spill from her eyes, staining the pillow beneath her. His conscience stirred again. This was the woman he loved. Or had loved. He didn't want to hurt her.

Did he?

"I'm sorry. I did love you."

He climbed fully onto the bed and curled himself around her. She didn't flinch away from him this time. She was done fighting. Resigned. David sighed and relished the familiar and comfortable feel of her nude body beneath him. He closed his eyes and concentrated on that for a while. He'd always liked the way their bodies fit together. It always felt right. Like coming home. It was just as nice now as it had ever been. He could almost imagine things *were* as they had been, that he and Janine were still going to have the future together they'd dreamed about.

But that wasn't possible now.

He opened his eyes and angled his mouth closer to her throat. The sight of her steady pulse beating there made his hunger flare anew.

He was a vampire.

She was human.

There was no way to reconcile the opposing sides of that equation. Nothing to do but drink her blood until—

His brow furrowed as he thought hard.

Wait a minute now.

What if . . .

He didn't know if he could do it. There was so much Narcisa hadn't taught him yet. It could go wrong. But what was the alternative? Suddenly David's mind was going a million miles an hour as he struggled to grasp all the implications and possibilities.

Impossible.

There was only one answer.

Go for it.

David snarled and flashed his fangs.

Then he buried them deep in Janine's throat and drank her blood.

~

Nightfall.

The last flickering rays of burnt orange leeched from the horizon. A black 2010 Volkswagen Jetta sped south down the interstate, headed for Florida. David watched the speedometer, careful to keep his speed just north of the 70 mph legal limit. He no longer feared the police, but he was determined to be more cautious from now on. About everything. He wanted to avoid any additional blackout scenarios if at all possible. And he didn't want to tangle with the cops again, so soon after their latest meal at that convenience store.

Janine stretched and groaned in the passenger seat. She leaned toward him and kissed him lightly on the cheek. She whispered huskily in his ear, "Hey, sexy."

He smiled at her. "You're the sexy one."

Another groan. Another exquisitely sexual twist of her body as she adjusted her position in the seat again. She was clad all in black now. Black leather pants. Black blouse. Black boots. Black belt with silver studs. Even her hair was black now, courtesy of a cheap dye job the night before. Her idea. She thought the "makeover" suited her lifestyle change. David had to admit she looked great.

Not just great.

Hot.

It hadn't been a sure thing by any means. He could easily have killed her. In the end, he'd done it by turning his thoughts off and allowing instinct to guide him. It had been sloppy. He had taken almost all her blood, but somehow he stopped himself in time, ripping his wrist open and forcing her to drink the blood from his veins. And it had worked. Somehow it had fucking worked.

He'd turned her.

And if anything, she'd taken to the whole vampire thing more easily—and with far fewer qualms—than he had. He was happy, content to be with her again. The blood-drinking and killing aside, much of the fundamental aspects of their relationship remained the same. They loved each other deeply. Her sense of humor still delighted him (though it was a little darker now). And they again were making plans to be together forever. The only difference was that now "forever" potentially meant literally just that—an eternity spent in each other's loving arms.

David smiled.

Who said there was no such thing as happy endings?

The only dark cloud on the horizon was the question of how Narcisa would deal with what he had done. He had no doubt she was furious at his rebellion. Though he tried not to let Janine see it, she knew he was scared. Narcisa was far more powerful than the two of them combined. They couldn't hope to successfully fight the older vampire if she chose to come after them. David secretly suspected a confrontation was inevitable. The one consolation he had, the one slim sliver of hope, was time. A week had elapsed since he'd turned Janine and there'd been no hint of pursuit.

Maybe she'd decided to let them go.

Perhaps she even secretly admired his display of independence.

Probably not, but it was something to cling to anyway and that was better than nothing. Wasn't it?

Another glance at Janine.

Another surge of lust at that sexy smile curling her blood-red lips.

Another glance at the rearview mirror.

Another moment spent waiting.

Watching.

Hoping.

Feeling the need to ride the rush again creeping up on him once more.

As the road ahead curled away into endless darkness.

THE
DIABOLICAL
CONSPIRACY

1

"WHAT HAPPENS HERE TONIGHT STAYS between us. Everything discussed stays between us. It is not to be debated or even spoken of outside these walls. As usual. Is this very clear?"

The speaker was a pale-skinned young woman with shoulder-length black hair. She wore black heels and a sleek black dress. Her skin was blemish-free and creamy smooth. A blood-red shade of lipstick compellingly contrasted the black and white goth-noir look. She was slender but shapely, with the curve of her hips and thighs emphasized by the way she sat with one leg crossed over the knee of the other. Her face, with its delicate lines and striking contours, was a study in beauty so exquisite it bordered on the otherworldly.

Mike Bradley had seen a lot of attractive women in his nearly thirty years of life. Beauty itself wasn't a rare commodity. All you had to do was venture into the world and soon enough you'd see plenty of it. But this girl . . . she was on a level beyond anything in his experience. She was . . . *perfection*. She was flawless. Elegant. Ethereal. And yet possessed of an electric eroticism that was staggering.

"I ask you again . . . is that clear, Mr. Bradley?"

Mike blinked rapidly and struggled to swallow a lump in his throat that felt roughly the size of a softball. He was so entranced by her that until that moment he had failed to realize she was looking right at him . . . and speaking to him. He coughed after finally managing to get his throat cleared. "I . . . uh . . . um . . ."

Her expression was blank, but there was a glint of something dangerous in her eyes. "Hmm . . . were you not giving me your full attention?"

Mike couldn't help squirming beneath the laser focus of her eyes. His heart started beating faster as he struggled for an acceptable answer to her question. Then he sighed as he realized the only real option here was confession. "I . . . ah . . . yeah, I guess my mind sort of . . . went off somewhere . . . while you were talking."

She stared at him for long, silent moments, each of which felt like a self-contained eternity as he sat there and listened to the increasingly loud thud of his heart. At one point it occurred to him to wonder why he was so uncomfortable. This was just a social gathering, albeit a bit of a weird one. This woman had no real authority over him. He could get up and walk out of here at any time. Nor was there any logical reason—beyond her unusual beauty—to find her so intimidating. Seated in folding chairs arranged in a loose circle in the strangely aseptic garage were eleven other people. Though most were strangers, a few were people he already knew. Nothing bad could happen here.

Right?

The woman then leaned forward in her chair slightly, causing Mike to instinctively press backward into his chair. "Mr. Bradley . . . may I call you Mike?"

Mike frowned. It surprised him that she would ask his permission for anything. "Uh . . . yeah. Sure. Why not?"

"Mike, it is imperative that you hear and comprehend everything I say tonight. This is your first time attending one of these meetings, so I realize you are not yet aware of what's expected of you. When I speak in my capacity as leader of this group, I deserve nothing less than your fullest attention. I'll say again, *hear and comprehend everything I say*. Got it?"

Mike forced himself to stop squirming. "I hear you. I understand."

Though he had managed to recover a degree of composure, visible evidence of his nervousness remained in the form of sweat on his brow. He would wipe it away, except he knew doing so would only draw attention to it.

The woman nodded. "Good. Our group requires a final member to complete the diabolical circle. A thirteenth member. Thirteen is one of the most infernally significant numbers. I do hope you will become our Thirteenth, Mike. We cannot move ahead with accomplishing our goals until the infernal circle is complete."

"Right, well, I . . ." Mike's brow furrowed as he trailed off, the strangeness of what she was saying finally beginning to register. "Hold on . . . is this some kind of, um . . . satanic cult or something?"

Sudden laughter erupted in the garage. Mike took a look at the faces of the people seated around him. They were all laughing, a few so heartily their faces flushed red. One man had a big hand slapped against his belly because it was heaving so hard. Even the ones he knew, his so-called friends, were laughing. The only exception was the beautiful leader of the group. Her focus remained solely on him, her gaze so studiously intent it was unnerving.

Mike loudly cleared his throat. "If someone could kindly explain to me what's so fucking funny, I'd appreciate it."

"Silence."

The laughter ceased at once at the woman's stentorian command. All of the grinning faces abruptly shifted expression, turning stony and sober. Mike found the instantaneous and unquestioning obedience of the others disturbing. It was clear everyone here respected and feared this woman. Which was more than a little creepy. Because none of this weirdness came across as some kind of prank or put-on, despite how absurd it seemed on the surface. No, whatever was happening here, these people were deadly serious about it. By now Mike was giving serious consideration to getting up and leaving. He had come along tonight at the invitation of Marnie, the cute blonde sitting to his immediate right.

He liked Marnie a lot. They were just friends, technically, and had been since becoming acquainted a little over a year earlier. It had been a very close relationship at various points over the course of that year. Though on average they only saw each other once every week or so, they talked a lot on the phone, sometimes for hours on an almost daily basis. And then there were the endless text conversations that invariably began almost immediately after one of the phone talks ended. These often continued deep into the early morning hours. They talked about everything imaginable. Everything in the world, seemingly. Every aspect of their personal lives. It was obsessive behavior, Mike knew, and they were both guilty of it. They were addicted to talking to each other. And yet she had rebuffed him the one time he made an overt romantic gesture. Not in a mean way, but in a way that made it clear he shouldn't do it again any time soon.

So he hadn't.

In fact, he hadn't talked to her at all in the three weeks since that feeble attempt at a seduction. Three weeks plagued by doubt and soul-searching. Just a couple days ago, he had arrived at the bittersweet conclusion that he was better off without Marnie in his life. He could move on now and maybe eventually meet someone who wouldn't string him along so inexplicably. So, of course, the very day after coming to that difficult moment of acceptance, she called him—seemingly out of the blue—and invited him to this meeting. After a brief hesitation, he initially turned down the invitation. The rejection startled her. She couldn't believe he'd said no to her. Some actual pleading on her part ensued, which a not-so-remote part of him found immensely gratifying. He finally relented when she told him he could take her on a "real date" if he agreed to come along with her to this thing. Even with the sting of the recent romantic rejection still fresh in his memory, he was unable to pass up this opportunity. His instincts told him it was a bad idea, that she was using him somehow, but saying no was impossible.

She had turned cagey when he pressed her for details on the nature of the group, telling him only that they were doing "important work" and that he would find the experience "literally life-changing." Yeah, right. He figured the group would be comprised mainly of pretentious weirdo snobs and the evening would be spent drinking wine and eating artisanal cheese while listening to the weirdoes spout a bunch of pseudo-intellectual claptrap. He still had no clue what these people were all about, but it turned out his prediction that he would find himself among a bunch of flaky oddballs had been bang-on-the-money. In addition to Marnie, he knew two other people here. Blake Carter and Cynthia Everson. They were friends . . . but friends he had met through Marnie. Blake and Cynthia seemed normal enough on the surface, but now he was questioning how well he knew them. They were obviously established members of this . . . whatever the hell it was. Which meant he had to be wary of them now.

Mike glanced at Marnie, but she wasn't looking at him. Like everyone else in the room, her gaze was riveted to the dark-haired beauty. He saw something like awe in her expression. More than that. Awe and . . . adoration. She worshipped this woman. They all did. He kept looking at Marnie, hoping his gaze would draw her attention in his direction. He needed some kind of reassurance, some indication she wasn't a hopeless flake. But, though she had to sense what he wanted, she kept staring straight ahead, never once sliding her eyes in his direction, not even for a fraction of a second.

So he gave up and looked at the group's beautiful leader, too.

The faintest hint of a smile briefly dimpled the corners of her scarlet mouth when their eyes met. "Please forgive the outburst of my fellow circle members, Mike. It has a rather simple explanation. You see, though your comment was likely made in jest, you came very close to guessing our true mission."

Mike frowned again. "So . . . you *are* Satanists?"

That tiny, almost imperceptible smile briefly surfaced again. There and gone in the space of maybe a full second. "Oh, yes."

Mike maintained a carefully composed expression at this revelation. But he thought, *Oh, awesome. Not just weirdoes, but satanic weirdoes.*

He glanced at Marnie again. *Now* she was looking at him. She was smiling. She was pretty to begin with, but, as always, he was struck by how a smile thoroughly transformed her face, making her not merely pretty but gorgeous. She looked incandescent when she smiled. There was a brighter light in her eyes and a brighter hue to her cheeks. Seeing her like this always made his heart race faster. But the bitch of it was she knew full well the effect it had on him. She was exploiting a weakness. To what purpose he did not know, but the knowledge of what she was doing added to his steadily growing unease. And though he knew he was being manipulated—and resented her for it—he knew he couldn't leave just yet. Not while the girl he maybe loved was looking at him that way.

"Look at me, Mike."

The leader again. Speaking in that stern tone that would brook no disobedience.

Marnie nodded and tilted her head slightly.

A gesture that said, *Do as she says.*

So Mike looked at the woman. "You know what? You keep telling me what to do and acting all mysterious and shit, but I don't even know your name."

"My name is Nadia."

"Great. Well, I hate to tell you this, Nadia, because I really like Marnie here and it seems like she's into this whole thing, but I've got no real interest in joining a satanic cult. You know, unless it's just some kind of goof."

Nadia's smooth brow creased slightly. "A goof?"

"Yeah. A goof. Like you're playing at being all dark and satanic, but it's an excuse to hang out and party with some freaky friends."

Nadia stared blankly at him for a long moment. Then her expression hardened some. "I see. I assure you, we are not *playing* at anything. Well, we do refer to our little group as The Diabolical Conspiracy, and there *is* a playful element to that. It sounds like it would be the name of a criminal organization in a spy movie parody. But it's something of an in-joke. It also functions as a means of deflecting scrutiny from certain authorities. Because who would take an organization called The Diabolical Conspiracy seriously, right? We are, however, *very* serious about what we do."

"And that is what, exactly?"

Nadia uncrossed her legs and scooted to the edge of her chair. This was a slow and exquisitely sensual process. Despite Marnie's proximity, he couldn't help but drink in every smooth twist and shimmy of this woman's delectable body. From the shifting of her hips to the way she exposed the finely toned curve of her calf when she briefly extended her right leg before scooting forward, it all compelled his complete attention. The hem of her dress rode up a little higher on her thighs as she moved, revealing more of that silken smooth flesh. By the time the process was complete, Mike was realizing how calculated every movement had been. He was being manipulated again. And, again, he had little to no control over either his physical or mental response. He ached to touch Nadia. To caress her body's shapely curves. To listen to whatever brand of oddball horseshit came out of her mouth so long as he could remain close to her.

Not for the first time, he noted that more than half of the group's members were young women. There were seven women and five men, not including himself. And, interestingly, not a single one of the women was remotely unattractive. The men were another story. Only two—Blake, and a guy he didn't know—possessed looks roughly approaching something resembling handsomeness. The other guys ranged from average-looking to, in one case, undeniably ugly. Mike was self-aware enough to know his looks placed him firmly in the average category. It seemed clear beauty was a requirement for female membership in The Diabolical Conspiracy. The reason couldn't be more clear—for precisely this kind of manipulation. But to what end?

It made Mike wonder what the women were getting out of this. Because it wasn't some quirky way of meeting hot, eligible guys.

Nadia was smiling again in that inscrutable way of hers. "You know, I can read people quite well. So well, in fact, I have occasionally been accused of being able to read minds. This is not true, of course, but my intuitive powers are so refined it may as well be true. Let's take you, for instance."

Mike fought an impulse to squirm again. He could feel everyone in the room looking at him. Studying him. Evaluating him. "Me?"

She nodded. "You. A part of you is still clinging to the belief our group is some sort of sophisticated adult role-playing club."

Mike shrugged. "Sophisticated" wasn't necessarily the right word, but her assessment was close enough to the truth. "Yeah. I guess. I mean, you tell me you're not playing at anything, but I look around at all the faces here and all I see is a bunch of adults. No grownups I know take Satanism seriously. It'd be a different thing if you were all dope-smoking teenage metalheads. Or maybe not. I mean, this is the twenty-first century. Satanism is a great plot device for horror movies, but that's about it."

Mike's gaze flitted about the room again as he became aware of the hostility being leveled at him from seemingly every direction. He looked briefly at Marnie. Yeah, from that direction, too. The air in the room felt suddenly stuffy and this time he couldn't help shifting around on the chair. He tugged at his shirt collar and looked at Nadia again. "But that's just, like . . . my opinion. No offense."

The corners of Nadia's mouth curved slightly upward. "Everyone . . . please cease staring daggers at Mike. We don't want our prospective new member to feel uncomfortable. We want him to feel welcome. *Wanted.* More than that, Mike, we want you to feel as if you are part of something special. We want you to feel a sense of belonging when you're among us. Wouldn't that be nice?"

"I . . . guess?"

"You don't sound certain."

"I'm not certain about much of anything at the moment."

Nadia nodded. "I thought as much. Allow me to reiterate a few points. We are a serious organization. What we do is in no way a goof. Nor is it an excuse to play naughty adult games. When we have orgies—"

"When you *what?*"

"Have orgies."

141

"That's what I thought you said. Excuse the interruption. Please continue."

Nadia made a soft sound that could have been either a quiet laugh or a grunt of disdain. With her it was hard to tell the difference. "As I was saying, when we have orgies, we do it in a ritualistic way. We treat it as something sacred. The expression of unrestrained physical lust symbolizes our freedom from God's laws and our joy in the liberation our devotion to Satan allows us. Do you understand?"

Mike smiled tightly and nodded. "Yep."

I understand that you're a bunch of goddamn fruitcakes.

"You think we're crazy."

Holy shit, she really can read minds.

He gave his head a single emphatic shake. "Nope."

"You're lying, but I am not offended. The first steps along the path to satanic enlightenment are always the most difficult."

"That's what I've heard."

Someone seated to his left sniggered at that remark. A glance in that direction revealed it was Blake, who was now trying hard to hide a smirk. Seeing this had the effect of relaxing Mike some. It was the first sign that maybe not everyone here took this shit as seriously as Nadia and Marnie apparently did.

This impression lasted until the moment Nadia rose smoothly from her chair and crossed through the open space within the circle of chairs to stand directly in front of Blake. There was no longer even the faintest trace of mirth on his face as he stared tremblingly up at her. His mouth was moving. He was trying to say something, but no words were coming out. From his demeanor, Mike guessed he was trying to apologize, but fear had temporarily paralyzed his vocal cords.

Nadia's right hand lashed out, snapping hard across his face. The sound was savage, like the crack of a whip on bare flesh. Then she nearly knocked him off the chair as she backhanded him. Mike grimaced at the display of wholly unexpected violence. Everything about the woman's demeanor had changed. Gone was the air of almost snooty composure. In its place was an animal ferocity that scared the shit out of him. And scared the shit out of Blake as well, who was sobbing now and blubbering barely intelligible words of contrition. She slapped him again, harder than before, and followed it up with yet another backhand. This last blow drove Blake from his chair. As soon as he hit the garage's cement floor, Nadia commenced kicking him in the midsection. She was screaming at him and kicking him over and over as he curled into a fetal ball.

An impulse caused Mike to rise hesitantly from his chair. He wasn't sure what his intent was. To intercede in some way, he supposed. But Marnie seized him by an arm and pulled him back down. To Mike's shame, he allowed her to restrain him. Stopping the assault was unquestionably the right thing to do. In truth, though, he was too shaken by what he was seeing to even attempt it. Too shaken and . . . too afraid. The realization made him feel like a coward. He didn't care for that at all, but it was a fact and he couldn't hide from it. And he knew one thing with absolute certainty now. Nadia wasn't playing around here. He took a fresh look at the faces arrayed around him, seeing them all in a different light than before.

This wasn't a game for any of them.

This was real . . . and very, very serious.

The people gathered here this evening were members of a genuine satanic cult.

Mike gulped.

God help me.

2

"THE PURPOSE OF THE DIABOLICAL Conspiracy is to promote and foster evil whenever and however we can. In this way, we celebrate our dark lord and do what we can to further his work here in the mortal realm. Do you have any questions?"

The violence of a few moments earlier had ceased as abruptly as it had begun. Nadia was in her chair again, with her left leg crossed almost primly over her right again. The look of wild-eyed, almost feral savagery had vanished. The Nadia he'd glimpsed in those horrifying moments was a woman completely capable of murder, he had no doubt. Now she was again exuding an air of cultured sophistication and class. That was certainly a part of who she was, but he knew now there was a darker truth behind the elegant veneer.

Did he have any questions?

Hell, he had about a million of them, but he was no longer sure how to ask them. Any lingering sense this was a game had utterly vanished during Nadia's assault on Blake. He could no longer couch his comments or questions in sarcasm. Offending Nadia was the last thing he wanted at this point. Because if he did offend her, what was to stop her from unleashing some of that fearsome rage on him? Any response at all had to be very carefully considered. More than ever, he wanted to get up and walk the hell out of here, but he had the creeping sense any attempt to flee would be doomed to failure. These people wouldn't allow him to leave. He tried telling himself this was just paranoia, he wasn't a prisoner here, but he didn't believe it. He was trapped here, stuck among this group of lunatics until the meeting was over. At least.

Nadia's expression softened some as she watched him. Was there even a trace of something like empathy in the cast of her features? It didn't seem likely in light of what she had done to Blake. Probably it was a trick of the light.

"I can tell you're troubled by what you've witnessed here this evening. Perhaps you're even afraid of me. But Mike, I want you to know you can speak freely here. You need not fear retribution for anything you say."

Mike's gaze flicked over to Blake for a moment. His friend was back in his chair, sitting on its edge, with his eyes trained on the cement floor and his arms clasped tight over his undoubtedly sore abdomen. It was obvious he remained in a considerable amount of pain.

Mike swallowed and at last found the courage to speak. "I appreciate what you're saying, Nadia, but you'll have to forgive me if I have trouble believing you. I just watched you stomp a man half to death because he laughed at something I said."

"That's different. Blake is a fully initiated member of The Diabolical Conspiracy. He has sworn his allegiance to Satan, to the club, and, yes, to myself. This is not the first time he's been impertinent at an inappropriate time. He has been warned and yet he couldn't help misbehaving. Everyone else here knows better." Her voice went up a sharp octave as her head swiveled in Blake's direction. "Isn't that right, Blake?"

Blake raised his head with some reluctance and flipped long locks from his forehead. "Yes. I'm sorry, I—"

"Shut up."

Blake fell immediately silent. Mike had to hand it to Nadia. In addition to being possibly the most beautiful woman he had ever seen up close, she was easily the most intimidating. Put this woman in a room full of world leaders and she'd have the gaggle of puffed-up old assholes quaking in their boots within minutes.

"Tell Mike what happened here tonight, Blake."

145

Blake looked at her and said, "I got—"

"I told you to tell Mike, not me."

Blake flinched, but he nodded and shifted in his chair to face Mike. "I got put in my place for disrespecting the covenant of the group, and for disrespecting Nadia's role as leader. Basically, I got what I deserved."

Getting that said appeared to take a lot out of Blake. His shoulders sagged and he went back to staring at the floor, his longish hair hanging in his face again.

Mike looked at Nadia. "So let me see if I have this straight. Blake got the crap kicked out of him because he's a member and disrespected your rules. But I can say anything I want and not get the crap kicked out of me because I'm not a member."

Nadia smiled again. "Not a member . . . yet. And, yes, that is essentially correct. As I have already said, you may speak freely without fear of retribution."

Mike nodded and put a hand to his mouth as he cleared his throat. He glanced at Marnie, who was watching him carefully, a very intent look on her face. But there was nothing troubled in that expression. The violence visited upon Blake—her friend—appeared not to have upset her in the least. And Mike again had to question how well he knew this girl. Nothing in all their countless hours of intimate conversation could have prepared him for her stoic acceptance of what had happened. He remembered feeling like he had never been so open with his thoughts and feelings with anyone else. And he had foolishly imagined it had been the same for her. But it was clear now there were large parts of her true self she was holding back.

He dropped his hand from his mouth and looked at Nadia again. "Okay. I guess I'll take your word for it. I can speak freely. Awesome. So let me ask you this—can I go ahead and leave now? Because this . . ." He waved his hand around at the circle of seated cult members. " . . . and again, no offense, but I want nothing to do with it."

This elicited a softly petulant sound from Marnie.

Mike didn't look at her, keeping his gaze resolutely focused on Nadia.

To his relief, the group's gorgeous leader did not seem angry with him. If anything, she appeared faintly amused. "No offense taken. Speaking just for myself, of course. Marnie, however, seems . . . displeased."

Yeah, well, tough shit for her.

"I feel bad for her, of course."

Mike frowned. "You do? Why?"

One corner of Nadia's mouth quirked slightly. Was that a smirk? "Because she expended so much time and energy cultivating your interest in her. She was so certain you would do absolutely anything for her. Apparently she was wrong about you. She'll pay a price for that."

He sensed Marnie leaning closer to him and felt that too-familiar physical tension he experienced any time that happened. His breath caught in his throat and he tried hard not to shake. And then he felt her warm breath against his ear and heard her hushed voice: "Change your mind. Now. *Please.*"

Mike sat forward in the chair. "Whoa. Hold on. What do you mean by that? What kind of 'price'?"

"I mean she'll be punished, of course. Severely."

"Because I don't want to join your group?"

"Precisely."

"Well, that's some fucked up shit. What are you gonna do to her?"

Marnie sniffled. "Let it go. It's too late now. You're only making it worse for me."

Mike felt a surge of anger at this. The feeling was intense enough to temporarily vanquish his fear of Nadia. "This is some bullshit. You're not doing a damn thing to her."

"Oh, but I am. And there's nothing you can do about it."

"We'll see about that."

Mike clasped hands with Marnie and began to rise out of his seat, intending to pull her along. He meant to get her away from these crazy people and God help anyone who got in his way. He was scared and his heart was going a million miles per hour, but he no longer felt like a coward. Not even the heartbreaking revelation Marnie had been using and manipulating him all along could break his resolve. It didn't matter that their "friendship" had essentially been a lie on the most fundamental level. He cared for her anyway and would not allow her to be hurt.

Except that, she had no interest in being rescued.

She jerked her hand free of his and folded her arms beneath her breasts as she stared up at him. "I belong here and I'll take the punishment I've got coming." Now she looked at Nadia. "I'm sorry I failed you." She looked around the circle. "Sorry I failed all of you."

Mike gaped at her, his eyes wide with disbelief. "You've gotta be fucking kidding me." He knelt toward her, pleading at her with his eyes as well as his words. "Come on, Marnie. Leave with me. It doesn't matter if you don't want me. Hell, I kind of knew that all along. But you're better than this, I know you are. You don't belong with this group of fucking head cases."

He heard Nadia laugh and turned in her direction. "Something funny?"

"Yes. It occurs to me I never directly answered your question."

Mike initially wasn't sure what she was talking about. He was so caught up in his anger and the desire to prevent any harm from coming to Marnie that everything else had gone right out of his head. "What fucking question?"

"You asked if you could leave."

"Oh. Right. *That* question. Well—"

"Here is your answer. You can't leave."

Mike frowned. "What? Are you fucking serious?"

A nod, followed by another faintly amused quirk of her mouth. "Oh, yes. Deadly serious. You're not going anywhere."

"And why not?"

"Because you know about The Diabolical Conspiracy."

"So what? You're gonna kill me now? Is that what happens? Are you people really that insane? Look, nobody cares about your silly little club. It doesn't matter if I know about your so-called evil conspiracy or whatever, because no one would ever take it seriously. I mean, you understand that, right?" This all came out in an almost overheated rush. Mike made himself slow down and pushed out each of his next words with deliberate slowness for extra emphasis. "You. Are. All. Fucking. *Ridiculous.*"

Nadia grunted. "You know what? I think maybe now I *am* offended. You should have kept your mouth shut while you were ahead."

Mike couldn't help laughing. "Well, tough shit, you crazy bitch. I'm outta here."

He turned away from her with the intention of exiting the garage through the open door to his right. The door led back into Nadia's house. He'd left his keys on the kitchen counter. He meant to retrieve them and depart this place through the front door, then get in his Hyundai and put a whole lot of miles between himself and these whack jobs very quickly. But before he could do that Marnie stood up and placed herself directly in his path.

Mike blinked at her in surprise. "What? You change your mind?"

There was a grim look on her face as she gave her head a slow shake. "No."

And then her fist crashed into his jaw before he could even begin formulating a response. She was a small, slender woman. He was stunned by the power contained in that punch. He staggered backward, feeling his knees go weak and he lost his balance. Then his feet went out from under him and he crashed painfully to the hard, unyielding floor. He cried out in shock as pain exploded throughout his body.

But his suffering was only beginning.

He blinked pain-triggered tears from his eyes and looked up to see them all standing over him, arrayed around him in a close circle. He felt vaguely like a patient on an operating table in Hell with all those people staring down at him. As his vision began to clear, he saw anger in each of their faces. Every one of them. Even Marnie. Even Blake. He had no real friends here. Never had. Any other impression had never been anything more than delusion.

Nadia was standing by his head. When he made eye contact with her, she lifted a foot and placed the sole of a high-heeled shoe against his throat.

She sneered at him, nothing but open disdain in her expression now. "Tell me if this hurts."

She lifted her other foot off the floor and balanced one-legged on his throat.

Mike tried to let her know.

Yes! Yes, it fucking hurts! Please stop!

But all that came out was a gurgle.

149

3

NADIA ONLY PERFORMED HER SADISTIC balancing act for a second or two. Any longer than that and she would have broken his neck. She came near enough to permanently crushing his windpipe. But then she removed her foot from his throat and he was able to drag in a single wheezing breath before the rest of them ganged up on him. They kicked him and kicked him, the points of their shoes connecting with his body from every direction. There was nowhere to go, no way to shield himself from the attack. The only thing he could do was lie there and take it. Which he did until they dragged him to his feet and started tossing him around the garage, using his body as a punching bag. Marnie didn't hesitate to mete out her fair share of abuse. If anything, she overcompensated, battering him more frequently and more savagely than anyone else. When he was no longer able to remain on his feet, she straddled him on the floor and rained an endless succession of blows down on his face. He felt his face turning puffy, felt blood oozing into his mouth from numerous open gashes. Toward the end, it dimly occurred to him this was how a palooka must feel after going ten hard rounds with the heavyweight champion of the world. Eventually things turned hazy and he lost consciousness.

When the lights came back on, he was flat on his back and tied to a bed in a dimly lit room. It was a small, sparsely furnished room. A guest bedroom, probably. The only illumination was a small lamp on the nightstand to his right. There was something in his mouth. Something made of cloth. A gag. The strip of duct tape stretched taut across the bottom part of his face made spitting it out impossible. His body ached in too many places to count. Moving even a little hurt a hell of a lot, so mostly he stayed still. On the plus side, someone had cleaned up his face. He could feel the little adhesive bandages covering the various cuts. It puzzled him. Why bother tending to his wounds if they didn't mean to let him go? It could only mean they weren't done with him yet, a realization that made him queasy with dread.

The bedroom door opened some ten minutes after he regained consciousness. Marnie stood framed in the open doorway for a second, her face expressionless before she came fully into the room and closed the door behind her.

Seeing her provoked a storm of emotions inside him. Before tonight, he had built a wall around his emotions where Marnie was concerned. It was a self-defense mechanism, a means of preparing himself for the inevitable letdown he'd always known would come. He'd known it because it was what always happened. He formed intense friendships with girl after girl and they rarely ever went much of anywhere. And at the beginnings of these things he always knew the end was already in the works, lurking somewhere out there just over the horizon. But he went along for the ride every time because he was hooked on the rush of fresh infatuation. Even so, a part of him had desperately hoped that maybe—just *maybe*—things might turn out differently with Marnie. That wall around his heart was more weakly constructed than usual, and tonight she had torn it down for him . . . just not in the way he had hoped. He loved her. Loved her more fiercely than he had ever loved anyone else.

And she didn't care a damn about him.

Not in any way that really counted.

Marnie settled gently onto the bed next to him and leaned over him. Her expression was still blank as she tilted her head side to side, carefully studying him. Then she sighed. "Look at you. You're a fucking mess."

He grunted.

She shook her head. "All you had to do was go along with it, you know. You could be making love to me right now."

His puffy eyes opened wide at that remark, the swollen eyelids trembling.

She nodded. "I'm not taunting you. I'm telling you how it is." She shook her head again. "Or how it *could* have been. If only you'd opened your mind a little bit. If only you had grasped the possibilities. I thought I knew you. Thought I understood you." Her voice softened as she spoke, became tinged with apparently genuine regret. "I never would have brought you into this otherwise."

She leaned in closer and pinched a corner of the duct tape strip between a thumb and forefinger and peeled it slowly away from his face. Mike spat out the wad of cotton—which turned out to be a woman's pink ankle sock—and coughed roughly a few times.

He looked at Marnie through eyes misty with fresh tears. "Thank you."

"You're welcome."

"You beat the shit out of me." He sniffled at the memory of her fist connecting with his flesh over and over again. The savage twist of her face in those moments would haunt him the rest of his days— assuming he had any days remaining to him beyond this one. "You wouldn't . . . stop . . ."

She nodded. "I had to. It was the only way I could save face after you rejected us."

"I don't understand. I don't get how you could do that to me. I . . ." He swallowed hard and forced the words out. "I . . . love you."

"I know you do." That tinge of sadness was back, though this time he wasn't sure whether it was real. It felt a little like she was back to manipulating him. Or maybe not. Maybe that was paranoia again. It was hard to tell the difference at this point. "I worked very hard at making you love me."

"So that's all it was? Work?"

She shook her head. "Of course not. Nadia tasked me with recruiting the group's thirteenth member because I've always been the best at identifying the special ones, the rare ones who have what it takes to be a part of what we do. After all, I was the one who originally brought her into the fold."

Mike frowned. "Huh."

"Does that surprise you?"

Mike would have shrugged had he been capable of it. But his arms were stretched taut to either side, his wrists bound to slats of the brass headboard with lengths of rope. "I guess I just figured this whole conspiracy thing was her idea."

Marnie shook her head. "No. In fact, it was more or less my idea. I was one of the three original founding members."

Mike squinted at her. "Say what?"

"You heard me."

"So what are you telling me? One day you decided to start a satanic cult because . . . why? It seemed like a fun thing to do?"

"I did it because I wanted to serve Satan, and because I grew up in the faith. I know that sounds funny to you, but it's the truth."

"Not much seems funny to me right now, I can tell you that. So who were the other two originals?"

"Blake was one of them. The other is . . . no longer with us."

"What happened to him?"

Marnie smiled. "What happened to her, you mean. You knew her, actually. She used to work with us at the call center. Nicole Simmons."

Mike stared at her for many long, silent moments while he mulled this over. At first the revelation rendered him almost numb with shock. This gave way to a flare of incendiary anger . . . which passed in a flash and was replaced again by fear. He let out a breath and said, "Nicole's dead. An accident."

Marnie touched his tender cheek. This time there was something almost pitying in her expression. "Part of that's right. I'll let you work out which part."

"This is crazy. You're talking about murder."

Marnie shrugged. "That's one way of looking at it, if you're viewing it through the prism of normal society's rules and regulations."

"Goddamn. What other fucking way is there of viewing it?"

Another shrug. Another brush of her hand across his wounded cheek, with firmer pressure this time, making him wince. "As a justified execution."

Mike wasn't sure whether to laugh or scream. He felt like doing a lot of both, actually. "Crazy. Fucking crazy." He was shaking his head side to side, over and over. His mind was reeling. "You're not sane. Do you know that?"

"Nadia handed down the death decree in her rightful role as leader of the group. Nicole was making preparations to leave us. She let it slip one night while we were up late drinking. Of course I had to tell Nadia. I loved Nicole, but I love the group more."

Mike's brow creased. "Did you know Nadia would order her death?"

"Of course. The only way out of the group is death. It's one of the rules we swear to obey when we pledge our allegiance to Satan and The Diabolical Conspiracy."

Mike stared at her.

Man, this just doesn't get any saner.

He searched her face, studying its pleasing contours for anything that might hint at the madness behind the pretty façade. But there was nothing. It was the same face he'd dreamed about for so many months. He thought about how much he'd enjoyed the simple act of talking to her, how often he'd savored that sweetly lilting quality in her voice. Reflecting on that now filled him with a deep, seemingly infinite sadness. He had thought she was a good person. A kind person. But it had all been an act. That person hadn't actually existed. She was good. Really, really good. It had been an Oscar-worthy performance, for sure. He didn't even want to talk to her now. Didn't care about anything she had to say. There was nothing she could tell him that wouldn't be more insanity. So his mind was made up. He would lie here quietly, ignoring her until she went away again.

Well, that was his intent for maybe half a minute.

But something was niggling at his brain.

"Hold on. How is it Nadia is in charge? Why not you or Blake? Surely one of you was the original leader."

Marnie shook her head. "No. Nicole was our leader in the beginning. But she lost her way."

Meaning she got tired of playing at being a devil worshipper, most likely.

"Nadia was always my finest discovery. She saw how things were going wrong and challenged Nicole. A vote was called. Nicole lost."

"And died."

Marnie nodded. "Yes. And died. It was the right move. The Diabolical Conspiracy has never been stronger. With Nadia at the helm, we are close to achieving many of our most important goals."

Mike considered querying her about the nature of those goals, but decided it was pointless. He'd only get more of that vague nonsense about doing evil stuff and didn't have the patience for listening to any more of that bullshit.

Marnie's hand came away from his face and moved slowly down

the length of his torso, stopping at the crotch of his jeans, where she cupped him and squeezed.

Mike thought, *Wait just a second here. This is interesting.*

Marnie smiled. "You like?"

Before he could answer, she squeezed him again, applying more pressure as she elicited a helpless groan from him.

She laughed. "You like."

Mike heaved a breath.

He liked. He liked a hell of a lot.

But even as he savored the sensations caused by her physical ministrations, he was cognizant of being manipulated yet again. She was too aware of how intensely he desired her and obviously had no qualms about exploiting that desire. On one level, it galled him that he could fall prey to those desires after all she had done. The more noble part of him screamed to rebel against what was happening, to fill his head with thoughts of the most un-erotic things he could imagine. But it wasn't working. She was too good. Too pretty. Too . . . too *Marnie*. She kept working at him and very soon had coaxed him to rigid, painful hardness.

Then her hand came away from him and her expression was carefully blank again. "Would you like to know why I'm doing this? Why I'm even talking to you?"

He was breathing hard and had to swallow a lump in his throat before he could speak again. "Not really. You're probably gonna tell me anyway, though."

She leaned over him, putting her face very close to his. He felt her breath against his cheeks and had to choke down another lump in his throat. "I had a talk with Nadia while you were unconscious. Haven't you wondered why you're tied to this bed? Why you're not dead yet?"

Mike let out a breath and struggled to focus on what she was saying. She was so close now. Almost close enough to kiss. The force of his desire for her was making him almost cross-eyed. "I . . . I guess it crossed my mind."

She shifted her position on the bed, stretching her body out as she rolled half onto him and angled a thigh against his swollen crotch. "I was pleading your case. I've been authorized to give you one last chance to join us."

She writhed against him, making him groan again.

Mike blew out another breath and said, "Jesus."

"Has nothing to do with this and don't you forget it." She nipped at his bottom lip and smiled at the way this made him shiver. "Would you like another chance?"

Mike thought about it. He still had no interest in joining up with a bunch of whacked out Satanists. But maybe he could play along with it for a while if it meant he could be with Marnie. He didn't believe she would suddenly become his girlfriend if he agreed to this, but it seemed likely she would at least let him have sex with her now and then if she believed it would cement his loyalty to the group. And maybe that would be good enough. It would be better than nothing. And it sure as hell would beat being dead.

She kissed him, darted her tongue between his swollen lips, and laughed. "Come on. What do you say?"

"What happens if I say no?"

"You know the answer to that."

He guessed he did. The same thing that had happened to Nicole. A staged accident of some kind. Or maybe he would just disappear. "And if I say yes?"

She kissed him again, harder now, pressing her breasts against his chest. Her face was slightly flushed as her moist lips came away from his own. "Then you get initiated into the group. You get to live." Her voice was huskier. She peppered his neck with light kisses. "And you get to make love to me."

Mike closed his eyes and groaned. "Well . . . that sounds wonderful. And it's as simple as agreeing to this?"

Marnie's face came away from his neck. Her cheeks were still flushed, but her expression was more solemn now. "Well . . . there *is* a condition."

"Anything. I'll do anything. Just don't stop kissing me."

A small smile touched the edges of her mouth. "It's a pretty big condition."

"Just tell me. Please. And then get back to what you were doing."

There was an almost playful glint in her eyes now. "You sure you want to know?"

Mike was becoming frustrated. "*Yes.*"

Marnie laughed. It was that same lilting, almost musical tone he remembered from their many long late-night conversations. How he had missed hearing it. She was definitely playing with him now.

And he loved it.

"You're positive?"

"Marnie, for the love of God, spill it."

"For the love of Satan, you mean."

"Fine. For the love of Satan. For the love of whatever the hell makes you happy. Just tell me and end my fucking misery."

Marnie smiled again. "Okay. Here it is. In order to earn another chance, you have to show us how serious you are and there's only one way to do that."

"Which is?"

Her expression changed again, the playfulness draining away. "You have to kill someone for us."

He gaped at her for a moment. Then he closed his mouth and swallowed. "What?"

"You heard me. You have to kill someone. You have to take another human being's life. And you have to do it tonight. Can you do that?" She put her face close to his again, so close the tips of their noses touched. "Can you do that for me?"

Mike couldn't say anything right away.

His mind was reeling again.

He felt lightheaded.

"Say you'll kill for me." Her voice had become husky again. Her lips were nearly touching his as she breathed the words. *"Say it, Mike. Say you'll kill for me."*

4

HE TOLD HER WHAT SHE wanted to hear. Of course he did. What else could he have done? The only other option, apparently, was immediate execution and he wasn't ready for that just yet. He had no desire to cause the death of another person, but merely saying he would do the deed didn't make him a bad guy or a murderer. Not yet. What it *would* do was maybe buy him a little time. Time he could use to possibly brainstorm an alternate way out of this mess.

It was a great idea in theory, but what Marnie did after he told her he would kill for her was so pleasurably distracting it made thinking about anything other than what she was doing impossible. She congratulated him on the wise decision and slithered down his torso to his crotch, where she opened his jeans and proceeded to do things with her mouth that made stars explode in his head. Hell, not just stars, but whole constellations. By the time he came, he felt like maybe he really could kill someone for her, which was probably the point. It was more manipulation, but this time he didn't give a damn. His head was swimming and it was impossible to think straight. Beaten mercilessly and later blown expertly by the same woman in the same night. It was goddamn surreal.

She worked fast after that, freeing him from his bonds and hustling him out of the guest bedroom and down a hallway toward the door to the garage. He glimpsed the living room through an archway as they hurried down the hallway. The living room looked so normal, so deceptively middle class, with the usual array of nice but not terribly expensive furniture. There was nothing about it that screamed, *Beware! Satanists live here!* Adjacent to the living room was a small foyer. The front door was there. From his vantage point, the living room appeared empty, which made him think the rest of them were back in the garage. Marnie was gripping him by an elbow. As he glimpsed the empty living room, an impulse to dash through that archway and make a run for it flashed through his mind. But Marnie must have sensed this because she tightened her grip on his arm in the same instant. He still might have jerked his arm free and tried for a getaway, but resurgent fear coupled with a case of paralyzing indecisiveness settled the matter. So he relaxed and let her guide him to the door at the end of the hallway and out to the garage.

The metal folding chairs were still arranged in a loose circle, but at the moment they were mostly empty. Nadia was the only one sitting, and she had her nose in a large, leather-bound book as he and Marnie reentered the garage. She didn't look up or otherwise acknowledge them as they returned. The other Satanists were standing near a table at the rear of the garage. The table was against the back wall. Upon it rested an assortment of refreshments, including bags of various kinds of potato chips, bowls of dip, and plates filled with cookies, doughnuts, and cake. Beneath the table were two large coolers containing cans of soft drinks and bottles of beer. Mike was amused by how quaintly mundane the scene appeared. It was like they were attending a PTA or neighborhood association meeting rather than a congregation of Satanists. Few of them would fit anyone's idea of how members of a cult dedicated to furthering the cause of evil would look. Nadia did sort of fit the bill, with her black attire and almost ghostly pallor. She also looked like she would be right at home amongst a coven of witches or whatever you called a bunch of vampires who got together and talked shop.

The sight of the glistening bottles of beer floating in ice made Mike's mouth water and he considered helping himself to one, but Marnie had other plans. She steered him toward the circle of chairs and told him to have a seat.

"Could I please have a beer?"

She touched the side of his head and ruffled his hair in a gesture that felt genuinely affectionate. Strange for someone who had made it clear she wouldn't hesitate to hurt or even kill him if necessary. "Maybe later. Stay there."

She left him then and joined the others at the rear of the garage. He looked across the circle at Nadia, whose attention was still focused on the oversized book. There was a large silver pentagram on the front of the book. Some kind of satanic text, Mike supposed. He wondered what kind of information it contained. Demonic summoning spells, maybe? Chapters on the basic principles of Satanism? Probably all that and a lot more. It looked like a very old book. The covers were weathered and the pages looked brittle with age. He had a feeling it wasn't the kind of book you'd find on the shelves of a chain bookstore. His gut told him there weren't many like it in the world. It was maybe even one of a kind. He had no factual information to base this on, but somehow it felt right. The book Nadia was reading was the kind of rare relic handed down through the ages, from one generation of cult leaders to the next.

"So . . . what's that you're reading?"

Nadia didn't lift her eyes from the page. "Shut up."

Though the volume of her voice was low, the words conveyed an undeniable weight and strength. He closed his mouth, deciding it wouldn't be wise to even verbally acknowledge the command.

His gaze went to the rear of the garage again. Aside from the occasional quick sidelong glance, no one else was watching him either. So he shifted slightly on the chair and craned his neck around to check out the rest of the garage. The garage door was closed and someone had blacked out the narrow windows inset in the metal at eye-level with spray paint. There were no cars in the garage, presumably to make room for tonight's meeting. But an examination of the cement floor made him wonder about that. It was virtually spotless, with no oil stains in sight. Weird. Did Nadia never park her car in here? Mike lived in an apartment and frequently had to park at the curb on public streets. If he had a garage of his own, he would sure as hell use it for its intended purpose.

"Look at me."

Mike jerked in his seat at the sound of Nadia's voice. She was looking right at him. The big book was closed now. She held it in her lap with her slender forearms folded over its cover. Good lord, but

the woman looked delicious. And glamorous, as if she had just returned from a photo shoot for a fashion magazine. He was again
struck by how perfect everything about her seemed. Hair, makeup,
outfit . . . everything. Why she was slumming it with a bunch of small-
town Satanists rather than living it up in some Manhattan or Parisian
penthouse was completely mysterious to him.

"Do you find me an enigma?"

Mike shivered.

There she went with that spooky mind-reading shit again.

"Uh . . . yeah. I guess I do."

"Good."

Mike grunted.

Good? That's all you've got to say to that? Fucking good?

"So you've accepted our generous second chance offer then?"

Mike shrugged. "Yeah. I guess I have."

She pursed her lips for a moment and regarded him in a coolly
appraising way that made him feel like bugs were crawling all over
him. "Guessing isn't good enough. You must be certain. You must
be truly and fully committed to performing as required. Are you?

Mike gulped. "Um . . . yeah. I am. Definitely. Fully, absolutely,
without reservation committed. No question about it."

She smiled. "I'm pleased to hear it. It would be a shame to lose
Marnie."

This comment made Mike's gut clench with sudden dread. "What
do you mean by that?"

"I mean your second chance is also a second chance for her. As
you may understand by now, we take a tremendous risk every time
we take the step of inviting a new member into our circle. An officer
of the conspiracy never extends an invitation unless she is certain the
prospective new member will unhesitatingly accept. Survival of the
group means not allowing even the slightest possibility of exposure."

"When you said earlier that she would be punished . . ."

Nadia nodded. "I meant she would die."

"Jesus."

"By agreeing to do as required, you have given her a temporary
reprieve." Nadia leaned back in her chair and caressed the old book's
cover with her fingertips. "If you do what has been asked of you, she
will live and continue to serve Satan." She glanced down at the book
and lightly ran one finger along the lines of the pentagram. "You
asked what I was reading." She looked up again and her eyes

projected an inner hardness that belied her exquisitely sensual feminine exterior. "This book is The Satanic Bible. The real one, not that piece of fluff written by LaVey."

Mike thought, *Who the fuck is LaVey?*

It was a question that went unanswered as Nadia continued: "It is one of only 666 copies produced long, long ago. Not many copies survive today. Perhaps only a handful. And this copy is the most sacred satanic relic in The Diabolical Conspiracy's possession. Any one of us would kill or die to protect it and thus preserve the knowledge it contains. Killing a man tonight will only be the first of many ways you'll prove you are worthy of being a member of our group. After tonight, you will be on probation. You will only become a full member when I am convinced you are as committed to the cause as the rest of us." She held up the book, displaying the cover for him. The faint and fading outlines of a goat's head were visible within the the the pentagram. "When I believe that you are truly willing to die for this book and what it represents, only then will you become our Thirteenth, thus completing the infernal circle."

Mike's frown deepened as he listened to her. The things she was telling him troubled him immensely. They still sounded insane to his ears. But he was trying hard to comprehend the twisted logic behind the words. He had to find a way to believe what she believed—or at least convince them all that he did—because the alternative was unacceptable. Because he couldn't—or didn't want to—imagine a world without Marnie in it, regardless of how she had used him.

He made the frown go away and looked Nadia unwaveringly in the eye. "Then let me start convincing you. You say I have to kill someone tonight. So let's get on with it."

Nadia's coolly appraising look gave way to another of her frosty, nearly invisible smiles. "As you wish." She pitched her voice higher for her next utterance, making the words heard over the din of conversation at the rear of the garage. "*It is time. Make the preparations. Bring out the sacrifice.*"

The conversational buzz ceased immediately and was replaced by sounds of activity. Mike heard a clink of bottles as they were dumped into a trash can. He glanced past Nadia and saw cult members quickly disposing of paper plates and napkins. Most then returned to the circle of chairs, but instead of sitting right away, they pulled the chairs outward, widening the circle. Two male cult members—including Blake—went into the house. Mike assumed the sacrificial victim was stashed away in there somewhere. Just thinking about that made his guts clench again, so he tried to stay focused on what was happening out here. Once the circle of chairs had been widened, most of the remaining cult members immediately seated themselves and bowed their heads. They also folded their hands in their laps and closed their eyes. Again, he was struck by how mundane the scene seemed on the surface. They looked like members of a prayer group instead of Satanists. Or, considering the circle of chairs, like attendees of an AA meeting in a church basement.

It was a little weird.

Another of the male cult members—the genuinely ugly one, who looked like Adolf Hitler and Joan Rivers had somehow gotten together and produced a deformed lovechild meshing distorted elements of each of their most unattractive physical features—dragged a large block of wood into the center of the circle. There was a curious narrow groove through the center of the top part of the block. Mike puzzled over this until he saw the ugly guy return to the rear of the garage and reach for the heavy-bladed axe hanging from a peg on the wall.

Then he understood.

Oh shit . . . that's a chopping block.

He had given no thought to *how* they expected him to kill this thus far unidentified person, but now that he was thinking about it, he realized there had been an unconscious assumption it would be something much cleaner than this. As far as any method of murder could be called clean, that is.

But this . . . this was just . . . *gruesome.*

He realized he was shaking again—and was doubting whether he could go through with this, regardless of the cost.

And then Blake and the other guy returned, dragging the bound and gagged intended victim along with them. It took every ounce of will Mike possessed not to scream during the shock of recognition that occurred then. Because the man he was supposed to kill was not a faceless, nameless stranger.

Mike knew him.

Knew him well.

I can't do this, he thought. *No fucking way.*

5

THE MAN WITH HIS HEAD on the chopping block was Donnie Wilkerson. Donnie and Mike's father had grown up together. When Mike had been a kid, he would occasionally see Donnie having drinks with his dad out on the deck behind their house. He hadn't been in the same room with the man in well over a decade, maybe closer to a decade and a half, but his memory of the man had not dimmed in the intervening years. The reason for that was that the man was rarely out of the public eye these days.

Mike's incredulity was off the scale. He simply couldn't believe what he was seeing. He looked at Nadia. "Oh, come on. You can't seriously expect me to kill the mayor."

Nadia's expression was placid, her posture relaxed. She looked as serene as a woman watching the ocean from a beach chair. "That is precisely what I expect. You will do it . . ." She lifted her shoulders in a small, unconcerned shrug. "Or you will die. And then Marnie will die. Regardless of what you decide, the mayor will also die."

"This is crazy."

Nadia said nothing, just continued looking right at him with that perfectly composed expression of a woman who didn't have a care in the world.

Blake and the other guy forced the mayor to his knees. Donnie Wilkerson was nude. He had the kind of ruggedly handsome face that projected an aura of strength and firmness of conviction. The kind of face voters liked. But the sight of his flabby, pasty middle-aged flesh exposed this way ruined that impression. He seemed vulnerable. Weak. Soft. Mike looked at him and was almost overcome with pity. His dad's old friend regarded him with dazed, uncomprehending eyes. Mike guessed the man had been drugged and he felt some relief at the knowledge. It would obviously be better if he didn't fully realize what was happening to him. Or know who was responsible. Though Mike doubted Donnie Wilkerson would have recognized him even if he hadn't been drugged. A lot of time had passed since they had last seen each other and Mike scarcely resembled the adolescent boy he had been in his mid-teens.

None of which made the notion of killing a man he knew—a man he believed was a good man—any less horrible.

Blake and the other man pressed Wilkerson's head to the chopping block. He didn't struggle. He stared at the cement floor and breathed raggedly through the gag in his mouth. Mike stared at the sprinkling of age spots and moles on the man's back and bony shoulders and felt another sharp twinge of pity. The ugly man who looked sort of like a diminutive Hitler stepped into the circle, approached Mike, and proffered the axe.

Mike's heart hammered away in his chest as he stared at the heavy, razor-sharp blade. The beating of his heart seemed amplified, almost deafening. He knew this was a false impression, a product of intense stress, but that hardly mattered. In those moments, it sounded to him as if his heart might explode. Which, given the circumstances, might not be the worst thing that could happen.

He glanced around at the faces of the others. They were no longer in those prayerful poses. They were all watching him now, their expressions expectant and . . . hopeful? Yes, hopeful. They wanted to see him do this awful thing. And why? Because they were all equally eager to see him join the cult as its thirteenth member? Maybe that was part of it. Nadia had repeatedly emphasized how important it was to complete the "infernal circle," whatever the hell that meant. But Mike suspected there was another layer to this and that was the simple, primal thrill of bloodlust. They wanted to look on as another human being met a grisly end right in front of them. Yes, he could see it in their eyes now, it was excruciatingly clear. These people were monsters. The worst kind of sadists. Suddenly he was seeing other things in a new light, as well. The chopping block, for instance. No one created or kept a thing like that around for a one-time use. They'd done this before. Maybe many times. And now he understood why they held their meetings in the garage rather than inside Nadia's house—because hosing blood spatters off a cement floor was much easier than getting those pesky stains out of a living room carpet.

Nadia sighed. "We're waiting. We understand this isn't easy, but our patience is not infinite. Take the axe. *Now.*"

The ugly man pushed the axe at him and muttered under his breath, "Take it. You won't get another chance."

Mike reluctantly accepted the axe and held it loosely by the handle. It was heavier than he expected. He had chopped firewood some as a boy. That was the last time he had used an axe. They were primarily intended as tools, of course, not as weapons. This one's axe head seemed heavier than normal, and larger. Of course. If these freaks did make a regular thing of decapitating people, they would want to have the biggest, baddest axe available.

Marnie leaned toward him, touched his arm. "Do it. For me. For both of us. Render glory unto Satan."

Fucking hell.

He was still stunned by how thoroughly Marnie was invested in this Satanism thing. Prior to tonight she had always seemed so intelligent and rational, but that had just been more role-playing. *This* was the real Marnie, this bloodthirsty devil worshipper. She believed in it all absolutely. Satan was her lord and she loved him. She had since childhood. The world was upside down. Nothing made sense anymore.

He looked at the mayor's slack-featured, drugged face. He still wasn't struggling.

Can I kill this poor bastard? Can I really?

Nadia cleared her throat. "You are out of time. Do it now. Or die."

Mike heaved a breath and got to his feet. He felt detached from his body as he approached the chopping block. The eyes of the others followed him as he moved. But he felt like one of them, just another observer, watching and wondering how this would play out. Because he still didn't know, not even as he raised the axe and placed the sharp edge of the blade against the exposed back of Donnie Wilkerson's neck.

He looked at Nadia. He felt like there were still things he had to know before this could happen. "Why am I doing this? Why this man? Why tonight?"

"To prove your worth, as you have already been told. And also because I fucking told you to do it. You don't need any other reasons."

The tone of her voice was sharper than it had been in a while and this was the first time she had seemed truly angry since her assault on Blake. It scared the crap out of him and he had to tighten his grip on the axe to keep from dropping it. He had the sense she wouldn't put up with further delay much longer.

Still, he hesitated. "This man is an elected official, which means this amounts to an assassination. This won't be the same thing as killing Nicole." He noted Nadia's look of surprise at the mention of that name and nodded. "Yes, Marnie told me about her. Nicole was a nobody. Just another citizen. This man's death will be big news. There'll be an investigation, possible risk of exposure. Surely—"

"Shut up."

Mike closed his mouth, swallowing the rest of his argument. Nadia's tone was more stern—and more laced with lethal, unforgiving intent—than ever. Saying anything else would be useless now. Everything he'd said had been useless. This woman couldn't be reasoned with, nor could her mind ever be changed.

Her expression was fierce as she addressed him again. "This man stands in opposition to the cause of evil. His own actions brought him to this point. He must die. He will die. Do it now. *Right fucking now!*"

She was on the edge of her seat now and her hands were clenched into fists. She looked ready to launch herself at him at any moment. The memory of what she had done to Blake made that a chilling prospect. Mike lifted the axe from the mayor's neck and propped the handle on his shoulder.

He looked at Marnie, saw her smiling and nodding her support.

And he looked around the circle one last time, at all those eager faces . . . at all these vultures masquerading as humans. One of the female members—a shapely blonde in a red party dress—had produced a gun from somewhere. Its barrel was aimed at his midsection. Insurance, he supposed, a safeguard should he abruptly snap and decide to wield the heavy axe on the cult members instead of the mayor.

But that wasn't going to happen.

His course was set now.

He truly had no choice.

Mike gripped the axe's handle tighter and lifted it high above his head. Then, with all his might, he swung the axe down.

6

LATER MIKE WOULD REALIZE HE should have taken at least another moment to accurately line up the arc of his swing with the back of the mayor's neck. The whole thing might have gone more smoothly if he had done that. But he didn't. So instead of chopping into his neck, the blade slammed into the back of his head, penetrating his skull but failing to instantly kill him. The shock to the man's system overrode the effects of the drug. His body spasmed and Blake and the male cult member assisting him struggled to keep his neck pressed against the chopping block. People were yelling. Screaming. One voice was louder than all the others. Nadia, of course. Ordering him to extract the axe from the mayor's head and swing it again, to finish the fucking job. Mike glanced at Marnie. She was screaming at him, too. In general, these crazy motherfuckers were making a hell of a lot of noise, which seemed odd for a bunch of people so worried about "exposure."

Mike dragged his gaze away from Marnie and focused again on the mayor's still-twitching body. About an inch of the heavy blade was buried inside the dying man's skull. A lot of blood was leaking out around its edges. He pulled at the axe handle, but it didn't budge. So he braced a foot on the edge of the chopping block and rocked the handle up and down until the blade came out. Then he repositioned himself and lined up the blade with the back of the man's neck again. This time he took a couple of careful practice swings, making sure he had the arc right before he swung in earnest again. There was still a lot of frantic noise in the garage as he did this. Everyone seemed anxious he finish killing the man as soon as possible. By now he couldn't blame them.

He let out a fearsome yell as he brought the blade down again. This second attempt was right on target. The blade met with some resistance as it hit Donnie Wilkerson's spine, but the force of the blow rendered the effect of the resistance essentially nil. The blade passed through the spine and thunked into the chopping block, successfully separating Donnie's head from the rest of his body. This time there was a lot more blood, a short-lived geyser of it shooting from the neck stump and spraying all over the cement floor. Now Mike understood why they had widened the circle of chairs. The body twitched another few times as the blood jetted, then finally went still.

A few moments passed before Mike realized all the screaming and yelling had stopped. But his ears were still ringing as he dropped the axe and staggered away from his grisly handiwork. He was dizzy as he banged into one of the chairs and only managed to remain upright with assistance from the chair's female occupant. Then he was out of the circle and stumbling over to a corner of the garage, where he braced himself against the wall with a forearm and hung his head as his stomach heaved and expelled its contents. Sweat formed on his brow and ran down his face as he continued to heave for a while. His teeth chattered and his body trembled. Tears stung his eyes as childhood images of Donnie and his father drinking on the deck again surfaced.

I'm a murderer, he thought. *A goddamn, no good motherfucking murderer. Inhuman scum.*

A harsh assessment, but an undeniable truth. It was how he'd always viewed others who took the lives of innocents. No way could he give himself a pass on that count. And it didn't matter that he had been coerced. The bottom line was he had committed an act of brutal murder. He was a killer. It was one of those horrible things that, once done, you could never take back. He would carry the label to his grave.

Then he felt a small hand at the center of his back. It was moving gently, stroking, caressing, soothing. Next he heard Marnie's voice: "It's okay, it's okay. You did good. I'm proud of you. So proud."

He sniffled and said nothing.

I'm not. I want to die. I deserve to die.

But even as he thought these things he knew he didn't mean them. He was deeply ashamed of what he had done, yes, but he wanted to live. And he wanted to get away from these people and back to his normal life, even if that meant he had to split town and disappear for a long time, maybe forever. Start over somewhere new and try like hell to avoid ever associating with Satanists again.

"She's right, Mike. You should be proud of what you've done."

Nadia. Right behind him.

He took a deep breath, slowly let it out, and turned to face her. He kept his face as blank as possible as she studied him, recalling her eerily accurate powers of intuition. He swallowed with some difficulty and made himself say, "Thank you. I . . . am."

She snorted. "I doubt that. I'm sure some part of you is thinking you'll keep playing the part of the willing new initiate until you can get clear of us and then you'll head for the hinterlands."

Mike managed to avoid a dramatic visual reaction, but he felt like shitting himself.

Goddammit, what's the deal with this chick, how does she do that?

Nadia smirked. "Just remember you are now as culpable as the rest of us. You have taken a life. Which means you can't expose us without sealing your fate. And I have a hunch you'd prefer not to spend a big chunk of your life behind bars. So you're not a threat to us. You'll be safe from us as long as that remains the case. Understand?"

Mike nodded, but he didn't say anything.

Nadia stepped closer to him and he had to resist an impulse to shrink back against the wall. She was almost close enough to touch. Had he thought she was intimidating before? She had been, of course, but at this range the effect was infinitely more intense. He had never been this close to anyone so mind-bendingly gorgeous. The feelings her proximity caused were nearly powerful enough to entirely blot out any memory of the horror that had transpired. His throat felt dry, constricted. He was shaking and felt like he might fall over if she came even one inch closer. She reached out and calmly flicked a speck of dust off the front of his shirt, making him flinch.

Then she touched his arm and said, "But I'm confident that won't be an issue. In fact, I'll make a prediction. By the time you leave here much later tonight, you'll be a genuinely eager convert." She stroked his arm and said, "And you'll be counting down the days until our next meeting."

Mike nodded again and forced out a sound meant to indicate a certain level of open-mindedness, if not actual agreement. But his throat was so tight it came out as a caveman-like grunt. Speaking was still not even a possibility.

Nadia laughed softly and touched his cheek. "You belong to us now, mind and soul. Never doubt it." She glanced at Marnie, who was still standing off to the side. Mike had almost forgotten she was there, he was so overwhelmed by Nadia. "I'll see you both inside. Hail Satan."

Marnie smiled. "Hail Satan."

Nadia walked away then. Mike kept his eyes on her until she disappeared through the door to the house. Only then did the rest of the world snap back into focus. The rest of the women had disappeared, too, except for Marnie. The men were busy with cleanup. Mike wondered vaguely whether he was expected to help, but the thought slipped away as Marnie insinuated herself against him and thrust a hand between his legs, making him gulp.

She rested her head on his shoulder and laughed. "My, hard again already. No surprise, really. Nadia has that effect on everyone." She made a purring sound. "Hmm, even on me. So what do you say, are you ready for the orgy?"

He at last managed to recover his voice. "The what now?"

She giggled. "The orgy, silly. Are you ready for it?"

All Mike could think about was that plentitude of buxom, beautiful women now lounging about somewhere inside the house. Including Nadia, of course. It was ridiculous to suppose he might at some point become physically intimate with her during this so-called "orgy" that was supposedly about to occur, but he couldn't help picturing it anyway.

It was a singularly powerful image.

He shivered.

He looked at Marnie. "Yes. I think I'm ready for it."

7

MUSIC WAS PLAYING AS THEY came back into the house. Some kind of haunting, dirge-y doom metal with sludgy, neo-psyche-delic guitars and an echoing female lead vocal that lent the music an even gloomier depth and edge. Mike didn't know what the music was, but it was something he would download if he happened across it online. It had a rich and interesting sonic texture. But in this con-text—in a house full of demented Satanists—the vibe the music pro-jected was more than a little creepy. As they neared the archway that led into the living room, he detected the flicker of a red strobe light. The pulsing light bled into the hallway and described strange, caper-ing patterns on the walls.

It was all a little weird. Mike felt like he was about to enter the lounge of a downtown goth club rather than a suburban living room. That impression changed somewhat as he followed Marnie through the archway. Only somewhat because the vibe was essentially what he expected, with the flashing red strobe eerily complementing the hypnotic rhythms of the music. And an early '70s horror film was playing on a large flat-screen television. Mike recognized it as *Twins*

Of Evil, a Hammer Films production starring horror legend Peter Cushing. The movie was playing with the sound off and was only on, presumably, to heighten the carefully cultivated spooky atmosphere.

But the resemblance to a downtown club ended right about there, unless the club in question was one of those private, invite-only things. The female cult members were all present and most of them glanced their way as they came into the living room. These were only fleeting glances, but a few of the women smirked as they made brief eye contact with Mike. The smirks were probably a result of his look of wide-eyed, slack-jawed astonishment. But Mike simply couldn't help it. These were all exceptionally lovely women—and every one of them was completely nude.

Including Nadia.

The cult's leader sat in a leather recliner with her eyes closed and her chin tilted toward the ceiling. She sat with her butt on the edge of the recliner's cushion and her legs spread wide. The blonde woman who had held the gun on him earlier was on her knees between Nadia's legs, her head moving rhythmically as she performed an act of very enthusiastic oral sex. The emphatic jut of Nadia's pink-tipped breasts was an equally entrancing sight. He couldn't tear his eyes away from her for many long moments. He felt hypnotized. And dizzy, as if his head might explode any second. Or as if *something* might explode anyway.

Mike was beyond flabbergasted. The other women were smiling and swaying to the music, elegant heads rotating slowly on slender necks, the eyes of some fluttering as if they were in a trance. Or on drugs. Which maybe they were. Mike's gaze roved over each of the sleek, shapely bodies as he wondered whether he might be on drugs, too. Maybe Marnie had dosed the soda he'd had upon arriving with acid. Or X. Or whatever it was people were taking these days. Because he definitely felt like he was tripping. How else to explain finding himself in a room full of beautiful, naked women who weren't demanding payment for the privilege?

His attention inevitably returned to Nadia, who was rocking in the recliner and clutching hard at the armrests as her head whipped side to side. The blonde between her legs was moving her head much faster now, her oral ministrations causing Nadia to cry out loud enough to be heard over the roar of the music.

Mike flinched when he felt a hand tugging at his jeans. He glanced down, saw that it was Marnie opening his pants. Again. Only days ago he'd resigned himself to never being physically intimate with her and now it was happening for the second time in the same evening. She had already shed her clothes while his attention had been elsewhere. It was his first time seeing her nude and the sight was everything he'd ever imagined and more. Okay, so maybe she wasn't quite Nadia's equal in the overall beauty department—who was?—but her unclothed body was a goddamn work of art.

He looked her up and down, shaking his head as he drank in all those lush curves. "You are so fucking beautiful."

She smiled. "I know."

He started to say something in response, but then her soft hand was gripping his hardness and he could only gasp.

She nuzzled his neck and groaned softly. "You like that?"

"Uh . . ."

It was answer enough.

She helped him strip off his clothes and guided him down to the carpeted living room floor. He slipped between her spread legs a moment later and entered her, gasping at that first plunge inside her exquisitely moist center. His face contorted and his nails dug into the carpet as he thrust against her again and again. He only belatedly realized he was fucking for an audience for the first time in his life. This moment of recognition happened less than a minute into the coupling with Marnie, occurring as he grimaced and twisted his head far to the right and saw a couple of the women staring down at him. One of them—a leggy brunette—had a hand between her legs and licked her lips as she made eye contact with Mike. Mike paused in mid-thrust, momentarily paralyzed by the attention. Marnie clutched at his back and thrust her hips at him, urging him to start moving again. For a terrible second or two he thought he would wilt inside her. He was as turned on as he had ever been, but during those seconds he also experienced an intense attack of performance anxiety. He was a shy guy and was way out of his depth here. The situation was exacerbated as the hideous memories of what he'd done in the garage only minutes earlier came rushing back in. What was wrong with him? What kind of monster could have sex so soon after doing something so awful to another human being?

Then he stretched his head to the right and saw Nadia watching him with obvious interest. She was still in the recliner, but the blonde was no longer going down on her. Instead she was sitting at Nadia's feet like an obedient pet and watching the show along with everyone else. Nadia was sliding her fingers through the woman's hair, heightening the impression of a mistress-pet relationship.

Mike felt a charge go through him as he locked eyes with Nadia. Her gaze was as intense and intimidating as ever. Then she smiled and her mouth was moving. Her lips opened, shifted, and opened again in the same pattern a few times before he realized she was repeatedly mouthing the same two words: *"Fuck her."*

Mike's heart seemed to skip a beat.

And from that point forward there were no more issues with performance anxiety. His cock felt like steel inside Marnie as he gave her a pounding that was at least as energetic as anything he'd ever managed before. By the end of it, Marnie was screaming so shrilly it sounded as if her vocal cords would surely snap from the strain. Her nails scratched groove after groove in his back and drew forth trickles of blood. It hurt like hell, but Mike didn't care at all in that last ecstatic moment of exploding orgasm.

Then he fell against Marnie and she clutched at him again and laughed and kissed and nuzzled his neck. After a few moments, he was surprised to find he was laughing, too. He felt so good, better than he had in longer than he could remember. He could blissfully, happily spend the rest of forever right here on this floor with Marnie. All of his self-consciousness was gone. He didn't care that he was nude or that they could all see every inch of his somewhat less than buff physique. He felt freer than ever.

Liberated, even.

The memory of the heavy axe blade biting into the back of Donnie Wilkerson's head tried to invade his consciousness a time or two, but pushing it away was easy. He knew it was another thing he would have to contend with sometime after the glow of this experience had passed, but he could worry about it later.

All he cared about right now was Marnie.

Marnie, Marnie, Marnie . . .

As he stroked her luxuriant blond locks, he stared into her wide blue eyes and felt as if he could get permanently lost in them. He held her and kissed her and stayed there on the floor with her for a time longer than he could guess—but not nearly long enough. The spell was only broken when a stray thought drifted into his head and instantly commanded his attention—*Oh, shit . . . no condom!*

He listened to his heart thud heavily for a few moments before relaxing again.

Oh well . . . too late now.

He met Marnie's gaze again and smiled . . . and then he felt someone's toe nudging him. He twisted his head to get a look at the interloper and saw Blake staring down at him.

Blake smiled and waved. "Hey."

Mike didn't say anything.

Blake laughed and tilted his chin. "Come on, dude. My turn."

Mike still didn't respond. Not because he didn't want to respond, but because he was temporarily incapable of coherent thought. For one thing, Blake had shed his clothes. His dangling junk was a little too close for comfort. But the bigger thing was that he was having great difficulty wrapping his head around what the guy had said.

Then he was frowning as he snapped out of it. "Turn? What do you mean *your* turn? The fuck are you talking about, man?"

"I mean I want to bang Marnie."

Mike's frown deepened as a surge of anger made his muscles tense.

So much for the fucking afterglow.

He started to rise, the urge to do violence overcoming him so swiftly he felt powerless to stop it. Not that he wanted to stop it. No, what he wanted to do was beat the living hell out of Blake, to pound that smiling face to a bloody fucking pulp.

But then Marnie gripped him by his shoulders and said, "Hey, look at me."

Still seething, he looked at her.

She smiled. "It's okay. Really. It's an orgy, remember? This is how these things work."

He didn't say anything, just stared at her in open-mouthed disbelief.

Her smile melted slowly away. "Mike. Seriously. Come on. Get up now."

Mike made no move to do as she asked. He kept staring at her and trying hard to understand what was happening here. This was special, what had happened between them. It *was*. Didn't she feel it, too? She had to, right?

Or . . . had he been used yet again?

His head was spinning.

The world was off its axis, off-kilter. Everything was wrong, wrong—

"*Mike.*"

Nadia's voice, rising effortlessly above the music and piercing his consciousness with the precision of a razor. He felt helplessly impelled to drag his gaze away from Marnie, even though it hurt to do so. He looked at Nadia, locked eyes with her, and waited for her to say something.

She crooked a finger at him and bent it toward her. "Come."

"But—"

"*Now.*"

No question of disobeying that tone. With tremendous reluctance, he disengaged himself from Marnie and got slowly to his feet. He started in Nadia's direction, sparing a murderous glance for Blake on the way. Blake was maddeningly unperturbed. He just smiled and dropped to his knees next to Marnie. Mike forced his gaze away from them. He had to, lest his rage turn volcanic, impossible to contain.

He stopped a few feet from the recliner in which Nadia still sat and said, "Yeah?"

She beckoned him to sit with a wave of her hand. He glanced at the leather sofa to his right and took a shuffling step in that direction before she said, "No. At my feet. With Carolyn."

Carolyn being the apparently multi-talented blonde, skilled of tongue and willing to use a gun. She smiled at Mike as he sighed and dropped to his knees at Nadia's feet. "Hi, Mike."

He had no desire to exchange phony pleasantries with this woman, but Nadia's frosty expression made it clear he'd better do just that. "Hi, Carolyn."

"You swing a mean axe."

"Um . . . thanks."

Nadia patted Carolyn's head. "Dear, go fetch us some drinks. And a bit of that special something. If you don't mind."

Carolyn shifted around on her haunches and kissed the back of Nadia's extended hand. The gesture was just another in an endless series of things that struck Mike as strange about this group. Nadia was more than just the leader of a weird little club to these people. They treated her like actual royalty. He supposed he'd better make an effort to do the same as long as he was involved in this Diabolical Conspiracy thing, regardless of how ridiculous it felt.

When Carolyn had departed, Nadia beckoned him closer still and he obliged, shifting around and pressing himself against one of her legs. She slid her fingers through his hair and then patted his head, just as he'd seen her do to Carolyn. He wanted to be mad about that.

There was something fundamentally demeaning about it. But that wasn't possible. Her incredible beauty negated any such resentment, just burned it away entirely. And the feel of her flesh against his was as electrifying as he imagined. Indeed, if he hadn't come so recently, he would hardly have been able to stand it.

He looked up at her. "Nadia—"

"Hush." She smiled. "Just relax and enjoy yourself. Let it all happen. Be happy in the knowledge that Satan loves you for what you've done in his honor tonight."

Mike didn't have anything to say to that.

Partly because it was fucking crazy. But mostly because what she had said also contained an element of wisdom. The only way through this was just to let it happen. To sit back and wait for the end of the ride.

So that's what he did.

His gaze went to the big flat-screen television as Nadia continued to absently stroke his hair. *Twins Of Evil* was still on. A bosomy vampire chick was flashing her fangs. He stared at the movie for a minute before letting his gaze flit about the rest of the room. Marnie and Blake were intertwined on the floor. Mike felt another twinge of anger, but made himself look away before it could spiral out of control. Nearly everyone else was also engaged in sexual acts. As he watched, people would disengage from each other and switch partners. The bodies met and connected in a wide variety of positions. Rather than being turned on, Mike experienced a disconnected kind of curiosity as he observed this carnal activity. He imagined it was like being on-set at a pornographic movie shoot.

After a while, Carolyn returned with glasses and bottles of wine . . . and a little vial of pills. The pills were X. Which Mike hadn't taken since his college days nearly a decade ago. But tonight he accepted the X with eagerness. It would make getting through this so much easier. His anger would melt away. For a while he would feel almost deliriously happy. A crash would come later, of course, but for now he needed this. And he consumed the wine—which was very good and expensive—with equal enthusiasm. In time, the substances worked their magic and he began to enjoy himself. The occasional resurfacing of the memory of what he had done to Donnie Wilkerson never lasted more than an insignificant moment. He got caught up in the music, the trance-y doom metal having given way to thumping industrial goth. He danced and laughed and whirled about the room.

THE DIABOLICAL CONSPIRACY

Before the night was done, he had sex again. First with Carolyn, then with the leggy brunette whose name he didn't know. And again with Marnie, but by then he didn't care who his partner was, just that he had another warm body against his own. The night lengthened toward dawn and still the party rolled on and on.

When he woke up later that morning, he didn't remember it having ended.

8

HE CAME TO WITH A jolt some hours later. There was an instant awareness of something horrible having occurred and he tried telling himself it had all been a drug-induced dream. But one look around the living room at all the passed-out nude Satanists brought the awful reality screaming back to the forefront of his mind. Here was irrefutable evidence of all the crazy sex stuff he hazily recalled. It wasn't much of a leap from there to acceptance of the more clearly remembered bloodshed in the garage.

The axe. That heavy blade. All that blood. The mutilation of Donnie Wilkerson's poor old body . . .

All real.

Thereafter his mind focused with laser intensity on a single, all-consuming goal—getting the hell out of this madhouse before anyone else woke up. As best he could tell, he was the first to regain consciousness, a supremely lucky break and one he meant to take advantage of without delay. Still, he would have to exercise considerable caution in order to slip away unnoticed, as there were many complications to overcome. He was still nude. And Carolyn was lying snuggled up next to him, with an arm draped across his midsection. He gently took hold of her wrist and lifted her arm slowly off his belly. He then shifted onto his hip and carefully rolled her onto her back. A panicky moment ensued when her eyes fluttered and seemed about to open. He still had hold of her wrist as he observed this potential complication. She yawned and stretched her body out, causing him to grimace as he maintained his loose grip on her wrist. Then she went still again and appeared to settle back into deep sleep. No more eye flutters. He lowered her arm as carefully as he'd raised it and got to his feet.

Aw, shit.

His head was swimming and his face was still sore from the pounding he had taken. Also, he felt sick to his stomach. Something was roiling around in there. He had a dim recollection of gorging on sloppily prepared food at some point during the night. Some kind of gruesome wee-hours culinary concoction involving meatballs, noodles, queso dip, and a jar of jalapeno peppers. Among other things. Some serious time on a toilet likely awaited him in his near future. It was only a matter of time before his body rebelled and started shooting it out one orifice or another. Yet another reason to make fucking haste.

Finding his clothes was the next order of business. He couldn't very well go running out to his car stark naked. Well, perhaps as a last resort. No way was he sticking around if anyone displayed signs of imminent wakefulness. In that event, he would say fuck this shit, grab his keys from the kitchen, and go. What was the worst that could happen? A citation for indecent exposure, maybe, but even that was unlikely if he moved fast enough.

Still, he hoped it wouldn't come to that. There were discarded garments seemingly everywhere. However, a frantic scan of the floor quickly turned up his jeans and shirt. He threaded his way through the naked bodies, snatched his clothes up, and hurriedly pulled them on, followed by his shoes. Another look around confirmed everyone else was still asleep. He was very close to pulling this thing off. Retrieving his keys from the kitchen was the only thing left to do.

The kitchen was a disaster area. Empty bottles and cans everywhere. Spilled food on the floor, the last remnants of that crazy Frankenstein meal. He nearly slipped in a puddle of milk—*milk?*—on his way to the counter. He pinwheeled his arms for a scary, vertigo-inducing moment before managing to right himself. Then he grabbed his keys from the counter and got out of the house as fast as he could. His plan was to drive somewhere far away. Far enough that he could sit somewhere in peace, with no expectation of being disturbed by anyone he knew and think about how to handle what had happened—and about what to do next. But as soon as he stepped out onto the porch out front he knew he wouldn't be doing that.

Marnie craned her head around and smiled up at him from the top step as he came through the front door. "Hi, Mike."

"Hi."

So he had been wrong about being the first one up. Marnie looked surprisingly bright-eyed and perky for someone who had been up partying all night. She was dressed and had even had time to fix her hair and makeup. He cursed himself for his shortsightedness. He hadn't even noted her absence in the living room. If he had just taken an extra moment or two to get a better lay of the land . . .

Well . . . then what?

Nothing, probably.

He would have been just as trapped as he was now.

"Shut the door and have a seat."

She patted the step beside her.

He thought about making a run for his car anyway but dropped the idea when he saw she was holding a partially concealed gun between her legs. He doubted Marnie would shoot him right out here in broad daylight, at least he didn't think she would. But it was hard to tell about anything anymore, especially where she was concerned. He figured the gun was there to encourage him to listen to her and do as she said. And at that it fulfilled its purpose.

He eased the door shut and lowered himself onto the step next to her. "Nice day."

She grunted. "Yeah."

The sky was clear and the air was alive with the usual sounds of a weekend in the suburbs. From somewhere nearby came the sound of a lawnmower. Dogs were barking and kids were playing. A minivan drove by in the street and turned into a driveway a few houses down, disgorging even more noisome kids. It was all so grotesquely normal. The things that had happened in the house behind him last night shouldn't happen in this kind of setting. It was an offense against all that was right and good in the world.

Marnie looked at him. "Trying to slip away, eh?"

Mike didn't deny it. Why bother with an obvious lie? He nodded at the gun. "Would you really shoot me?"

She didn't answer that question. Didn't say anything at all to him for a few moments as she watched the minivan mom down the street get her rambunctious kids together and hustle them inside the house.

Then she stood up and held a hand out to him. "Give me your keys."

Mike stared at her.

"That wasn't a request."

He stared at her a moment longer, then heaved a resigned sigh and handed over the keys. "What now?"

"Get up. We're going for a ride."

9

IT WAS A STRANGE THING being driven around in your own car. There was something almost emasculating about it. He wondered if that might not be part of the point. Or maybe it was a way of illustrating how he had surrendered control of his life over to the cult. But as they traveled to various locations within the city it became clear there was a simpler explanation—Marnie knew exactly where she was going and didn't want to be bothered with the tedium of giving him directions.

That sick feeling of dread he remembered from the night before recurred as he watched her turn down a familiar series of streets leading to an inevitable destination. Their first stop was a small apartment building. She parked at the curb outside and opened her purse to remove a crumpled pack of cigarettes. Menthols. She smoked one down to the filter without saying anything. Mike normally didn't allow smoking in his car, but this time he made no protest. He was too disturbed to care. His sister and her new husband had moved into this building only a month ago. He was pretty sure he had never mentioned this fact to Marnie during any of their recent conversations.

Marnie flicked the cigarette butt out the window, put the car in gear, and drove across town to another familiar location. She pulled into the parking lot outside the retirement complex where his mother lived on the second floor. Again, she didn't say a word as she lit another cigarette and smoked it all the way down. After that, she drove him to a handful of other locations scattered about town, each of which held a personal significance for him. He wanted to tell her there was no need, because by then he was getting the point, but his anxiety was such that he kept his mouth shut as she finished her tour of the town.

She remained silent until she returned to Nadia's neighborhood and parked in the same spot at the curb they had vacated an hour earlier. She patted her purse and looked at him. Her gun was nestled in there next to the cigarettes. "I won't shoot you. I like you too much for that. Truly. But I don't have the same level of affection for your sister, your mother, your fucking grandparents, or your goddamned childhood best friend. Got it?"

Mike was trying hard not to hyperventilate. "Yeah. I . . . listen—"

"Be quiet."

Mike closed his mouth and winced as his upset stomach churned again.

Marnie reached out and touched his knee, making him jump a little. "You're one of us, and you will be until you die. There is no escape. Ever. Understand?"

He nodded, but he was shaking.

This wasn't fair. It wasn't right. He was a free man. A citizen with all the rights and liberties of anyone else. And like any other free person, he should be allowed to determine the course of his own life, including the people with whom he chose to associate. But even as he thought these things, he understood they were no longer strictly true. He belonged to this cult now. This goddamned Diabolical Conspiracy. They owned him. It made him want to scream, to rage against the injustice, but he knew no amount of screaming would change anything.

"If you ever give me reason to doubt your commitment to the cause, I'll return to each of those places we visited today. And the next time you see any of those people, it'll be in a fucking casket. Understand?"

He looked at her, trembling as he met her unwavering gaze. "Have you killed people before?"

"Yes."

No hesitation. And was that even a hint of pride he detected in her tone? He thought it was. For sure there was more than a trace of smugness in her hard expression. She had killed people, hell yes, and she was *proud* of it.

She removed the key from the ignition and tossed the key ring to Mike. "It's like Nadia told you last night. Just give yourself over to this. Embrace it. You truly have no choice. And don't think of warning your loved ones because we'll definitely get wind of it." She smiled and touched his knee again. "You can pick me up at six tonight."

His brow creased at that last remark. "What?"

"Pick me up at six. At my place. Is there a problem?"

"Um . . ." He sighed and shook his head. "No problem . . . so to speak. I'm just curious as to why I'm picking you up. You guys aren't having another meeting already, are you? I couldn't handle this shit on a nightly fucking basis, no matter what."

"Relax, there won't be a meeting for a while." She squeezed his knee and winked at him. *What the fuck?* "You're picking me up because you're taking me to dinner. And then to a movie. My choice, of course."

Mike had no idea what to say to this. A real date with Marnie was the thing he had wanted most for many months. But now that it was actually happening, it was just about the last thing in the world he wanted. It was strange how the world turned sometimes. Actually, it was pretty fucked up. How in hell was he supposed to make polite dinner conversation with someone who had threatened to murder his entire family?

She touched his face, stroked his cheek with her fingertips. "I know what you're thinking and you need to relax. You're only getting what you always wanted, after all." She leaned toward him as her hand slipped behind his neck and pressed him closer. "Now kiss me, bitch."

He kissed her.

There was nothing else he could do. It was like she said, he had to embrace what was happening.

The kiss became heated, unexpectedly passionate under the circumstances. She broke it off briefly at one point and searched his face, her eyes blazing with intensity. "Say you love Satan."

He told her what she wanted to hear.

"Say it like you mean it."

THE DIABOLICAL CONSPIRACY

So he said it again, striving to infuse his voice with a conviction he didn't really feel. She made him repeat it several more times.

And each time it got easier to say.

10

Three months later

THE LAST CALL OF THE day came through at six minutes before quitting time. Mike knew the person on the other end of the line would be a problem caller before she even uttered a word. Three and a half long, soul-killing years on the job had honed his instincts to a sharpness that bordered on telepathy. It was very similar to the way Nadia seemed able to read the minds of conspiracy members, except along a narrower, more specialized path. He heard it in the quick little intake of breath the caller took before launching into a high-volume, barely intelligible tirade about supposedly poor customer service. The moment he heard that he knew what was coming and knew chances were strong he wouldn't be clocking out for at least another half hour. And he was right. Of course he was. By now he knew every customer type so well he could almost recite everything they might feasibly say ahead of time. This included anticipation of inflection of voice and at which juncture in the conversation they would insert certain stock phrases, including—but certainly not limited to—all-time top-of-the-charts favorites such as "I want to speak to a manager!", "Isn't there anyone there higher up than you?", "I'm reporting you to the Better

THE DIABOLICAL CONSPIRACY

Business Bureau!", and (his personal favorite) "I'll never do business with your company again!"

One could only hope.

Thirty-five hellishly tedious minutes later he was able to wrap the exchange up after offering the customer free shipping on her next order and a one-time-use twenty-percent discount code. He counted this as a personal victory, as he always did any time he was successfully able to avoid allowing a customer to badger him into giving them something they didn't deserve. Because he did consider himself at war with the legions of spoiled, entitled assholes out there. Most of them figured they could get something for free if they screamed loud enough, and maybe they could if they lucked into talking to a newer—and more easily intimidated—rep. But Mike was a battle-hardened veteran of the customer service wars and would not put up with that shit. Every now and then someone would call in with a legitimate gripe. Those were equally easy to instantly recognize and, funnily enough, those people were usually far calmer than the sanctimonious, screeching pricks he had to deal with much of the time. He was happy to accommodate the people in this sadly smaller category of callers, and he treated them with the respect they deserved. But when it came to the screamers, he did not fuck around. He allowed them to scream and vent for as long as they liked—and often that was a very long time indeed—but he never budged from the position he knew to be right.

It was a tough, hard-earned mindset.

So it was a pity that mental toughness didn't carry over into certain other areas of his life, such as dealing with The Diabolical Conspiracy. That was how he thought of it in his head, with capital letters—with the same emphasis all the other conspiracy members used when they spoke the name aloud. He followed their lead in that regard, just as he did with every other aspect of cult membership. But every day he wrestled with the urge to stand up and take some kind of action against the group. His conscience told him he should do something. Maybe even take his story to the cops, as daunting as he found that prospect.

The mayor's disappearance was big news and the source of endless speculation. The host of theories offered up covered a wide spectrum of highly unlikely fates for a small city mayor. Some posited that Donnie Wilkerson had been the target of a Jimmy Hoffa-style mob hit, while others said he had split town with a secret mistress and a stash of embezzled city funds. It didn't matter that there was no evidence to support any of this. The media abhors an information vacuum—particularly when the vacuum exists at the center of a major story—so sometimes it simply manufactures "facts" of its own. Mike found it morbidly amusing that none of the wild stories circulating even approached the sheer insanity of the truth.

He could put a stop to it all any time. Today, even. Right now. He was thinking of this yet again as he finally exited the call center and trudged across the now half-empty parking lot toward his car. Though there was a veritable sea of open spaces now, his car was where he'd left it early this morning, at a very distant corner of the lot. The first shift was always the most fully staffed and the lot had been nearly full then. There was a lot of noise and bustle in the morning as his co-workers hurried to make it inside and be ready at their desks before the start of their shifts. Now, though, all was eerily quiet. The dismal gray sky overhead and the slight nip in the air contributed to an atmosphere of oppressive gloom. It made him uptight. And paranoid. He glanced over his shoulder more than once, half-expecting to see Diabolical Conspiracy spies shadowing his every move. Which was absurd, but he couldn't help it. Ever since that disturbing morning drive with Marnie following his first conspiracy meeting, a large part of him had felt like he was living in a deeply strange satanic version of an espionage novel.

And, yes, he could put a stop to it any time.

Today, he reminded himself yet again.

Right now.

Soon he would be behind the wheel of his car, engaged again in that most liberating moment of his work day routine. Ensconced once more inside his vehicle, he would feel free again, unburdened at last of all the daily stresses that were part and parcel of his profession. He was no longer tethered to a desk. He could go wherever he wanted. Home. To the store for groceries. Or to a bar or a movie. It didn't matter what or where, really, just that his time was his own again and he could do as he pleased. For instance, instead of heading home now, he could turn in another direction and drive to the police station. He could spill everything he knew. He could offer to wear a wire to the next Diabolical Conspiracy meeting. And he could put an end to this crazy fucking shit that had engulfed his life once and for all.

But every time he worked himself up nearly to the point of

thinking he would do just that, he would remember that chillingly quiet morning drive with Marnie and shelve the idea. He suspected she had exaggerated the conspiracy's reach and ability to anticipate and eliminate threats. The rational part of his mind told him it was ridiculous to believe they would systematically begin murdering every one of his loved ones the moment he showed up at the police station. But they had gotten their hooks too far inside him. He believed the hype, despite its surface absurdity. They had gotten away with murder many times before and had never been exposed. In the end, he simply couldn't stomach even the remote possibility of the people he cared about being harmed.

So he was trapped.

Unless . . . well, unless he killed himself. Speaking of remote possibilities. But he hadn't entirely ruled it out. If the situation ever reached the point of feeling completely untenable, it might become a feasible exit strategy.

Until then . . .

He started to frown as he drew closer to his car. There was something clipped behind the windshield wiper on the driver's side. A white slip of paper, perhaps, or an envelope. There was something ominous about the way the edges of it flapped in the steady breeze, as if it were calling his attention. More paranoia? A quick scan of the scattering of other cars nearby showed no other white slips of paper clipped to other windshields. Of course not. Security would have chased off anyone attempting to distribute flyers on company grounds. No, whatever else this might be, it was undeniably an attempt to communicate directly with him.

Fuck.

A tight knot of dread formed inside him as he reached the car and saw that it was an envelope clipped behind the windshield wiper. Somehow a sealed envelope felt even more ominous than a folded sheet of paper. He opened the car and chucked his backpack inside before snatching the envelope from the wiper. That knot of dread tightened several more degrees as he saw the block letters printed across the front of the envelope—TDC.

The Diabolical Conspiracy.

Mike slapped the envelope against the palm of his free hand and kicked at a pebble on the asphalt, sending it skittering across the lot until it disappeared beneath a blue Lexus. Which was what he would like to do about now. Fucking *disappear.*

Fuck! Fuck, fuck, fucking double goddamn fuck!

He had known it. On some level, he had known from his first glimpse of the thing clipped to his wiper that it would in some way be related to those evil fuckers. He didn't know how he had known it, but he had, even though things had stayed mostly quiet on that front since that first horrible night. There had been a couple more meetings, but they had been uneventful, almost mundane. There had been no more murders. No more orgies. And the last meeting had been more than a month ago. Yet something within him had accurately divined the true nature of this thing almost instantly. It was as if something in the universe had been speaking to him. Trying to warn him. Which he couldn't interpret as anything other than a bad sign.

He sneered at the letters written on the envelope a moment longer.

Then he got in the car and tore it open.

The note it contained was terse and also written in block letters:

GO TO FAT SAM'S ON FRONT STREET. ASK FOR JAS-PER. SAY YOU'VE COME TO PICK UP THE PACKAGE. TDC.

Mike read the note several times over, the crease in his brow deepening each time his eyes scanned the cryptic message. Fat Sam's was a popular burger joint. Locally owned with two locations, one near where he lived and this one, on the opposite side of town. He couldn't imagine what kind of business The Diabolical Conspiracy could have with Fat Sam's, nor did he *want* to know what that business might be.

He shook his head and swore softly: "Fuck me."

For one wild, heady moment, he considered disregarding the note and heading home. But he knew he couldn't do that. When he failed to perform as instructed, he would be punished. Somehow. Some way. Nadia would probably flog him or some damn thing at the next conspiracy meeting. Also, Marnie was waiting for him at home. She had moved in with him at the beginning of the month. Her idea, and one he'd had little choice but to accept. It was possible she already knew of the note and the purpose behind it. Hell, it was even possible *she* had clipped the note to his windshield. The writing didn't look like hers at first glance, but the block printing had been done with obvious deliberation, perhaps to disguise the author's identity. Which begged some obvious questions. Why leave a note at all? Why not call him on his cell?

He shook his head again.

More spy novel bullshit.

THE DIABOLICAL CONSPIRACY

Ridiculous or not, he had no real choice here. He could only do as he had been told. So after crumpling the note in a ball and tossing it aside, he started the car and headed for Fat Sam's.

11

MIKE WALKED INTO THE FAT Sam's location on Front Street at just after 5:30 that evening. He would have gotten there sooner if not for the painfully slow rush hour traffic, which more than tripled the normal drive time. Paranoia again tinged his thoughts and made him increasingly twitchy for the duration of the ride. The big thing driving these feelings was his late departure from the call center. The person who had arranged this mystery mission would have been aware of his shift's normal end time, but would not have been able to anticipate today's egregious delay. What if whatever he was expected to accomplish tonight hinged on him doing so within a very tight, preset time frame? In that case, he might already be too late. Terrible things might already have been set in motion, things he would likely be powerless to stop.

His luck took a slight turn as he entered the restaurant. The waiting room was empty and there was one couple ahead of him. The perky blonde hostess grabbed a couple of menus and escorted them to a nearby table. She returned in under a minute and greeted him with a dazzling smile.

"Hello! Just one tonight?"

Mike tried on a brittle smile, but he immediately knew it was a mistake. Though she struggled not to show it, something in his expression disturbed her and the wattage of her smile dimmed considerably.

So he made the phony smile go away and said, "Um, I'm here to see Jasper?" His voice rose in pitch at the end, rendering it a question rather than a statement. He sounded nervous and unsure of himself. Ridiculous. He was a grownup. He loathed sounding like an unconfident, stammering fool in the presence of this stunningly pretty young girl. Why this should matter, he didn't know, but it did. "I was told—"

"This way."

A tilt of her head indicated he should follow her, so he did, his gaze zeroing in on her sumptuous backside as she led him through the main dining area and then into the bar. The bar was a little more noisy and crowded, thanks to it still being happy hour. People were laughing and joking, but little of what he heard penetrated as he admired the sway of the hostess's hips and the way her ass moved in those tight orange shorts. She looked so ripe, a tender, juicy fruit ready for the picking. He guessed she was a student at the university, probably no more than a year or two out of high school. Watching the way her body moved was almost painful. The urge to reach out and touch her—to slide his hands around her slim waist—was nearly too powerful to resist.

The erotic trance lasted until he realized she had come to a stop and was knocking on an office door. He looked around and saw that they were no longer in the bar, though they were somewhere adjacent to it. He could still hear laughter and the constant clinking of glasses and bottles. A glance over his shoulder showed him a glimpse of the bar area at the opposite end of a short passage. About halfway down the passage on the right was a set of flapping double doors. He guessed the kitchen would be on the other side of those doors. His head snapped around again when he heard the office door come open.

"That man is here to see you."

There was the sound of someone clearing their throat, followed by a familiar voice saying, "Send him in, Angelique."

Angelique stepped aside and waved Mike in. Mike was unable to resist a glance at her breasts as he walked by her. It was a helpless male reflex. Nothing he could do about it. They were nice breasts, and they pleasingly strained her tight top. She caught his eye for an instant as he entered the office. Her expression in that moment was somewhere tantalizingly between a smirk and a smile. And then she shut the door to the office and was gone.

Holy shit. I want her so bad.

That throat-clearing sound came again and the world abruptly came back into crisp focus. He was in a cramped office. A laptop was open atop a small desk. A scattering of paperwork obscured much of the desk's surface. There was a calendar on the wall behind the desk, with the picture for this month showing a group of smiling restaurant employees. There was little about the office that was not nondescript. If he had been asked to picture the office of a restaurant's manager, he likely would have imagined something very like this—staid and boring.

By far the most compelling thing about it was the ugly little man sitting on the other side of the desk. This was The Diabolical Conspiracy member who always reminded him vaguely of Hitler. He had the same beady, creepy eyes as the deceased genocidal maniac. The mustache and short, greasy brown hair also contributed to the impression. But Hitler, not exactly a pretty man himself, had been positively dashing compared to this dude. In fairness, it was the fault of biology rather than any failure of grooming or hygiene. It had a lot to do with the shape of his face. Nothing seemed properly symmetrical. One eye looked like it was higher up on his face than the other, which had the effect of throwing his other features out of perspective. His nose looked too small, while his perpetually protruding lower lip made his mouth look too big. Simply put, he was not an attractive man. At all.

And his name definitely was not Jasper.

"Um . . . I was told to ask for—"

Edward Olson nodded. "Yes. Jasper. I know. It was code. Have a seat."

Mike glanced at the metal-framed chair sitting opposite the desk, shrugged, and dropped into it. "So what's this about? The note I got said something about a package."

Olson steepled his fingers as he leaned back in chair. "We'll get to that in a minute. You seemed distracted when you walked in here. Is something wrong?"

He had been distracted, all right, but it wasn't the memory of the hostess's sensational little body that was making him so twitchy. No, that was all thanks to the mysterious summons from the conspiracy. He could confess to the true nature of his unsettled demeanor. Surely Olson would understand. Still, Mike was of the opinion he should keep feelings like that close to the vest where other conspiracy members were concerned. He didn't want any of them suspicious of his motives or potential future behavior, after all. Playing it off as purely a byproduct of his intense attraction to Angelique was the way to go. They were both guys. Olson would get it. He could even crack a sexist joke or two and they could have a moment of phony male bonding.

"Angelique. Jesus, man, that ass of hers is pure perfection. What I wouldn't give to take a bite out of it."

"Oh?"

Mike grinned as he started to get into it. After all, he wasn't faking anything here. His lust for the hostess was sincere. "Definitely. Too bad I'm shacked up with Marnie these days. If I could get with Angelique, I wouldn't let her out of bed for days. If ever. It would just be nonstop, Olympic competition-level sport fucking."

Olson's expression didn't change as he said, "She's my daughter."

"Say what now?"

"She's my daughter."

That's what I thought you said, but it doesn't fucking compute.

Mike felt his face grow hot. He shifted in the chair and felt twitchier than ever as he said, "About what I said—"

Olson waved it off. "Relax. Of course you feel that way. Who wouldn't want her? You can have her if you want. I'll arrange it."

Mike stared at him in open-mouthed shock for a longish moment. He pictured himself actually fucking Angelique and for a space of many seconds he was incapable of thinking coherently of anything else. But then the sleazy, sick reality of what Olson was suggesting finally registered and the lust consuming him withered and died.

Good lord, he thought. *Is this guy really talking about pimping out his own daughter?*

The notion disgusted him on numerous levels and elicited shame for his lustful thoughts. The attraction he felt for Angelique was normally understandable, but it was now tainted by this loathsome proposition.

Olson surprised him by laughing. "The sneer on your face tells me you think my suggestion reprehensible, which I find amusing." He leaned forward and rested his arms on the edge of the desk. "We're

Satanists. Perverting the natural order and offending God is what we're all about." He smiled. "At least in part."

Mike tried to think of an appropriate response and failed.

Olson smirked. "Would it help at all if I told you she's not my biological daughter, that she's adopted?"

It doesn't help a goddamn thing, but it explains a lot, including the mystery of how a toad like you produced a goddess like that. Should have known that shit wasn't possible.

Mike regained some of his composure and sat up straighter in the chair. "Maybe. We could talk about it some other time, though. I'd like to know what the deal is with this package. I was late getting off work and now I'll be even later getting home. I'd like to get whatever this is over with."

Olson nodded. "Understandable." He scooted his chair back from the desk and stood up "Let's go for a walk."

Mike followed him out of the office and down the short passage until they arrived at the flapping double doors. Olson pushed through the doors and Mike hurried in after him. As he suspected, this was the kitchen. There was a lot of noise, the clank of dishes and the rapid-fire talk of the staff. The kitchen workers remained focused on their work and barely acknowledged the intrusion as Olson led Mike to another set of flapping double doors at the other end of the kitchen. Beyond those doors was a storage room and doors to freezers.

Mike was more confused than ever. He couldn't imagine why a package of interest to The Diabolical Conspiracy would be stashed in the bowels of a restaurant. If it was anything especially sensitive, wouldn't it make more sense to keep it somewhere less public? Well, yeah, of course that would make more sense. The Diabolical Conspiracy did many things that made little or no sense on the surface.

Olson led him to a far corner of the storage room, where he stopped and looked at Mike. "Here's your package."

He slapped the sealed top of a blue metal barrel. There were three small holes drilled through the barrel's lid. Seeing them retriggered the gnawing sense of unease that had gripped Mike during the drive here, though at first he wasn't sure why.

He frowned. "What is this?"

There was a crowbar lying across the barrel's lid. Olson grabbed it and used it to pry the lid open. After setting the lid aside, he beckoned Mike to take a look inside, which he did with extreme reluctance. He suspected he was about to see something either unspeakably abominable or otherwise disturbing.

He was right about the disturbing part.

A little girl of about six or seven stared up at him with dazed eyes. She was wearing a torn polka-dotted dress. One cheek was smudged with dirt from leaning against a side of the barrel's interior. She was bound and gagged.

Mike stepped back and choked back bile. He hadn't felt this sick since the night of his first conspiracy meeting . . . since the moment he buried the heavy blade of that axe in Donnie Wilkerson's neck. "Oh my God."

Olson replaced the lid and looked at him with a quizzical expression. "You all right?"

Mike couldn't say anything at first. All he could think about was the fact there was a tied-up little girl in that barrel—and that Olson had closed her up inside it again. Just knowing she was in there was worse than anything else that had happened since he had become mixed up with these conspiracy assholes. Worse by far than the murder of Donnie Wilkerson. This little girl was a pure innocent. This thing being done to her—whatever its ultimate aim was—was an offense against everything right and decent in the world. No question on that count. And Mike was again seized by the idea that it was within his power to end this. He could grab that crowbar and beat this despicable, grotesque excuse for a man to fucking death. And then get that girl out of that goddamn barrel and head straight for the police station.

Olson nodded. "Forget it. You think we're alone here?" He pointed to a security camera in a corner of the room. "You're being watched. Acting against me would be futile. You might overpower me, but you'd never make it out of the restaurant alive."

Mike glanced at the camera then looked at Olson again. "Who's watching us?"

Olson shook his head. "Doesn't matter. What matters is that you leave here with the package tucked away in the trunk of your car and that you then proceed directly to Nadia's house. I'll call Nadia as soon as you're on your way. If you don't arrive at her house within twenty minutes of that call, she'll make some calls of her own."

Mike tensed. "Calls to who?"

Olson's expression turned hard and pitiless. "Again, doesn't matter. What *should* matter to you is that those calls will result in a lot of heartache for you. By which I mean a lot of people you care about will die. And you won't be able to stop it."

Mike was again reminded strongly of that first night of this madness. He felt caught. Trapped. Helpless. He could act to help this girl now or he could do as he had been told. Either way, it would probably result in something unacceptably tragic.

He shook his head. "Why me? Why does it have to be me? Any of you could have delivered this . . . *package*. Goddammit, why are you making me do this sick fucking thing?"

Olson remained unperturbed by this display of emotion. "I understand you're upset. But you need to set that aside for now. Nadia will explain everything once you get to her house."

Mike didn't say anything to that. He shook his head again and continued the struggle not to fall completely apart.

Olson grunted. "I'll take your silence as compliance. You know damn well you're not going to risk the lives of all your family and friends for one little girl. Now help me get the barrel up on this dolly."

12

THE DRIVE BACK ACROSS TOWN to Nadia's house was even more nerve-wracking than the tension-fraught drive from the call center to Fat Sam's had been. It didn't help that he seemed to be hitting every red light en route to her subdivision, thus lengthening the ordeal by untold minutes. He had never been particularly superstitious until recently, but now it was easy to see this as additional evidence of some force in the universe working against him. The way the day was playing out definitely felt like the handiwork of an unseen malevolent cosmic joker, with an array of perfectly timed roadblocks popping up at intervals designed to drive him crazy from frustration and anxiety. He didn't know what the overarching joke actually was yet, but he was pretty sure he was an integral part of the eventual punch line.

And at no point did he cease being aware of the living human cargo stashed in the trunk of his car. It was bad enough he had her at all, but the drive might at least have been marginally less tense if the barrel had not been too big to fit in the trunk. Initially this had been a source of relief, as he assumed Olson or Nadia would simply summon someone else to transport the "package," someone with a vehicle that had ample trunk space. He should have known he wouldn't get off the hook so easily. Olson consulted with some employees and procured some bungee cords. Several of these were used to secure the trunk lid after they had wedged the barrel in as far as it would go. Mike's protests that this was too risky fell on unsympathetic ears.

"What if I get pulled over?" he'd asked the portly restaurant manager, struggling to keep the pitch of his voice from rising to a whine. "The cops might want to know what's in the barrel."

"Well, you better hope you don't get stopped," was Olson's less than helpful reply.

His personal safety was part of it. Yes, he had killed a man after being threatened and backed into a corner by these people. That was a bad thing and a stain on his soul he could never erase. But there was a huge difference between doing monstrous things because you enjoyed doing them and doing them because you were being coerced. He wasn't a bad man, not at heart. True, he didn't wish to encounter representatives of the law just now, but he also didn't want any harm to come to this girl. Yet if he didn't take action of some sort, harm certainly *would* come to her.

As always, however, his options seemed limited, if not nonexistent. There was the time limit for reaching Nadia's house to contend with, for one thing, but the bigger complicating factor was Olson's confiscation of his cell phone prior to his departure from Fat Sam's. Nadia's orders, according to Olson. She didn't want him phoning his relatives with warnings and then making a last-ditch dash to the police station. And the time limit meant he couldn't risk stopping somewhere to find another phone to use. Other than doing precisely as he had been told, there was nothing he could do that wouldn't endanger the people he cared about.

Marnie was waiting for him out front when he arrived at Nadia's house. It was dark by then and external house lights came on as he pulled into the driveway and switched off the engine. Instead of getting out of the car right away, he watched Marnie come toward him down the sidewalk. She was smiling as she made eye contact with him. He hadn't known she would be here, but her presence didn't surprise him. She was essentially Nadia's second-in-command. Whatever sick thing they had planned for the unfortunate girl in the barrel, it was clear it was something of great importance to the group. So of course

Marnie would be here for the arrival of the precious "package."

She circled the car and opened his door for him. "Hey, sexy. What are you waiting for? Get your ass out here."

Mike forced a smile. Then he drew in a calming breath, undid his seatbelt, and got out of the car. His smile became a frown as he glanced out at the curb. On meeting nights, cars usually lined the curb bumper-to-bumper outside Nadia's house. But the only other cars around belonged to Nadia and Marnie. "There not a meeting tonight?"

Marnie slipped her arms around his waist and pulled him close, mashing her breasts against his chest. "No, baby. It's just you, me . . . and Nadia."

"Huh. I just figured, you know, what with the, uh . . . package you had me bring here that . . . well . . . there'd be some kind of freaky satanic sacrifice scenario happening."

Marnie laughed and kissed him lightly on the mouth. "Freaky satanic sacrifice. You're silly." More lilting laughter from his "girlfriend." "And you're right, actually, but that's all happening tomorrow."

Mike's heart sank at those words. He'd hadn't fully realized it, but on a subconscious level some part of him had harbored a naïve hope The Diabolical Conspiracy had some non-fatal intent in mind for the little girl. What that might have been he couldn't imagine, but it didn't matter now, because Marnie had emphatically put the matter to rest. They meant to kill the girl and as of this moment she had maybe a day left to live.

Unless he did something.

But what?

What, goddammit!?

Marnie kissed him again, a touch more hungrily this time, then stepped back. "Nadia will give you the lowdown soon, but first let's get that thing in the garage."

That thing.

He stared at Marnie for a moment and tried hard not to show the disappointment he was feeling. She was a bad person. Very bad. He had known that for some time now. But somehow it still stung when something happened to remind him how utterly soulless and unforgiving she was. This being one of the more blatant instances of that. The girl in the barrel was nothing to her. She wasn't a human child. She wasn't something precious. She was just a *thing*.

That was the real turning point.

He was going to do something to stop this and damn the cost. He didn't know what he would do yet, just that he would do something. The decision lifted a mental weight and allowed him to relax some. His smile in that moment was even genuine. He would do something. And he even had a little bit of time to figure out what that might be.

Marnie tilted her head to one side, her eyes narrowing some as she studied him. "You look almost . . . happy."

"Something wrong with that?"

She smiled and shook her head. "Not at all." She leaned into him again and gave him another kiss. "It's just nice to see. It's been a long time. You're finally feeling like a real part of this, aren't you?"

Mike laughed and made himself nod. "Yeah. That's it. That's it exactly."

She gave him a fierce hug. "I'm so glad. You had me worried for a while."

Mike put his chin on her shoulder and breathed a weary sigh. "Me, too." He closed his eyes and tightened his arms around her. "But everything's gonna be all right now."

They held each other a few moments longer. For Mike, they were moments tinged with bittersweet nostalgia as he recalled his former intense affection for Marnie. At last, though, they broke the clinch and got to work on getting the barrel out of his trunk and into the garage. Once they had accomplished that, Marnie used the crowbar to pry the lid off and peek in at the girl. The child still looked dazed, which wasn't surprising given the bumpy ride she'd endured and the drug still circulating through her system.

Marnie smiled. "She's perfect. Nadia will be pleased."

She replaced the lid, took Mike by a hand, and led him into Nadia's house. There were no pulsing strobe lights in evidence this time, but the house was dimly lit in every room but the kitchen, with floor lamps on instead of overhead lights. This was par for the course. Every time he came here he felt like he was walking into a haunted house. Nadia liked to keep things dark and spooky.

Speaking of . . .

"Where's Nadia?"

Marnie tugged at his hand and kept moving. "This way."

A woman of mystery, as always. But Mike was resigned to that now. So he let Marnie drag him through the kitchen into the living room and then up a set of dark, crimson-carpeted stairs to the second floor. There was a short hallway at the top of the staircase. At the end of it a door to a bedroom stood partially open. Red-tinted light spilled through the opening.

Marnie paused outside the door and waved him in ahead of her. "You first."

Mike frowned, feeling a touch of apprehension, but he didn't know what to do other than what he'd been told. As usual. So he pushed the door open and stepped into the room, his eyes widening at the sight of Nadia lying languidly upon a large, plush-looking wood-framed bed. She was stretched out at an angle across the bed and lying on her side, with a side of her head propped in an upraised palm.

She was wearing a tiny black negligee.

She smiled when she saw him. "Hi."

Mike gave his head a dazed shake. "What . . . uh . . . ."

"Get undressed, baby."

That was Marnie, speaking from somewhere behind him. He turned to look at her and saw she had already begun shedding her clothes. Her pants were bunched around her ankles and she was undoing the buttons of her form-fitting blouse. She laughed at his astonished expression.

Nadia slid off the bed and embraced him from behind, her hot breath against his ear making him shudder as one of her hands went to the zipper of his trousers and tugged at it. "Relax. This is your reward for a job well done. And for earning our trust. Let yourself enjoy it."

Mike's state of arousal was off the charts. It temporarily blinded him to everything else. He'd fucked multiple women the night of the orgy, but Nadia had not been one of them. She hadn't seemed interested in the male members of the cult and he had assumed the reason was strictly a matter of sexual preference. But maybe he had been wrong about that.

Nadia writhed against him from behind as she pushed his pants down past his hips. Marnie, fully undressed now, approached him from the front and tugged his pants the rest of the way down. Then she stood again and ripped his shirt open, sending buttons flying. After that, they were both wriggling their lithesome bodies against him, peppering his flesh with wet, hot kisses as they moaned and caressed him with their soft hands.

Mike started getting lost in the sensual overload of it all even as an increasingly remote part of his brain kept thinking about what an amazing and singularly unlikely thing this was that was happening to him. The orgy had been another kind of thing. A heady, delirious combo of drugs, sex, murder, and madness. It had felt like something barely connected to reality, almost like fractured memories from a fever dream. But now he was completely sober and experiencing something out of his wildest fantasies. He was in the middle of a hot girl sandwich, that ever elusive three-way combo that was the ultimate holy grail of sex for most guys. It was the kind of thing that never happened to ordinary dudes like himself. But it *was* happening. It was real. And it was impossible not to get lost in it, even so soon after being made to facilitate the first phase of something vile and horrendous.

But he could think about all that later.

Acting on some apparently sub-aural signal only women could hear, they each simultaneously seized him by a wrist and dragged him toward the bed—and then threw him down upon it and pounced on him.

Yes, he thought. *Whatever it is I need to think about, I'll think about it later.*

Later, later, late—

Nadia did something to him that made him gasp and thrash on the bed.

And soon after that he was screaming.

13

THE EVENING UNFOLDED AS A relentless and fearless exploration of flesh and the numerous wondrous ways three willing and eager bodies could intertwine in the pursuit of unending carnal bliss. After abandoning himself to this extended interlude of decadent indulgence, thoughts of the girl in the barrel rarely strayed into his consciousness. And every time that did happen, either Marnie or Nadia would send the troubling images fluttering away with yet another expert manipulation of his body. They were the most skilled bedroom partners of his life, each possessing apparently endless knowledge of ways to bring him soaring to the heights of senses-melting ecstasy, as well as equal skill in how to ease him back from the precipice and further delay the inevitable release his body cried out to achieve. After a while, it became nearly a form of torture, the way they repeatedly made him scream and beg for the mercy of orgasm. And they delighted in his "suffering," frequently laughing at him and taunting him. He didn't come for the first time until nearly an hour after they had stripped him of his clothes. When it finally did happen, he lay gasping on the bed for many dizzy moments as he struggled to put the scattered fragments of his consciousness back together.

But that was far from the end of the festivities. They plied him with wine and pot and had him watch while they went at each other with an invigorating animal ferocity that soon enough had him ready for action again. It went on that way for hours more. By the time they finally did allow him to rest and drift off to sleep, it felt like a miracle he had managed to hang on to any shred of sanity. Thoughts of the girl in the barrel remained at bay as he began the spiral down into unconsciousness. There was room for little else in his mind beyond exhausted reflection on what these women had done to him. If, over the course of his entire lifetime, he had managed to bed just one woman capable of doing the things Nadia and Marnie had both done tonight, he would have counted himself as extremely fortunate. Yet, somehow, he had bedded two such women *at the same time.* Just now. Tonight. It was nearly impossible to believe, even as his gaze roamed over the sleek, nude forms of the goddesses snuggled up to either side of him.

A moment of reckoning was bearing down on them all. But whatever happened within the next twenty-four hours, there was one thing he would never be able to deny—sex with fully committed gorgeous Satanists was unquestionably the best kind of sex anyone could ever have. And this was the last conscious thought that followed him into the shadowy abyss of sleep and unremembered dreams.

When he awoke, sunlight was filtering in through the gauzy curtains above the bed. Nadia was still asleep—and still nude—next to him. Marnie was missing and for a moment he absently wondered what had become of her. But then the sound of a shower running somewhere nearby penetrated his consciousness. Mystery solved. The girl was a machine. Regardless of how hard she partied the night before—or how little sleep she'd had—she was always the first one up and always seemed none the worse for wear. One morning he asked her how she did it and she told him she'd made a deal with the devil. It was a sign of how upside-down reality had become for him that he wasn't completely sure whether the comment was a joke or a statement of fact.

A glance at the bedside clock made his heart lurch.

7:07 a.m.

Less than an hour before the start of his shift at the call center and he was still in bed. He gingerly disengaged himself from Nadia. She groaned and stretched out a little, but she did not wake.

Thank God.

The last thing he wanted now was to have to deal with all the potential distractions a nude and fully awake Nadia would present. Getting his shit together sufficiently to make it to work on time was going to be an iffy proposition as things stood now. So he did his best not to jostle the bed as he got up and searched the floor for his clothes. As he dressed, he couldn't help staring at Nadia's gloriously unclothed body. He remembered that old adage about how some things are better left to the imagination. Nadia was emphatic proof this was not always true. Seeing her nude did nothing to dispel his original impression she was possibly the most beautiful woman he had ever seen. To the contrary, it enhanced the impression. She was a goddess. It was too bad about the whole servant of evil thing.

After patting his right hip pocket to verify his keys were still there, he walked out of the bedroom. In the hallway, he paused next to a closed door to the left. Here was the source of the running water sound. He imagined Marnie in there, standing beneath the shower nozzle as the hot water spray needled her nude body. It was another erotically powerful image and for a moment he felt almost irresistibly compelled to go in there and join her in the shower. He even put a hand on the doorknob for a moment, then jerked it away as he realized what he was doing. Acting on the impulse would be insane. He would be late to work for sure if he let that happen. But that wasn't the only reason it would be a bad idea. He needed some time away from these women so he could hopefully start thinking straight again and maybe begin figuring out a plan of action. But even knowing that didn't send him running out of the house right away. He stared at the closed door a few moments longer and thought some more about Marnie's dripping-wet flesh. It baffled him he could be so horny again so soon after last night's prolonged indulgences, but then it occurred to him he was experiencing a kind of sex hangover. And what did they always say was the best way to recover from a night of indulging in powerful intoxicants?

Have a little hair of the dog that bit you.

In this case, that would mean another taste of Marnie's sweet flesh rather than a nip of booze. His hand drifted to the doorknob again as he moved closer to the brink of surrendering to his basest instincts.

But then he thought of the girl in the barrel.

Shit.

She had spent an entire evening sealed away in that goddamn

thing. Bound and gagged. Helpless. Deprived of food and water. Who knew how long she had already been in the barrel prior to his arrival at Olson's restaurant? Way too long was the only real answer to that. He wondered whether she had voided her bowels or bladder during the night. It was a disquieting thought that made his face twist in disgust. It was very possible. And maybe she had spent the entire night literally stewing in her own juices while he was busy fucking Marnie and Nadia. The thought filled him with an intense self-loathing and extinguished the remnants of his lingering horniness.

He turned away from the bathroom door and hurried down the stairs, pausing at the bottom to stare briefly at the front door. He could still get to work on time—making it in just under the wire—if he walked out of here now and got in his car and got moving without further delay. Rescuing the little girl remained his ultimate aim, but now he was wondering whether he should wait until tonight's meeting of The Diabolical Conspiracy to make his move—as he'd originally assumed he would do—or instead do something right fucking now.

A sudden squelching sound told him water was no longer running through the pipes overhead. Marnie had finished her shower. If he had a window of opportunity here, it was closing fast. A mental image of the girl squatting in a puddle of her own piss decided the issue for him. He glanced at the front door one more time, cursed under his breath, and headed for the garage. Once he was there, he eyed the blue metal barrel with increasing trepidation as he approached it. What if she had died during the night? It didn't seem likely. She was young. Healthy. But there could have been complications arising from the conditions of her captivity. Maybe she had choked on the gag. Maybe whatever drug they had used on her had overwhelmed her system. The possibilities deepened his already considerable anxiety. It was too easy to imagine the girl dead inside the barrel. But one way or another—and regardless of whether he wanted to—he was going to find out.

He used the crowbar to pry the lid off the barrel. He closed his eyes and issued a desperate prayer before taking a look inside.

Please, please, please let her be okay.

He put the crowbar down and slid the lid aside to look in at the girl, flinching at the acrid piss stench that drifted out. The odor shamed him and made him wish he had acted last night. The good news, though, was that the girl was alive. She peered up at him with eyes that didn't look as dazed as they had the night before. A good thing, of course, but the downside to that was seeing the obvious terror in her expression, which hadn't been there before. She whimpered and cringed away from him as he peeked in at her.

"Don't worry," he whispered in what he hoped was a reassuring tone. "I'm not going to—"

The rest of it went unsaid as he heard the door to the garage open again.

Aw, shit.

"Sneaking another look at the vessel, are we?"

Mike frowned.

The what?

Mike glanced to his right and saw Marnie approaching him. She was smiling and her tone was light and carefree. Either she didn't suspect him of rebelling against the conspiracy or she was exceptionally good at concealing suspicion.

She sidled up next to him and looked in at the girl. "My, but she is a cute one. Stinks, though." She laughed and waved a hand in front of her face, then nudged Mike with an elbow. "We'll have to clean her up before the ceremony. I bet Olson volunteers for that duty. That'd be right up his alley, the fat little perv."

Mike was still holding the barrel's lid and now he gripped it tighter as he struggled to keep his disgust at that comment from showing. A voice in his head was shouting at him now, urging him to smash the lid against Marnie's head, then grab the girl and get the fuck out of here. Incredibly, though, a reluctance to physically harm Marnie lingered. It was insane. She wasn't just a bad person. That had been understating it by quite a lot. She was a horrible, despicable person, possessed of an almost indescribably vile excuse for a soul. And yet, she was still Marnie, his former all-consuming obsession. It might not be enough to stay his hand, but it *was* enough to make him hesitate.

Marnie nudged him again. "Aren't you gonna be late for work?"

"Fuck work."

She laughed again. "Wow, that's so unlike you." Another laugh. "I dig it, though. You don't need to be Mr. Responsible all the time."

"The ceremony tonight . . . what's it all about? You said Nadia would tell me last night, but that never happened."

"Gosh, I wonder why? We were all kind of otherwise occupied, you know. Speaking of that . . . I take it you had a good time?"

The girl in the barrel kept staring up at him. She wasn't looking at

Marnie at all, as if she sensed there was no hope of help from that direction whatsoever. Her eyes were openly pleading with him. It made Mike nervous. What if Marnie noticed and somehow realized he'd given the girl reason to believe he might help her?

He had to distract her while he worked up the nerve to act.

"Yeah . . . a good time. Definitely." He glanced at her. "So come on already, give me the lowdown. What's up with this ceremony? What did you mean when you called this girl 'the vessel'? And why was it so goddamn important that I be the one to transport her here. That was some stressful shit, by the way, and I'd love an explanation."

Marnie pursed her lips for a moment as she appeared to think it over. Then she shrugged and said, "Nadia really meant to tell you last night, but we got sort of carried away with all the drinking and fucking. I guess she forgot." She smirked. "Hazards of the lifestyle."

"The satanic lifestyle, you mean?"

"Yeah. What else? Anyway . . ." Marnie flipped long blonde locks from her face and looked him in the eye. "That shit with you yesterday, the whole transport thing, was a crucial piece of the puzzle Nadia has put together. It's all based on stuff from the Satanic Bible. You're the Thirteenth, remember? Your initiation into the group completed the infernal circle. As the Thirteenth, it was necessary for you to deliver our vessel." She flicked a glance at the girl in the barrel and smiled again. "This little sweetheart being the vessel. Delivery of the vessel by the Thirteenth opens a direct channel with realms beyond this world, including the infernal hierarchy of Hell. But opening the channel is just the first phase. When you kill the vessel tonight, we'll be able to request an audience with Satan himself. Imagine it. A chance to communicate with the single most powerful entity in the universe. The lord of darkness. Our beautiful master. It's an incredibly rare opportunity for those of our faith."

Marnie radiated a palpable live-wire excitement throughout this speech. Mike had never seen her anywhere near this enthusiastic talking about anything else. She sounded like a person breathlessly discussing the imminent occurrence of some massively historical event. From her point of view, of course, a summoning of the devil would be on that level. Mike didn't believe Satan himself would actually be present in Nadia's garage tonight, mainly because he didn't believe in the existence of such a being. But Nadia was a master manipulator. It was possible she had some kind of theatrical trickery in mind to make the rest of these loonies believe it was happening. How she meant to pull the deception off was an interesting thing to contemplate, but it didn't matter much because the ceremony would not be happening. Not tonight and not ever.

He looked at the girl in the barrel again. She was still watching him in that beseeching way. "So I'm supposed to kill . . . the vessel?"

"Of course." Marnie was still going on in that bubbly, giddy tone. How could she sound that way when discussing something so monstrous? "You still don't understand how integral you are to everything as the Thirteenth. I envy you so much, baby. Tonight, when you slit this thing's throat and bathe in her blood—"

There was a cracking sound as the edge of the lid's barrel connected with the center of her face. Blood jetted from her nostrils as the blow broke her nose and sent her stumbling backward. Mike pursued her as she crashed against a work table and then pitched forward, dropping to her knees. He swung the lid again with all his might and it smacked into the side of her head with a resounding thump. She toppled over and stared up at him with dazed, uncomprehending eyes. A flicker of sick sympathy flared within him as he took a good look at the damage he'd already inflicted. He experienced a moment of terrible doubt. She had never seen it coming. It stunned him to realize how completely she had accepted the sincerity of his immersion into her "faith." This was a betrayal. Didn't matter that it was a righteous one. It was a betrayal nonetheless. But he understood there was no taking it back now. He'd chosen his path and the only thing left now was to see it through to the end. So he dropped to his knees next to her and choked back bile as he raised the lid above his head and brought it down again. Tears blurred his vision as he watched her body convulse and then stop moving.

Oh, Marnie. Oh, God. I'm so fucking sorry.

Though a voice of reason reminded him of Marnie's grievous shortcomings and told him this horrible thing he had done was right and necessary, the grief he felt was real. And he couldn't bear to look again at what he had done to her, at the wreck he had made of her beautiful face.

Oh, Marnie. Jesus, what have I done?

There was a moment there where he might have crumbled completely, but that same strident voice of reason spoke up again, reminding him there was still work to be done and that everything might yet be lost if he didn't get his ass in gear. So he got shakily to his feet and stumbled over to the barrel. The little girl peered up at him again and when he looked into those terrified but hopeful eyes, his resolve to do what needed doing returned and strengthened.

He reached into the barrel, grasped the girl by her armpits, and pulled her out, setting her gently down on the garage's cement floor. Holding her gently by the shoulders, he strove for a comforting tone as he said, "You're gonna be okay now. Hold on while I find something to cut you loose."

Tears spilled from her eyes, but she managed a nod to show she understood.

He forced a smile. "Good girl. This is almost over, I promise."

He stepped over Marnie's prone form and scanned the work table for something he could use. There were knives aplenty in the kitchen, of course, but he couldn't risk going in there yet. It was possible Nadia was up and moving around by now and he didn't want to deal with her until he'd set the girl free. There wasn't much on the table's surface, so he started rooting through the drawers beneath it. He hit pay dirt with the second drawer, finding a pair of garden shears with sharp-looking blades.

After freeing the girl from her bonds and removing the gag from her mouth, he gripped her by the shoulders again and said, "What's your name?"

She sniffled and her bottom lip trembled, but she managed to spit it out. "Buh-Brittany."

"Okay, Brittany. Listen close. I know you're scared, but it's important that you do as I say. Do you understand?"

She sniffled again and nodded as she wiped tears from her eyes.

"I'm gonna open the garage door in a minute. When I do, I want you to *run*. Okay? I'd take you back to your parents or to the police myself, but I've got some things I have to do. There are some more very bad people out there and I have to act fast to make sure they'll never hurt you or anyone else again. Knock on a neighbor's door, tell them somebody bad took you and dropped you off in this neighborhood. But please don't send them this way, okay? At least not right away. This is super important. If the police get here too fast, I won't be able to do the things I need to do. Understand?"

Her brow creased with confusion and her lower lip jutted out in a pout, but she nodded again. Mike wasn't at all sure the message was getting through, but there was nothing he could do about that other than hope for the best. He got to his feet again, did a quick scan of the garage, and spotted what he was looking for over by the door to the house. A punch of a button mounted on the wall there resulted in a rattling of gears as the garage door began to retract.

Mike met Brittany's gaze one more time. "Run. Now."

She ran.

Mike watched her as she dashed through the opening, the hem of her pee-stained polka-dotted dress flapping wildly around her skinny legs as she ran. Then she hooked a right and kept on running, disappearing from his vision. Once she was gone, Mike felt a small degree of inner peace return. He had done the right thing. Finally. For once. But it was just one piece of the puzzle. Much hard—and dangerous—work remained.

He reentered the house and stood inside the short hallway that led to the kitchen on one side and the living room on the other. Holding his breath, he listened for sounds of activity. But several moments passed and he heard nothing but the hum of the refrigerator from the kitchen. He let the breath out and got moving again, cognizant of that diminishing window of opportunity. Maybe Nadia was still asleep, but that wouldn't remain the case for long.

He slipped into the kitchen and treaded lightly over the tiles as he crossed to the counter, where Marnie had left her handbag the night before. He opened it and felt his heart speed up at the sight of the nickel-plated automatic pistol resting in there against a makeup case. The same gun she had threatened him with that morning three months earlier. Had it been just three months? It felt more like a lifetime. Everything had changed. The mundane world he had known prior to the night of his forced initiation into The Diabolical Conspiracy was lost to him now. Part of him wanted to believe he could yet get it back somehow, but the larger part of him knew better. Odds were he wouldn't even survive the day. A return to normality was a pipe dream, nothing more.

Taking the gun with him, he left the kitchen and climbed the stairs to the second floor. Nadia was still stretched out on the bed. She was still nude and the sight of her lovely body quickened his pulse, in spite of everything. Her head turned in his direction as he came into the room, her eyes fluttering open as she blinked blearily at him for a few moments. Then the world seemed to come into focus for her as her gaze locked on the gun in his hand.

She sat up. "That's Marnie's gun."

He didn't say anything.

"Where is Marnie?" She squinted and leaned forward a little. "Is that . . . is that *blood* on your shirt?"

Mike pointed the gun at her. "Marnie's dead. Get dressed."

Nadia's expression didn't change. The implied threat of the gun didn't seem to bother her. "So you killed Marnie? That's too bad. I liked her a lot. Are you going to kill me, too?"

Mike jabbed the gun in her direction. "I told you to get dressed. Shut up and do it."

Still no visible fear on her part, not even the slightest flinch. Nothing more than a mild curiosity. It disturbed him. "But why am I getting dressed? If you've gone this far, you and I both know you have to kill me. You know I'd never let you off the hook for this. So why not just kill me now?"

"Because I need your help."

She laughed. "Oh, really? With what?"

He took a step closer to her and aimed the gun point-blank at her face. "I need you to help me kill the rest of them."

14

THE PARKING LOT BEHIND FAT Sam's was mostly empty when Mike pulled in just before nine that morning. The only other vehicles present were a van, two compact cars, and a delivery truck. The delivery truck was backed up close to the restaurant's rear entrance, while the other vehicles were parked by a Dumpster in the same vicinity. Mike drove to a far back corner of the lot and backed into a space to watch for the arrival of a black Jaguar. All the empty space made him feel conspicuous, but parking any closer to the restaurant would increase the likelihood of being spotted by his quarry too soon. No, back here was the best position for surveillance. If the information Nadia had fed him was correct—and he believed it was—Olson would be arriving within the next few minutes. In the unlikely event of someone else from the restaurant approaching him to inquire about his presence or to tell him the restaurant wasn't open yet, he had a cover story prepared. He would say he had arrived early for an interview and was killing time. It was a plausible-sounding excuse, but as it turned out, he didn't need it.

Olson's black Jaguar pulled into the parking lot six minutes after the hour. Mike hit the gas and roared up to a stop next to it as Olson was stepping out of his car. He threw his door open and popped out, aiming Marnie's gun over the roof of his car at Olson's stunned face. The portly freak threw up his hands in an instinctive protective gesture but, perhaps paralyzed by shock, made no attempt to run. Mike let out a breath and squeezed the trigger. The bullet was on-target, punching through the center of his face and sending a cascade of red out the back of his head. Olson fell back against his car and slid toward the ground. Mike was back in his car before Olson's corpse hit the dirty asphalt. He dropped the gun on the empty passenger seat next to him and burned rubber out of there. The whole thing went down so fast he was reasonably certain there had been no witnesses. No one had come running out of the restaurant at the sound of the gunshot, nor had he seen anyone on foot nearby. A lucky break. He would need more of them if he hoped to accomplish this insane mission he'd embarked upon.

His next stop was an apartment complex a few miles away from Fat Sam's. He drove slowly through the maze of buildings until he arrived at the one marked with a large black G. After pulling in next to a red Volvo, he grabbed Marnie's gun again and tucked it in his waistband as he got out of his car. He pulled out the tail of his shirt to conceal the weapon and climbed a set of stairs to the second floor, where he knocked on the door to apartment 3G.

Blake Carter worked second shift at a department store. The Volvo parked out front belonged to him. So he was almost certainly home. The only question was whether he would be awake yet. Mike didn't want to attract unwanted attention by having to repeatedly bang on the door.

His luck was in again.

The door came open perhaps a minute after he knocked. Blake, clad only in boxer shorts, peered blearily out at him. "Mike? Dude, what are—"

Mike shoved his way in and kicked the door shut behind him. Blake made a sound of surprise and stumbled backward. However, despite the abrupt nature of the intrusion, he didn't seem alarmed yet. It was amazing. You would think a bunch of bloodthirsty, crazy Satanists would have sharper survival instincts, but apparently they were as apt to responding with bewildered confusion in moments of unexpected violence as anyone else. Mike pulled out the gun and shot his friend in the chest. The look of hurt surprise on his face triggered an instinctive pang of regret, but this feeling was even shorter-lived than the grief he'd experienced in the wake of assaulting Marnie. He was over it by the time Blake's body hit the carpeted floor. Partly this was because of the sense of cold determination he was fighting to hold onto as a necessary component of making it through this whole blood-drenched process.

But it was primarily because another crisis had immediately popped up to occupy his attention in the wake of Blake's death, this time in the form of a slender blonde woman clad only in black panties and a black bra. She stood in the short hallway beyond the little living room, regarding Mike with an expression of shock and terror. He didn't recognize the woman. As far as he knew, she was in no way associated with The Diabolical Conspiracy.

"Shit."

Hearing his voice snapped her out of the paralysis of terror gripping her. She screamed and fled back down the hallway, disappearing into a room on the left and slamming the door shut behind her. Knowing he didn't have a choice, Mike hurried after her, opening the door with a single swift kick that sent splinters of wood flying from the jamb. She stood cowering against the far wall with a cell phone pressed against her ear.

He aimed the gun at her. "Put the phone down."

Instead of doing as she had been told, she screamed.

And screamed again.

Goddammit.

He rushed at her and she cringed away into a corner of the room. She almost slipped past him when he briefly stumbled after trying to adjust his trajectory to account for her movement. But he managed to remain on his feet and lunged after her as she went flying by him. He tackled her and drove her to the floor, effectively pinning her beneath him. She squirmed and cried out, but he pressed the gun against the side of her head and said, "Stop."

She stopped moving as she felt the cold kiss of steel against her flesh. And now she was sobbing. "Please. Please don't rape me."

Jesus. So this is what it's come to.

He sighed. "I'm not going to rape you."

Another sob. "Oh, God. Please don't kill me."

"I'm not gonna kill you, either."

She sniffled. "Please. Please. I barely even knew Blake. I don't give a shit about him. I won't tell the cops about you. I'll lie. I'll tell them you were big and black. I'll make them believe it. I swear. You don't have to kill me."

Mike rolled his eyes. "For the love of fuck. Look, I already told you, I'm not gonna kill you. Unfortunately, I do have to hurt you. I'm sorry."

He whipped the butt of the gun across the back of her head before she could say anything else. It made her whimper and squirm beneath him again. Mike felt ripped off. That shit always worked on TV cop shows. So he hit her with the gun again, harder this time. And then he did it a third time. She never quite lost consciousness, but she did seem to have been rendered insensible. He got to work fast while she was out of commission, binding her wrists and ankles with electrical cords. He sealed her mouth shut with a strip of duct tape from a roll he found in the kitchen. That done, he gave her a once-over before departing. The electrical cords wouldn't hold her as securely as rope. Eventually she might be able to twist her way free. But there was nothing else he could do other than hope they would hold long enough for him to do what he needed to do.

All was quiet outside as he exited the apartment. He heard no sirens and saw no one walking around or loitering in the vicinity. Evidently most of Blake's neighbors worked first-shift jobs. The many empty parking spaces in the apartment complex testified to this. His heart was still galloping from the close call with the girl, but he began to relax a little as he got back inside his car. Despite the unexpected complication, things were still going according to plan. He felt bad about having to hurt the girl. Actually, he felt like shit for it. She had bled a good bit from a gash the gun's butt had opened up behind one of her ears. But all might have been lost if he hadn't done it. So he put his guilt aside and moved on to the next target on his list.

Who, fortunately, happened to reside in the same apartment complex. He backed out of the space outside Blake's building, changed gears, and headed over to building K. In a few moments, he stood outside the door to apartment K2 with his right fist poised to knock. But the door opened before he could rap his knuckles against the wood.

Cynthia Everson, wearing only pink pajama bottoms and a white bra, aimed the barrel of a shotgun at him from inside the apartment. Her blonde hair was tied back in a loose knot and she stood with her weight shifted to one side. She smirked. "Surprise, asshole."

Mike gaped at her and felt his insides curdle. The shotgun's barrel looked like a cannon. He imagined a shell fired from it ripping through his guts and felt like crying.

Cynthia stepped back and waved him in. "Get in here and shut the fucking door, traitor."

Mike stood still. He was breathing hard. Was this how Olson had felt in that last moment before the slug from Marnie's gun destroyed his face?

Probably.

Run. It's your only chance. Do it now.

Cynthia adjusted her aim, raising the barrel so it pointed directly at his face. "Go ahead. Run. I'd love an excuse to blow you away."

Instead of running he stood there, shaking as tears sprang from the corners of his eyes.

Cynthia laughed. "That's what I thought. Now get in here, you fucking coward."

She moved back a few steps as Mike reluctantly shuffled into the apartment and pushed the door shut.

"Now turn around."

Mike did as instructed.

"On your knees."

Again, he did as he was told.

Cynthia chuckled. "Brace yourself. This is gonna hurt."

She didn't lie.

The butt of the shotgun slammed into the side of his head with devastating force and the lights went out.

15

AN INDETERMINATE TIME LATER, HE awoke tied securely to a chair in Nadia's garage. Given what he recalled from his last moments of consciousness, this did not surprise him. It made a twisted kind of sense that he had been returned to the group's nominal headquarters. Here was where he would be judged and sentenced. The fact he had been stripped of his clothing surprised him only a little. He doubted he would be participating in any more of their orgies. It was likely his clothes had been removed to in some way further facilitate whatever horrible punishment they had in mind for him.

However, seeing Marnie seated in a chair opposite the one he was in surprised him a great deal. Her face was badly bruised and bandaged in places, but she was very much alive. The intensity of the hatred shining from her eyes might have made him hate himself more than ever had it not been for the sickening thing she held cradled in her lap.

Marnie nodded at that moment of recognition. "You should've made sure I was dead. If you'd done that, she might still be alive."

Mike screamed.

Marnie laughed and stroked the blood-streaked hair of the severed head in her lap. The head of his sister, one of the many people he had hoped to save by killing off every member of The Diabolical Conspiracy. The sight of those horribly still, pain-contorted features made him want to vomit. And then he did, leaning his head forward to spray chunks of partially digested meat on the cement floor. After that, he retched and dry-heaved until his throat was burning, crying bitter tears of failure and loss the whole time.

She was right. He should have confirmed her death before moving on to the next phase of his mission. But in the emotion of the moment he had failed to do so. Maybe because of the reflexive regret he'd felt after hitting her with the heavy lid of the barrel. He'd been reluctant to even look at what he had done to her. And maybe the oversight had something to do with the way her body convulsed before going still. But now he wondered whether that might have been a bit of playacting on her part. She had been weakened and defenseless. A moment of convincing theatricality might have been a deliberate attempt to forestall any further blows. It seemed an absurd notion. It was difficult to believe anyone could be that coldly conniving when facing probable violent death. So maybe he was giving her too much credit. Either way, it didn't matter now. He had failed on every level. The Diabolical Conspiracy would endure after all. And its members were busy murdering the people he cared about in retaliation for the things he had done today.

Marnie lifted the head to her face and kissed it on the lips. "Mmm, cherry lipstick." She licked her lips and lowered the head. "Haven't tasted that flavor lipstick since I made out with that high school girl we killed last summer. Lisa Thomas. You remember her, the one the media made a big deal about when she disappeared."

Mike did remember. He started to feel queasy again.

Marnie rolled the head gently between her hands and smiled in a wistful way. "She was a feisty one. Screamed a lot, especially when we set her on fire. And of course I got a kick out of how the local law pinned the blame for her disappearance on that pathetic sex offender." She sighed. "Good times."

Mike cleared his throat. "So what happens now?"

Before Marnie could answer, he heard a clack of heels on the cement floor. Nadia strode into his field of vision and took up a position next to Marnie. She rested a hand lightly atop Marnie's head and ruffled her hair. Marnie smiled and leaned into the touch. Nadia's expression was oddly serene for a person who had spent much of the morning stashed away in the trunk of his car. She didn't look like a woman bent on vengeance, but Mike knew better than to trust this impression. His sister's severed head was proof enough of her intent. They were going to kill him. This was a given. The unknown part of the equation was how much torture he would have to endure before that happened. It was going to be hellish. Unbearable. He would be screaming his lungs raw long before they were done with him. Just thinking about it had him close to hyperventilating. He didn't know how he could face it. For the first time, he truly wished he had set aside his so-called goddamn morals and let them go through with their evil little ceremony.

Nadia smiled. "How are you feeling?"

He laughed softly.

Nadia cocked her head to one side and peered at him quizzically. "Something funny?"

"No. Nothing's very fucking funny right now."

She chuckled. "Depends on your perspective. Before we decapitated your sister, we made her eat her own vomit. That was amusing. At least I thought it was."

Marnie's bruised expression conveyed a savage amusement of her own as she glared at Mike. "I laughed so hard it hurt my broken fucking nose. I laughed even harder when I told her how what was happening to her was your fault. That made her cry and cry her little head off. Oops." She put a hand to her mouth in a mock display of regret. "Just a figure of speech. Forgive me."

Mike said nothing.

Nadia moved away from Marnie and approached Mike, taking care to avoid the splattered vomit on the floor. "Look at me."

Her tone was sterner now, very similar to the one she had used prior to beating Blake the night of Mike's first conspiracy meeting.

He looked at her.

She still had that serene look, but there was a faint smugness in her expression now, too. "That was quite the wild west undertaking you set out on earlier today. You were foolish to think you could succeed, of course, but I do admire the audacity."

Mike held her gaze, but he still didn't say anything.

"I must say, however, I didn't much enjoy the ride in your trunk. *So* filthy." She crinkled her nose at the memory. "Nor did I care for the repeated threats to shoot me between, quote, my 'evil fucking eyes' if I didn't guide you to the locations of every conspiracy member so you could kill them." She snapped a hand across his face, rocking his head hard to the right. "Look at me."

He sucked in a breath and turned his head to look at her again. Amazingly, despite the violent outburst, she still looked unbothered. "I don't guess it'd do any good to ask you to kill me now."

She laughed. "Why on earth would I grant so absurd a request?"

He shrugged. "Didn't figure you would. Couldn't hurt to ask, though."

"And why do you say that?"

Another shrug. And then a sigh. "I know you plan to torture me mercilessly. I'd obviously prefer a quick death. So I asked even though I knew you'd say no."

"I see." Nadia's eyes narrowed as she gave her head a slow, thoughtful nod. "Well, this is yet another case of you not knowing nearly as much as you think you do. In fact, I'd prefer not to kill you at all."

Mike was caught off-guard by the comment. He felt a flicker of hope even as he chastised himself for being naïve enough to even for a moment think she was being sincere. "Bullshit."

Nadia glanced at Marnie. "Am I bullshitting him, dear? Tell the boy the truth."

Marnie was smirking again, which did nothing to counter the gut instinct that told him this was merely cruel deception, a bit of psychological torture prior to moving on to the physical aspect of his punishment. "She's telling you the straight up truth, Mike. Look at you. Look at us. We don't have to play fucking games at this point." Her smirk deepened. "But there's a catch."

Of course there is.

Mike swallowed and said, "So what's the catch?"

He flinched as Nadia extended a hand toward him, expecting another vicious slap. Instead she caressed his cheek with the back of a hand. "You're very lucky. Anyone else in your position would be dead already. But I have a special feeling about you. I still believe you can make important contributions to our group. And, believe it or not, I harbor a very real affection for you." She glanced at Marnie. "We both do. Isn't that right, Marnie?"

"Oh, yes." Marnie's smirking expression shifted, became something close to an actual smile as she again began stroking his deceased sister's hair. "*Very* real."

Nadia focused on Mike again. "So we've had a debate. Examined the whole issue from every conceivable angle. And we had a vote. I regret to say the vote did not turn out in your favor. Many of the other members are not happy with what you've done, to say the least. I do not blame them, of course. They are right to feel angry and betrayed. However, in my position as unquestioned leader of The Diabolical Conspiracy, I have overruled the vote and you are indeed being given a conditional second chance."

"What do I have to do?"

Nadia kept her gaze on him as she moved away from him and again took up a position next to Marnie. She raised her voice significantly as she said, "Everyone into the garage now. Except Carolyn, of course."

Mike's head turned toward the door to the house, which stood open. As he watched, the surviving members of The Diabolical Conspiracy began to file into the garage. The expressions on their faces ranged from carefully blank to open hatred. Second chance or not, Mike couldn't fathom ever winning some of these people over again. Most of them moved into position behind Marnie and Nadia. One of the last people into the garage was young Angelique Olson. Mike couldn't conceal his shock at seeing her. She smiled with apparent warmth as their eyes met. Either she didn't yet know he was the one who had killed her adoptive father or she simply didn't care. But this was secondary to his surprise at her mere presence.

"Angelique?"

She kept smiling. "Hi. Thanks for killing my fucking father."

"Um . . ."

Mike didn't know what else to say to that. Maybe her gratitude was sincere, but he doubted her take on Olson's demise mirrored that of many people in the room.

Nadia said, "We need to act fast to fill the vacancies you've created in the infernal circle. Angelique is being taken in as a legacy initiate."

"And she knows all about what you do?"

Angelique answered for her: "I know everything. Hail Satan, motherfucker."

Mike sighed. "Right. Of course. Hail Satan."

His eyes moved away from Angelique as two more people came into the garage. A male member entered pushing a bound and gagged woman ahead of him. It was the same woman he had overpowered in Blake's apartment. She was still clad only in her black underwear. Mike's heart sank upon seeing her. He had tried to spare her, but in the end it hadn't mattered. She was going to die. More blood on his hands.

The man pushing her into the garage steered her toward Mike and made her stand in front of him. In the man's hand was a big knife, the kind used for gutting animal carcasses in the wild. After making the woman stand still, he slipped the blade inside the band of the woman's panties and cut the flimsy scrap of fabric loose with a single flick of his wrist. The trembling woman whimpered at this, but she made no attempt to rebel against what was happening to her. The dark bruises on her face were stark evidence as to why. She had already learned the folly of fighting back against these people.

Next the man used the big knife on Mike, quickly freeing him from the lengths of rope binding him to the chair. He then pressed the hunting knife into Mike's hand and moved away from him.

"Stand up, Mike."

Nadia, in that stentorian, commanding tone again.

Mike stood up.

Nadia smiled. "You have to prove yourself all over again. Except now you'll have to go farther than ever to demonstrate the depth of your allegiance. This is phase one of your redemption. Kill this bitch. Do not hesitate."

Mike stepped forward and rammed the blade deep into the woman's abdomen, then quickly yanked it out and plunged it in again. She dropped to the floor as he stood gasping over her with the bloody blade. She was still clinging to life, with her cheeks puffing behind the gag in her mouth. Mike felt something painful wrench inside him as he stared at her pitifully pleading eyes.

It felt like his soul tearing loose.

Nadia clapped her hands slowly together twice. It was what his father had called a "golf clap." She was still mocking him. "Bravo. Nice job. But you're still not done with phase one. Quickly, before she dies, defile her. Again I'd advise against hesitation."

He did not hesitate this time either. And he did as instructed. It was so much easier now, without a soul. By the time he was done, the woman was dead. He climbed off her and examined the faces arrayed behind Marnie and Nadia. "There. Is that sick enough for you? Am I evil enough yet?"

Nadia smiled. "Almost. By the way, have I ever mentioned that

Carolyn lives next door to me?"

Mike's grip on the hunting knife's handle tightened.

No. No. She isn't saying what I think she's saying. No way.

Nadia was still smiling as she raised her voice. "Carolyn, you can come in now."

Mike's heart was pounding again as he stared at the door to the house, a desperate part of him pleading not to see what he dreaded seeing most.

But, as was so often the case, his prayers went unanswered.

Carolyn came into the garage.

She wasn't alone.

Mike screamed and dropped to his knees.

Brittany looked dazed as she stumbled hesitatingly across the cement floor. They had drugged her again, which was a small mercy at least. It wasn't much, but at least it was something. At least she wouldn't know to be scared again until it was too late.

Probably.

He looked at Marnie.

And he looked at Nadia.

They had been right, after all. The devil was among them tonight. Multiple devils, actually, all wearing human masks.

Nadia leered at him. "Are you ready for the final phase? Can you do what needs to be done?"

He could.

And he did.

He couldn't rescue this child. The pragmatist within him recognized the impossibility of that. But perhaps he had been premature about pronouncing his soul dead. Because this was one defilement that was happening without him. He acted quickly, before anyone could move to stop him, by placing the sharp edge of the hunting knife against his throat and ripping open his jugular vein. He had a final few moments of consciousness as he watched his blood arc across the garage and spatter across Brittany's smudged face.

The other conspiracy members were applauding.

And cheering.

Mike's eyes rolled back in his head as he toppled over and stared up at the ceiling. The rest of them moved into view, huddling over him as his vision faded. He heard them talking about him as the world dimmed.

"I didn't think he had it in him."

"Hell, I knew he'd do it."

"I'm proud of him."

"Good riddance."

"I think I really loved you, Mike. Goodbye."

Mike's eyes fluttered as his last thoughts sputtered across his fading consciousness—*Something's wrong. What's happening? Why*—

EPILOGUE

Eight years later

MARNIE WAS EXHAUSTED AS SHE pulled into the driveway outside Nadia's house. Her house too now, actually, had been for a long while, but she still always thought of it as belonging to Nadia. Deeply ingrained mental habit. Another long day at the General Assembly had at last drawn to a close not a half hour earlier. Fourteen endless hours had elapsed since she had left home this morning and she counted herself lucky to be back this soon. There were many days when she regretted her decision to get into politics. She was always so damn tired. In the end, though, she knew it was worth it for all she was accomplishing on Satan's behalf. There were so many subtle ways you could hurt people when you had the ability to shape policy. She was making a real difference in advancing the cause of evil on a daily basis. It was something to be proud of, as Nadia liked to remind her at the end of especially trying days like this one.

The TV was blaring as she entered the house through the front door. Brittany and Jason were on the couch facing the TV, but they weren't actually watching it. Jason was playing with his iPad and Brittany was texting away at somebody on her smart phone. Probably her little boyfriend, Alex.

"Hey, kids."

"Hi, Marnie," was Brittany's reply.

Jason said, "Hi, Mom."

Neither of them looked up from their gadgets.

Typical.

Marnie rolled her eyes and continued into the kitchen, where she slung her purse off her shoulder and dropped it on the dining table. Nadia, wearing an apron, was at the counter, busily working at something in a mixing bowl.

She smiled warmly. "Hey, honey."

Marnie walked up behind her and slipped her arms around her waist. "What are you making?"

"Something special."

Marnie kissed the side of her neck.

"Ohh, that feels nice."

Marnie did it again, eliciting a giggle.

"Come on, tell me what it is."

Nadia gave a resolute shake of her head. "Sorry, it's a surprise for later. But I'll give you a hint. Blood of an innocent is a key ingredient."

Marnie made a sound of approval. "Sounds promising."

She kissed Nadia again and slid a hand inside her apron. Nadia turned away from the mixing bowl and allowed Marnie to kiss her on the mouth. Then she pressed back against the counter and smiled. "Feeling frisky today, are we?"

"What can I say? Treading on the rights of the little guy makes me horny."

Marnie felt a tug at her arm and turned around to see the round face of her son peering up at her. She smiled and ruffled his hair. "Hey, Jase. What's up?"

"Want a piece of pie."

She figured he was referring to the leftover lemon icebox pie Nadia had made for dessert the day before. She couldn't blame him. It was very yummy indeed. "Maybe after dinner."

He protested at this, but she sent him back to the living room with another admonition to wait until after dinner for his dessert. Marnie sighed and watched him go, feeling the usual aching tug at her heart. "He reminds me so much of his father sometimes."

Nadia snorted. "Let's hope he turns out better than that."

Marnie's expression turned thoughtful. "He will. We're raising him in the faith, after all. He'll never know another way."

As if on cue, Brittany came into the kitchen next, climbing onto a stool on the other side of the counter. "So when are you guys having another orgy?"

Marnie and Nadia exchanged wary glances.

Marnie said, "We're having another *meeting* next week."

Brittany pouted. "Like I don't know what's really going on when you send us over to Aunt Carolyn's for the night. I've sneaked in and spied on you guys a few times, you know."

Nadia shot her a sharp, disapproving look. "Brittany!"

Brittany smirked. "Whatever. You can't shield me from grownup stuff forever. I'm not a fucking kid anymore. When do I get to join in? I wanna get freaky for Satan, too."

The adult women exchanged glances again and this time those looks were tinged with resignation and weariness. Nadia reached over the counter and touched her adopted daughter's hand. "Your time is coming, sweetie. I promise."

Brittany slid off the stool and started slouching back in the direction of the living room. She was already texting again as she got off her parting shot: "Fucking *better*."

Nadia shook her head. "They grow up so fast." A dark look briefly crossed her features and she lowered her voice as she said, "I love her so much. When I think of how close we came to—"

"But we didn't. Things worked out the way they were meant to. The way Satan really wanted." Marnie opened a cabinet above the counter. "I need a drink. Want one?"

"Fuck yes. Make it a double."

Marnie poured the drinks and they toasted each other.

"To us."

They clinked glasses.

"To us."

Marnie poured out more liquor and lifted her glass again. "To evil."

Another clink of glasses.

"To evil."

After a few more toasts, Marnie let Nadia go back to her cooking and carried the bottle of whiskey outside. She sat on the ground above where Mike Bradley lay buried in his unmarked grave and had a few more quiet, thoughtful drinks. Before going back inside, she tipped out a tiny dollop of whiskey and watched it seep into the dry ground.

THE DIABOLICAL CONSPIRACY

And she thought the same thing she always thought in moments like this—*We could have had something special, you asshole.*

If only he had been a true believer.

Like his son.

Marnie screwed the cap on the bottle and went back inside.

BIO

Bryan Smith is the author of numerous novels and novellas, including *Depraved*, *68 Kill*, *Slowly We Rot*, *The Killing Kind*, and *Dead End House*. He's a two-time Splatterpunk Award winner, once for best novella (*Kill For Satan!*) and once for best collection (*Dirty Rotten Hippies and Other Stories*). He is also the co-author of *Suburban Gothic*, written with Brian Keene. A film version of *68 Kill* was released in 2017. He'll have a story in the forthcoming Simon & Schuster anthology *The End of the World As We Know It: Tales of Stephen King's The Stand*. He lives in TN with his dog Mac. Signed copies of his books can be purchased at https://bryansmithhorror.bigcartel.com/

Other Grindhouse Press Titles

www.ingramcontent.com/pod-product-compliance
Lightning Source LLC
Chambersburg PA
CBHW011516240626
47154CB00010B/3057